THE JANUS GROUP SERIES

Rath's Deception
Rath's Gambit
Rath's Reckoning
Rath's Trial
Rath's Rebellion
Rath's Redemption

Rath's Trial

PIERS PLATT

ISBN: 1533447209
ISBN-13: 978-1533447203

CONTENTS

1

"Here they come," Paisen whispered over her tactical radio.

Through the thick jungle vegetation, she saw a convoy of four off-road vehicles appear on the twisting road below her. She scanned the high branches around her, but could see no sign of the rest of her team, even when she switched to thermal vision on her eye implants. *Good,* she thought. *They're learning.*

Like her, the other contractors were heavily camouflaged, each harnessed into a tree perch nearly a hundred feet up in the canopy. Paisen turned her attention back to the approaching vehicles. *A jeep, a cargo truck, and another jeep. That truck worries me. If it's carrying a squad of foot soldiers, we're outnumbered.*

But it's too late now.

She sent a signal through her internal computer, and a countdown appeared in her heads-up display, synchronized with the other contractors' displays. When it reached zero, she squeezed the detonator in her hand. A smaller tree several yards away toppled over, blocking the road in front of the lead jeep. Simultaneously, she saw camouflaged forms detach from the trees around her, descending rapidly toward the forest floor. The only noise she heard was the sound of their climbing ropes sliding smoothly through karabiners. Paisen kicked backwards off her perch, swinging out into free air and bringing her auto-rifle up to her shoulder as she followed her team down.

Below, she saw the driver of the lead jeep open his door and climb out to inspect the fallen tree, cursing. Paisen shot him while still descending, and saw him topple over, stun round buried in his shoulder. She hit the ground moments later, legs wide, rifle scanning for targets. There were two other passengers in the jeep, but Vence, who had landed on the far side of the jeep, had already tagged both of them with stun rounds from her own weapon, and Paisen saw them slump over in their seats.

"Lead vehicle clear," Vence reported, her voice cool and collected.

"Rear vehicle clear," another voice responded.

Paisen heard a burst of gunfire, and saw a gun barrel sticking out the back of the cargo truck, firing wildly.

Shit.

A camouflaged contractor flew across the road, riding his rappelling rope like a rope swing. The arc of his swing took him directly past the open rear of the truck, and Paisen saw him lob a stun grenade inside, before swinging into the bushes on the far side of the road.

Fucking Tepper, that cowboy.

She shook her head in annoyance. But the grenade detonated a second later, and two other contractors ducked around the back of the truck hot on its heels, firing stun rounds continuously.

"Truck's clear," one reported. "And Tepper's stuck in a thorn bush."

"Serves him right," Paisen grunted.

It took them less than five minutes to drag the unconscious soldiers from the vehicles, bind them, and lay them out of sight of the road. The contractors each stripped off their camouflage gear and climbing harness, picked a soldier's face to mimic, and then boarded the vehicles. Vence finished cutting through the fallen log moments later, and Paisen helped the shorter woman haul the pieces aside. Less than ten minutes after the convoy had first appeared, it was back on the move, with the contractors at the wheel.

They wound their way through the jungle for several miles, the trucks making slow progress on the crumbling dirt track. Paisen heard the radio crackle to life.

"So there I was," Tepper said, broadcasting to the entire team.

"Christ, here we go again," Vence said to Paisen, smiling and shaking her head in mock annoyance.

"… sophomore year of high school, flunking all my classes," Tepper continued. "When they announce a contest, for the entire school. Whoever writes the best essay gets an all-expense-paid trip to Earth. Earth! The mother planet, can you imagine?"

The trucks continued on through the jungle, passing through patches of sunlight and shade.

"Now I'd always been a little obsessed with Earth, so I figured out a way to rig the contest. I hacked into the contest submission website, read all of the other kids' papers, and picked a really good one, and then changed the name on it so I would get credit for it. Then I went through and fucked with all of the other papers, you know – typos and grammar errors, that kind of thing. I changed one kid's paper so that it just started swearing randomly in the middle of sentences, like he had Tourette's or something."

"You're an asshole, Tepper," Vence radioed back, laughing.

"Oh, for sure. It was a total dick move, I know. But I wanted to go to Earth *so bad*."

"Did you win?" another contractor asked.

"Yeah! I fucking won! Greatest day of my life. This was

gonna be the thing that turned little Tepper's life around, you know? I would go to Earth, and see our heritage, and become famous and make lots of money somehow – this was my golden ticket."

"What was Earth like?" someone else asked.

"Well … here's the thing," Tepper said. "It turns out if you sleep through your shuttle flight, and all of the other shuttles are fully booked, you miss your spaceliner and you don't get to go to Earth. Still haven't been, actually. But someday … someday."

Vence laughed out loud. "Jackass."

"We're closing in on the objective," Paisen radioed. "Clear the net."

They crested a small rise and the prison camp appeared, a cluster of rough wooden bungalows sitting on bare, red clay, surrounded by rows of razor-wire fencing. Guard towers stood at each of the camp's four corners, looking out over several hundred yards of cleared forest land, tree stumps still showing in the low grass. The sight reminded Paisen of her last experience at a prison colony, back on New Liberia – of hauling scrap through the irradiated city, and her encounter with the Warrior gang. She shook her head as if to clear away the memories.

Focus on the mission.

The convoy stopped at the camp's entrance, where two guards waved to Paisen in the passenger seat of the lead truck. She saluted them lazily, and they lowered an electrified net out of their path, swinging the gates open. The trucks drove down the main thoroughfare of the camp, inmates shuffling hurriedly out of their way. Paisen checked her mirror, and saw Tepper and Jacque jump casually off the back of the truck as they passed a row of barracks huts. The two men sauntered over to the nearest hut, and ducked inside.

"There's the motor pool," Paisen said, pointing out the windshield.

"I got it," Vence confirmed, her voice gruff and

masculine, in keeping with the male driver she had mimicked.

The vehicles made a slow loop of the parking area, and Paisen ensured they were parked facing back toward the camp's entrance. She swung her door open and stood, stretching slowly as if weary from a long journey.

"Found him," Tepper announced over the radio net. "Ready for extract."

Paisen ducked back into the jeep. "DNA match?"

"Confirmed, boss, it's him," Tepper said. "We're getting him into his guard uniform now."

"On our way," Paisen said. She whistled loudly, and the rest of the contractors turned to look at her. "Mount up," she said. "Change of orders."

There were a few convincing grumbles, but the team moved quickly, and the convoy pulled off again, retracing its steps. Paisen saw a man exit one of the administrative buildings up ahead of them. He flagged them down with a frown, and Paisen recognized him from the intelligence brief as the camp's commandant.

"Pull up a little farther, and then stop," Paisen muttered to Vence. She drew her sidearm and held it low in her lap, aiming it through the door. In her heads-up display, a red reticle appeared over the commandant's frowning eyebrows, wavering slightly as the jeep rocked to a stop.

"Where the hell are you going?" he asked. "You're supposed to replace Bravo Company for the next month."

She shrugged, and pointed at the jeep's radio. "Just got orders to report back to base," she told him. "Call it in if you want."

"Damn right I will," he seethed. "Don't go anywhere." He turned on his heel. Paisen caught movement in her rear-view mirror, and saw Tepper and Jacque escort their target out the barracks door. The commandant must have seen it too: he slowed and glanced toward the truck, where Jacque had stopped and cradled his hands, helping the target up into the bed of the truck. The man, looking gaunt and tired in his new guard uniform, looked up briefly, and then disappeared into the truck.

A flicker of recognition crossed the commandant's face.

Tepper leaned around the edge of the truck and shot him quickly and without ceremony, a single stun round in the middle of the chest. The suppressed weapon's noise registered as a loud cough, barely audible. The commandant tumbled forward onto the floor of the building's porch.

"Goddamn it!" Paisen swore.

"We're in," Tepper called, a second later.

"Nice and easy, head for the gate," Paisen ordered. "So far no one's noticed."

Vence started up again, glancing nervously up at the guard towers looming over them.

"Slow it down," Paisen told her. "We're not in a rush, remember?"

"Sure," Vence replied, easing off the accelerator.

"Be ready to go loud," Paisen told her team over the net. "Truck team, you suppress the towers. We'll handle the guards up here."

"Someone else just walked out of the commandant's office," Tepper reported.

Paisen rolled down her window as the jeep came to a stop at the gate. She grinned sheepishly at the two guards.

"Leaving already?" the nearest asked.

"Afraid so," she told him. She watched as his hand reached for the switch to open the gate. And then the alarm klaxon blasted out across the yard.

Paisen and Vence fired at nearly the same instant, their rounds punching through the jeep's armored sides. Paisen was out the door before the guards' bodies had hit the ground – she took three steps, slammed her hand down on the gate control lever, and the electric net swung down to the ground. Behind her, she heard Tepper's crew in the truck open up, auto-rifles peppering the guard towers with rounds.

"Go!" Paisen yelled, yanking the jeep door closed.

Vence floored it, and the vehicles raced across the open meadow, back toward the safety of the jungle. Paisen risked a glance back toward the camp, but Tepper had done his job well – neither guard tower was returning fire.

Which in no way makes up for the rest of the shit you've pulled on this mission, Tepp.

They had covered five of the six miles to the landing zone, bouncing haphazardly along the rough forest road, when the missile streaked in and hit the truck's cab, the explosion knocking the truck over onto its side. The sudden blast made Vence jerk the jeep's wheel, and the vehicle slammed hood-first into a tree trunk just off the side of the road.

"Jesus Christ!" Vence said.

"Get out!" Paisen yelled. "That came from a drone, there'll be more inbound." She released her seatbelt, wincing at the bruises it had left across her torso, and tumbled out her own door.

She pushed her way through a bush, then started toward the truck. *Gotta get to the target, get him out of here.*

She had taken no more than three steps when another missile hurtled in, and impacted the jeep directly behind her. The blast engulfed her, and her vision went dark.

2

His heads-up display flashed a proximity warning, and Rath pulled his air car over, parking at the side of the road. He pushed open the door and then stood, stretching and surveying the rolling cemetery grounds in front of him.

Last one, he thought. *Number 49.*

Technically, Senator Reid had been his final – and fiftieth – Guild-assigned kill. But Rath had visited Senator Reid's grave the week before, in order to save Arthin Delacourt III for last. His photographic memory surfaced the images of Delacourt's final moments: the Suspensys pod dropping from the spaceship's cargo hold, the old man sleeping peacefully under the clear canopy. The streak of orange-white flame as the pod hit Scapa's upper atmosphere, then broke up into flaming pieces. Rath shook his head.

It was quick, and he died in his sleep. I gave him that much, at least.

He set off across the manicured lawn, weaving his way between the granite headstones. The day was hot, consistent with Scapa's desert climate. Rath wondered how much water they needed to keep the grass in the cemetery green. He followed the map in his heads-up display toward Delacourt's grave, and noted that a middle-aged man was near the site already.

Someone else paying their respects, or visiting a loved one.

Rath zoomed in on his eye implants, frowning as he read the marker in front of the man.

That's Delacourt's grave.

He stopped at a random grave and knelt, keeping the man in his field of view, and pretending to clear a patch of overgrown grass from the base of the headstone in front him.

Bad timing. Guess I'll have to wait my turn.

As he watched, the man broke into a fit of sobs and leaned over, his hand on the top of the gravestone. Rath winced.

Watch him, he chided himself. *Look at what you caused.*

The man straightened after a time, and gave the headstone a final caress. "I miss you, Dad," he mumbled, but Rath's enhanced ears caught every word.

"Dad …?" That must be Delacourt's son. That's odd … I always assumed his son was the one who hired me, in order to get his inheritance.

The man headed off through the cemetery, toward his own vehicle, and Rath waited until the car was out of sight to stand and walk over to Delacourt's grave.

Lots of visitors today, old man. Rath knelt with a sigh. *I can't ask for your forgiveness … and you probably wouldn't give it, even if you could. But I am sorry for taking your life. I made some bad decisions, and now … well, now I think perhaps I should have let them kill me instead. I don't think my life is worth the lives of fifty others. So I'm sorry. All I can do is promise to make my life worthwhile now, to make your death – and Vonn's death, and all the others – mean something.*

Rath stood. "I don't know how I'm going to do that. But I'll try. I promise you that," he told the silent grave.

He turned and walked back to the air car, sweating in the afternoon heat. A hydration warning from his newly-installed hemobots flashed in his heads-up display, nagging him to drink more water. Rath silenced the notification, thinking instead about Delacourt's son. *If his son ordered the hit in order to get his father's fortune, why is he visiting his grave? What I saw didn't look like remorse ... it looked like genuine sadness.*

Rath shut the car door, and then flipped the air car's auto-pilot on. The engines hummed to life, and the car rose onto its hoverjets.

"University Hospital," he ordered.

"We will arrive in eighteen minutes in current traffic conditions," the car replied, spinning on its axis before gaining altitude.

Eighteen minutes. Then it's time to find out if Jaymy really loved me.

3

Patriarch Thomis Rewynn reached the top of the pulpit, and surveyed the congregation below, the thousands packed into their pews throughout the cathedral. The elderly priest's gnarled fingers gripped the marble on either side of the lectern, but he ignored the datascroll that held his notes. He knew what needed to be said.

"We live in the darkest time in mankind's history. The old ways are dying, forgotten amidst a torrent of mass media, instant gratification, and pop culture. Godlessness and corruption run rampant, to the highest levels of our government."

Rewynn eyed a portly middle-aged man in the front row, who sat between two Senate Guards. "But there are those who still stand up for tradition, like a beacon in a storm. Determined men, like Scapa's own senator, Gaspar Foss. Men who are willing to fight to restore the values we hold dear. Thank you, Senator, for all that you do. We're honored, as always, to have you with us."

The senator nodded gravely in reply.

"And what are those values? Three simple rules, you know them well. Repeat them with me."

As one voice, the congregation recited the litany with him: "Man chooses woman, woman serves man, and both serve God and Church."

"Yes," the Patriarch said, nodding. "It is the ancient way of humanity. A simple system that created the nuclear family, a perfect, self-contained unit. Until society abandoned it, replacing it with foolish notions that ignored millions of years of human evolution and biology, and led people astray."

He took a sip of water from a glass on the lectern, and then set the glass down.

"Many people think that our church's symbol features water because it is meant to represent our intent to purify society, to wash it clean of sin. Or, they say, it is the unstoppable tide of our advance. Perhaps it represents the lifewater we drink, the elixir that imbues us with God's powers. But those interpretations miss a key element of the symbol: there are *three* waves bisecting the circle. That is not a mistake. They symbolize those three values that you just recited. Man, wife, church … and God the circle that surrounds all. Simi Quorn passed these values down to us when he founded this great church nearly a hundred years ago. They're the same values that he had to rediscover, when his own life fell apart – divorced, an addict, a criminal, a con-man, the lowest of the low. But when God spoke to him, he listened. And he rejected the wickedness of his former life, and started a new life, and a new church. He knew that God was not only the path to redemption, but also to a higher order of consciousness.

"And you've all experienced it – here in God's house. When you drink his lifewater, you feel your mind expand, and grow. We feel closer to God in that instant, and capable of more than we ever thought possible – and we *are* capable of more. We are smarter, more dedicated, more moral beings – that is part of Simi's gift to us. To be better than the average human. We are his chosen children, and through the power he gives us, we can achieve miracles.

And we *must* achieve those miracles, for it is the only way we can save the galaxy from itself. From the wickedness that spreads, like a plague, across the galaxy."

He pointed at them, scowling. "You see that plague spreading every day. But ask yourself this: What have you done about it? Have you fought for our values, like Senator Foss? We are in a war over humanity's soul, and wars require sacrifices. So when you hear God's voice, telling you to take a stand … when the Church asks *you* to play *your* part … be sure you listen, and do your duty. God is watching, and he knows who is a faithful soldier in his crusade."

Rewynn turned and descended the steps, and made his way to the ceremonial well that stood at the front of the church. The congregation rose silently, expectant. At a signal from the Patriarch, an acolyte beside the well began turning a well-worn crank, and a series of buckets rose from the depths of the well, spilling a clear, sparkling liquid into a carved marble trough that ran for several yards along the front of the altar.

The old priest held his hands aloft. "Let us now drink of his lifewater, that we may believe again in the power of his teachings. In the power of ourselves. Simi brought us lifewater," he intoned.

"Through it we are cleansed, and transformed into a better version of ourselves," the masses responded. "We live to serve his values, and the Church."

Acolytes standing at the end of the pews directed the first row of seats to approach the well. Senator Foss was among them, though his Senate Guards remained seated in the pew. At the gate leading to the well, another set of acolytes received each church-goer's donation. Each person swiped their holophone across a reader device before being allowed onward. The senator paid his tithe, too, then knelt at the marble trough, and dipped his hand once in the ice-cold lifewater. He raised it to his lips and appeared to drink. Then he returned to his pew and sat, closing his eyes and breathing deeply.

The ceremony continued for close to an hour as each member of the congregation paid, passed through the gate, and took a drink at the well. As the line drew to an end, a whispered argument broke out between a disheveled-looking woman and the acolyte manning the payment reader station. Rewynn crossed over to them, frowning.

"What is the matter?" he asked, quietly, checking to ensure that his microphone was no longer live.

"Patriarch, this woman has no tithe for the church," the acolyte whispered, worry creasing his face.

"Where is your husband?" Rewynn asked the woman. "Surely he can pay for you?"

"He left me, sir," the woman protested. "He renounced the Church, but I would not." Rewynn's scowl deepened. The woman's eyes were desperate, roving – the old priest had seen it before. "I tried to get the money in time, I really did. But the Church says I'm not allowed to have a job. And without my husband—"

"Without your husband, you are of no use to the Church," Rewynn told her curtly, cutting her off. "Find him and bring him back, and once your family is whole again, *then* you may return."

"I don't know where he is – I think he left the planet," she replied.

"Then find another husband, and recruit him into the Church," Rewynn told her, impatiently.

The woman eyed the lifewater thirstily. "May I drink again? It would give me the power I need to find him."

"No," Rewynn told her. He gestured to several acolytes who were watching over the people drinking at the well. "See her out, immediately."

The woman broke into a wail of dismay, but the acolytes ignored her, and took her under the arms, dragging her down the church's aisle. The great doors slammed shut a moment later, silencing her crying.

* * *

Rewynn showed no hint of surprise when he entered his private office and found Senator Foss seated in a deep leather armchair, waiting for him. The senator wore a well-tailored suit that nevertheless stretched tight across his ample belly, and his hair was thinning and greying at the temples.

"Gaspar," the priest said, by way of greeting. "How are things proceeding at Anchorpoint?"

"Slowly," Foss replied, with a grunt. "The NeoPuritan coalition is still too few in number. We just aren't a big enough voting bloc to sway policy."

"The numbers will come, in time," Rewynn stated. He sat down behind his desk, and sighed.

"I'm going to try to elevate our visibility," Foss told him. "I'm making a play for membership on the Intelligence Committee."

Rewynn raised a single grey eyebrow. "That would be quite a coup."

"It would be. I think it's achievable, but it will take some maneuvering."

"And some funding?" Rewynn asked.

"Potentially," Foss replied. "I'll let you know."

Rewynn shrugged. "The Church stands ready to aid you, as ever."

"I obtained a copy of the classified report on the Janus Group," Foss said, changing subjects.

"And?" Rewynn asked.

"And I'm concerned that Contractor 621 will come back to Scapa," Foss said.

"Why would he come back?"

"A woman," Foss said. "According to the detective who aided him, 621 carried a necklace that he had purchased for a woman he met. He intended to find her again."

"You think he means to give it to the nurse he met

here?" Rewynn dismissed the notion with a wave of his hand. "That necklace could be for any number of women, on a thousand planets."

"No," Foss said. "My friend, it was a multi-colored crystal bead necklace, quite distinctive."

Rewynn stroked the wood desktop in front of him idly. "One of those trinkets they sell to tourists at the Rainbow Desert?"

"That is my fear. If he returns, he could uncover the role we played in his assignment here."

Rewynn pursed his lips. "Are you sure you're not being paranoid, my friend?"

"Just prudent," Foss protested. "Remember, this man exposed the Janus Group, and brought the entire organization to its knees. We should not underestimate him. And we don't know what the Group told him."

"They told him nothing but what he needed to know, and certainly not who hired him," Rewynn scoffed. "That's how the Janus Group has always operated."

"I hope so," Foss agreed, unconvinced.

Rewynn examined the senator. "You're still worried," he observed. "Gaspar, I agree that there is some risk. But he's still a guildsman, with all of their abilities. We can't exactly follow every male traveler that arrives on Scapa carrying a backpack."

"We could put surveillance on the nurse."

Rewynn considered this in silence, then nodded. "Very well. I have an acolyte-in-training who would be ideal. He'll shadow her, and keep us apprised of her activities."

"And if 621 does return?"

"We'll dispose of him."

4

"All systems are online. The prototype is ready."

The old man seated at the ship's command station looked up slowly, and then cleared his throat.

"Initiate the test," he growled.

The technician turned back to his console and entered a command into the computer. On the ship's viewscreen, a live-streamed image of a factory appeared, two silent smokestacks rising from a jumble of run-down buildings squatting in the midst of a grassy plain.

"Precision kinetic darts launched," the technician reported. "Impact in thirty seconds."

The old man focused his gaze on the factory. His eyes caught movement – a truck had appeared on the viewscreen, approaching the factory's gate in the distance. The technician saw it, too, and glanced at the old man questioningly. The man wavered for a minute, and then shrugged.

"Proceed with the test," he said.

* * *

The truck slowed to a stop at the closed gate. Beyond the fence, the abandoned factory's twin smokestacks loomed high in the cloudy sky. The passenger hopped down, jogging around the cab of the truck and pulling at the gate.

"It's locked," the man reported, letting the heavy chains drop back into place.

The driver of the truck grunted. "I got a key right here. Hop back in."

The driver waited until his passenger had clambered back into the cab, then slowly drove forward, pushing against the gate with the grill of the truck. The padlocked chains held, but the chain-link fence itself quickly bent under the pressure, and the truck rolled over the collapsed fence a moment later. The driver accelerated on toward the factory.

"Radiation readings still pretty low," the passenger commented. "Surprised no one's tried scavenging this place yet."

"It used to be a chemical plant," the driver explained. "That probably scared 'em off."

With an ear-splitting shriek, a tight cluster of objects rained down onto the buildings ahead of them, throwing off sprays of sparks as they tore through the metal roof of the factory. One of the objects punched a neat hole through a brick chimney and then slammed into the cracked pavement ahead of the truck, throwing up a cloud of dust. The driver pumped the brakes instinctively.

"What the fuck!"

The dust settled, and the two men saw a deformed metal dart at the center of the impact crater. As they watched, the metal began to glow: red at first, then white-hot.

And then everything went black.

* * *

On the viewscreen, the factory appeared to shudder, and then the buildings erupted in a massive explosion. A split second later, the explosion's shockwave reached the camera's location, and promptly knocked the recording device over, sending it tumbling through the grasses of the plain. When it came to rest, it showed a massive plume of dust and smoke. There was no sign of the factory.

"Well?" the old man asked.

"We'll need to analyze the readings, sir," the technician reported. "But it looks like several kilotons in yield for each dart. The device is as powerful as advertised."

The old man rubbed his chin. "That's the final piece, then," he said. "Recover the surveillance drones, and then prepare for our next FTL jump."

"Yes, sir."

The old man stood slowly, wincing as he straightened. "And wake the other council members," he said.

"Which ones, sir?"

"All of them."

* * *

Through the binoculars, the woman watched as the sheriff gathered up the yellow tape marked *POLICE* that had cordoned off the burned hulk of the truck, and then stuffed it into a plastic trash bag. The sheriff threw the bag into the bed of his truck, then climbed in and started up. He was out of sight less than a minute later.

The woman tucked a stray strand of curly black hair behind her ear, and refocused the binoculars. She scanned the ruined factory again, slowly working over the crumbled buildings, searching for any signs of movement. Satisfied, she stood, brushing dried grass from her utility coveralls and slipping the binoculars around her neck. She pulled the camouflage netting off of her hoverbike, folding it and tucking it into one of the bike's saddle bags. Then she righted the vehicle, levering it off of the grassy plain, and swung her leg over and throttled up. As she approached the ruins, she checked the pistol in her hip holster, reflexively.

She parked next to the truck and pulled out her holophone, starting up the phone's camera.

"Video evidence log: September eighth, 2415. Detective Atalia il-Singh reporting. Southern hemisphere of New Liberia, grid coordinates M 782 003. Former chemical factory." She panned the phone over the ruined buildings. "Will submit photo and chemical analysis in addition to this log. Factory has recently sustained massive damage from an explosion of unknown origins, on the order of a nuclear weapon, but no radiological after-effects are present. Local law enforcement believes a chemical reaction from materials remaining inside the factory may have caused the blast, but I don't agree with their assessment. Aerial imagery suggests external explosions." She walked around the truck, stopping at a large crater in the road in front of it. "And this crater was clearly caused by a high angle impact, something dense traveling at high velocity."

She swung the phone around to capture the destroyed truck. "Two men were killed during the explosion; they appear to be scavengers, likely searching for scrap metal."

She zoomed in on the crater. "In short, I'm filing this report in accordance with recent instructions to investigate any and all large explosions in our assigned areas. If you can give me a bit more context around that order, like *why* I'm doing this, I can do follow-up work as needed. Until then, I'm returning to my regular assignment."

She stopped the recording, encrypted the file, and then sent it via email to her supervisor.

Now maybe I can get back to doing actual work.

5

Dasi slid the magazine into the pistol and pulled back on the slide, chambering a round. She lifted the weapon, gripping it tightly between her hands, and aligned the front and rear sight posts over the man's silhouette. Wincing, she pulled the trigger. The gun roared, and she let the barrel drop, squinting to see down the range. A small hole had perforated the paper target several inches to the right of the illustrated man's torso.

"You're jerking the trigger," a gruff voice said from behind her, shouting to be heard over the din of other recruits firing.

"What?" Dasi asked, sliding the ear cups off her ears and turning around.

"Keep your weapon pointed down range, Cadet!"

Dasi started, and reacted automatically, turning back to face the target.

"Jesus Christ, Apter. Pay attention. And keep your ear protection on."

"Yes, sir," she sighed.

"You're jerking the trigger," the instructor repeated. "Just squeeze it. Gently, slowly."

"Yes, sir." *How did I ever manage to hit Contractor 700?* she wondered. It seemed like a lifetime ago that she had stood in the senator's office, picked up the pistol, and saved Paisen's life. *It was a lifetime ago.* Her shoulders slumped as she contemplated the target. *I thought maybe a life in the Interstellar Police would be a new start … but it's not what I expected.*

"Whenever you're ready, Cadet Apter," the instructor said, testily.

Dasi lifted the pistol again, and slowly squeezed the trigger for what felt like a lifetime. Finally, the gun bucked in her hand, and another hole appeared in the target. This time, it was to the left of the silhouette, and low.

"Yeah, the trigger pull was good, but you forgot about your sight picture this time," the instructor said, exasperated. "Try again."

The pistol was heavy in her hands – her muscles were still sore from the morning's physical training session. Her stomach grumbled, too, in hunger. It was nearly noon, but she had been up for seven hours already, and breakfast had been a long time ago. Something about the non-stop activity and stress of training made her hungry constantly, but she knew the food awaiting her at lunch was a far cry from what she would have found in the senate cafeteria where she used to eat.

Dasi concentrated on the target again, calming her breathing, and lined up the sights. *Okay, now pull – squeeze – the trigger.* She squeezed slowly, but the gun began to waver in her grip, her tired muscles struggling to hold it rigid in front of her. She hurried to squeeze the trigger before her arms gave out, and the gun fired.

"Where did that one even go?" the instructor asked, rhetorically. "I don't think you were even on the paper. Again."

Dasi felt tears brimming in her eyes, behind the plastic safety glasses. *Don't you cry,* she chided herself. *Not again.*

"Cadet Apter!" Her platoon's command instructor

appeared at her lane. Dasi kept the gun pointed at the target this time, and looked over her shoulder.

"Sir?" Dasi asked.

"Phone call for you. You can take it in the Range Safety office."

"For me?" Dasi asked, confused. *Only my parents know I'm here, and I spoke to them last night.*

"Did I stutter?" The command instructor frowned. "Go. Be back in five minutes."

"Yes, sir," Dasi said, relieved to have a brief respite. She put the pistol down on the lane's tabletop and turned to leave.

"Clear that weapon!" the command instructor thundered.

"Yes, sir," Dasi said. Trembling, she dropped the magazine out of the chamber – it fell on the floor. She hurried to pick it up, and then completed clearing the weapon. She looked at the instructors when she had finished.

"What do you want, a medal? Your weapon is clear, now go!"

"Yes, sir," Dasi said. She jogged past several lanes of fellow cadets, who were all firing steadily into their targets.

In the range's office, Dasi found a desk phone showing a line on hold. She sat at the desk and picked up the headset, touching the screen to take the call.

"Cadet Apter," she said, through force of habit.

"Dasi Apter?" a woman's voice asked.

"Yes, speaking," Dasi said. "Who is this?"

"Hi, this is Marga, I'm an artificial intelligence customer service avatar at CloudBase Storage. Miss Apter, I'm calling because your ninety day free trial is about to expire next week."

"My what …?" Dasi asked. "What company did you say you were with?"

"CloudBase Storage," the avatar repeated.

"I've never heard of you," Dasi said. "I'm sorry, I think

you must have the wrong person."

"Let me verify that," the avatar said. "Dasi Apter, Apartment 119B, Portside Bay 4, Anchorpoint?"

That's my old address, Dasi realized, frowning. "Yes, that's me. But how did you reach me here?"

"Your contact information was recently updated. Let me just take a minute to walk you through our storage tiers. You're currently using a little over six hundred terabytes of data, so that would place you in our Enterprise Silver Tier, which is five hundred dollars per month. That comes with unlimited read and write access—"

"How much am I storing?" Dasi asked, confused.

"Six hundred terabytes," the avatar repeated.

"I think someone may have stolen my identity," Dasi said, rubbing her forehead. "I honestly have no recollection of ever using your service. I don't know what all of that data could be."

"Did you lose your login credentials, ma'am?" the avatar asked. "I can send those to the email address we have on file: dasi-dot-apter-at-memail-dot-com?"

"That's my email," Dasi said. "But I still don't—"

"I've sent a temporary password to that address, along with a link to your files. May I take the liberty of sending along a few digital brochures, as well? Then you can review our storage plans in more detail at your leisure, and decide which you'd like to purchase in the future."

"Okay," Dasi said.

"Great! You can contact me by clicking on the link in those emails, at any time, day or night. Do you have any other questions at this time?"

So many questions, Dasi thought. She checked her watch. *Gotta get back to the range.* "Ah … no. No more questions."

"Well then, thank you for choosing CloudBase for your storage needs. We appreciate your business."

"Sure, thanks," Dasi said, hanging up.

What the hell was that?

* * *

Dasi let the hot water pummel her back, closing her eyes and savoring the feeling as some of the soreness left her aching body. Beside her, one of her fellow cadets laughed, sharing a joke with another of the women in their platoon.

"Lights out in fifteen," a voice called.

I used to look forward to my shower every day. Now it's just another chore that takes away from time I could be sleeping.

Dasi flipped the water off and grabbed her towel, drying off as she made her way through the bathroom. She slipped into her pajamas in the changing area, and then hurried to the upper floor of their barracks, padding quietly down the center of the bay in her flip-flops, until she reached her bunk. She stowed her towel in her wall locker, hanging it over a clothes hanger in the vain hope that it would dry overnight. Then she pulled out the battered datascroll the Academy had issued her, and lied down on her bunk, propping her pillow up behind her.

She opened the study guide labeled *Arrest Procedures*, but after nearly ten minutes of reading, she realized she was nodding off, reading the same passage over and over in her exhaustion. She sighed, and moved to turn off the device, then paused. On impulse, she opened the web browser, and accessed her email account. A new message from Marga at CloudBase was waiting for her.

Dasi copied the temporary password, and then opened the link, logging into the account. She frowned at the screen, scrolling for several seconds across what looked like hundreds of files. She stopped scrolling, and peered more closely at the screen, reading several of the file names. *Interplanetary Census from Year 2400. Galactic Weather Aggregation Bureau – Historical Models. Federacy Budget Breakdown – Fiscal Year 2410.*

Dasi shook her head. *What is this stuff? It just looks like random datasets. Definitely not my files.*

Dasi scrolled back to the top of the folder, and then sorted the files by date, but they all appeared to have been uploaded on the same date.

A couple months ago. Back when I was still in Anchorpoint.

She sorted by size next, and found a single file that took up several hundred terabytes of space. The file was labeled *5Sv11.3b*. Dasi clicked on the file.

A text reader program opened, showing a file full of unfamiliar words interspersed with brackets and special symbols.

I think that's programming language – code. It's some sort of program? She sighed. *I wish Khyron were here. He would know.* She felt a knot of grief rising in her throat, and took a deep breath. *Keep it together, Dasi. Remember why you're here.*

She thought back to the hotel room on Wayhaven, where she had watched as the media descended on Guild Headquarters. *I sent those reporters to Headquarters – and I knew they'd come looking for me as soon as they could. Beauceron promised me I wouldn't be arrested for my involvement in that whole thing, but … I killed a man! And I didn't want to be thrust into the limelight like Beauceron was.*

Sitting there on the floor of the hotel room, as a janitor worked to disassemble the desk Rath had handcuffed her to, she had recalled her conversation with Rath, back on the *Hurasu. Find a job where you can help people,* he had said. *That's what you got you into politics in the first place.* On the TV feed, Dasi had seen the police arrive on the scene at Headquarters, Beauceron among them, and she had had a sudden epiphany. *What better way to help people than becoming an Interstellar Police officer? And six months of training at the Academy is not a bad way to disappear for a while.*

In her barracks bunk, Dasi snorted at her own naiveté. *Brilliant idea, Dasi. You're worried about being arrested, so … go join the police?* And Academy life had been quite different from what she expected – she had thought it would be like college again, but it turned out to be a strange mix of exhausting, frustrating, and demeaning. *And hard. Much harder than I thought. Admit it, Dasi: this was a mistake.*

"Lights out!" an instructor called, and a second later, the lights were off. Dasi rolled up the datascroll, tucking it away on a shelf in her wall locker, and then slid under the covers, staring up through the gloom at the metal springs of the bunk above her. Down the bay, one of her classmates was already snoring loudly. Dasi was bone tired, but now that the lights were out, sleep eluded her. Tomorrow their training schedule included more range time, and Dasi felt her heart rate accelerate with anxiety.

I'm going to quit, she thought. *'Cause if I don't quit, I'm going to fail out anyway.*

6

Jaymy's shift in the Emergency Room ended in the early evening. Rath was reading a book on his datascroll at a bench across the street, but he caught sight of her exiting the hospital's main entrance with several other nurses. The women stopped and talked briefly, laughing, before heading their separate ways. Rath rolled up the datascroll and slid it into his pocket. He followed Jaymy as she walked, staying on the opposite side of the street to avoid detection, per his training.

She looks tired. Working in the E.R. is probably a tougher gig than working up at Suspensys.

She walked for several blocks, and then entered a bistro. Rath waited for a few minutes, but when she did not emerge, he crossed the street and pretended to study the restaurant's menu near the front door. Through the window, he saw Jaymy seated alone at a small table, ordering her dinner. Just to be safe, he slid an EMP grenade out of a pouch on the outside of his Forge, and tucked it into his jacket pocket. Rath took a final look at himself in the reflection of the bistro's window, checking that his facial features matched the ones of the cover identity he had used when he had first met Jaymy.

When you first seduced her, he corrected himself. *And tried to recruit her to be an accomplice to murder.*

Inside, the babble of voices threatened to overwhelm Rath's enhanced hearing – the bistro was nearly full from the dinner rush, and most of the tables were full of diners eating and talking. Rath dialed back his auditory implants, noting security cameras in two corners of the room. The maître d' asked for his name, and Rath pointed over at Jaymy's table.

"I'm joining someone," he said.

"Very well, sir."

He took a deep breath, and walked over to her table.

"Hi, Jaymy," he said.

She looked up, and shock and surprise registered on her face. "Rob …?"

"Can we talk?" Rath asked. He pulled the empty chair out, and raised an eyebrow.

"I don't know," she said.

"Jaymy, it's taken me months to work up the courage to come back here. To talk to you." Rath's mouth was dry. "I know you probably don't want anything to do with me, but I just want a chance to tell you the truth."

Her eyes narrowed, and she bit her lip. "How would I know you're telling the truth?" she asked.

"You'll know," Rath assured her. He sat, and let his Forge rest on the floor.

"You still carry that backpack everywhere, I see," she pointed out.

"Yeah," Rath said. He set a battered jewelry box on the table. "I carry this, too. I tried to give it to you."

"I remember," she said.

"It's a necklace that I bought for you," Rath continued. "From the time we visited the Rainbow Desert together."

"If you think some jewelry—" she started, but Rath held up his hand.

"No, I know. Just let me talk for a minute." He rubbed

at a stain on the table with his thumbnail. "Okay, here goes. My name's not Rob."

Jaymy crossed her arms. "You lied about your name, too? Somehow that doesn't surprise me."

He cocked an eyebrow at her, and dropped his voice. "My real name is Rath Kaldirim … but you've probably heard my other name on the news: Contractor 621."

Jaymy studied him for a second, and then sighed, shaking her head sadly. "Thank you."

"What do you mean?" Rath asked.

"I spent a while trying to get over you, Rob … or Rath, or whatever you want to be called. When you walked back in here, it brought all those emotions flooding back, and I thought, 'Well, Jaymy, you're clearly *still* not over him.' But now that you've reminded me what a colossal liar you are, I think I'm finally done with all that. So thank you for giving me that closure."

"I'm telling the truth," Rath protested.

"Really?" she asked. "With all the lies you've told, now you expect me to believe that you're the famous guildsman that was all over the news?" She snorted. "Prove it."

Rath's mind raced. *Shit. I kind of figured she would just believe me.* He glanced around the restaurant to ensure that no one else was watching, and then slid the grey counter bracelet past the end of his sleeve and triggered it, watching as the golden '50' appeared in the air above it, rotating.

"I don't know what that is," Jaymy said.

Rath shut it off as a waiter approached them carrying a plate of food. He set it in front of Jaymy.

"Can I get you anything?" he asked Rath.

"No," Rath shook his head. "Thanks." The waiter headed back to the kitchen. "That was my counter bracelet. The Guild gave them to us to help us track our kills. Jaymy, I *am* a guildsman. Or I was. That's why I approached you – I needed to recruit you to kill Delacourt for me. Why do you think you got fired from Suspensys?"

"I didn't get fired, they had a round of layoffs after the break-in, and I volunteered to go. I wasn't all that happy there to begin with."

"Oh," Rath said. "Are you happy now?"

"I'm pretty happy, yeah. I'm doing what I was trained to do – helping the sick and injured. Not just watching over a bunch of sleeping billionaires."

"Did they interview you about the break-in?" Rath asked. "About me?"

"Yes," she admitted. "The cops interviewed all employees, and asked if anyone had approached us before the attack. I told them about you. They asked me to let them know if I saw you again. Which I'm seriously considering doing," she noted.

Rath ignored her remark. "Why do you think they asked you to do that?"

She shrugged. "They thought you might have been involved. But that doesn't prove that you *were* involved, or that you're the rogue guildsman on the news."

"Okay, how about this," Rath said. "About a month before we met, did Suspensys suddenly roll out mandatory cyber-security training? Did they ban the use of all plug-in data drives on the station?"

Jaymy frowned. "Yes."

"And they fired a janitor, too. That's because I hired him and tried to hack into the Suspensys computers."

"If you say so," Jaymy said, still unconvinced. "That still doesn't prove anything."

"It proves I know an awful lot about what happened at Suspensys during that time." Rath gave her a half-smile. "Try this: the security personnel on the station got in a gunfight with the attacker, when he broke in. They shot him twice: in the right leg, and the left shoulder."

"Okay, but that was on the news. Everyone knows that."

Rath pulled his shirt to the side, exposing a faint scar on his left shoulder. "You want to see the one on my leg, too?"

Jaymy's frown deepened.

"You still don't believe me," Rath stated.

"What would you think, if you were in my shoes? What's more plausible: that I dated a famous secret assassin, or that I dated a pathological liar?"

Rath glanced around the bistro at the other diners, and the security cameras on the walls. "I could shift my appearance, but … not here. Not in public."

Jaymy squirmed in her seat. Her plate of food sat cooling in front of her, untouched. "Let's suppose, for a second, that you are who you say you are. And just to be clear, I still don't think you're telling the truth. But hypothetically, if you were being honest: what did you think I would say?"

"I don't know," Rath admitted. "I was hoping it would help you understand why I did what I did. I didn't have a choice. The rules are: you have to complete your mission, or they kill you. I'm not saying it was right, but … I seduced you because I had to. And I wish I could change that. I wanted you to know that I *did* love you – I still do."

"I loved you, too," Jaymy said, her voice softening. "But … now you're either the galaxy's biggest liar, or a serial killer. And I don't know which is worse."

"Being a killer is worse," Rath said, grimacing. "Trust me."

"Yeah, probably." Jaymy studied him for a minute. "I get the sense that you wanted this to be a big moment, like you could swoop in and confess, and suddenly everything would be different."

"I was hoping …," Rath admitted, with a faint smile.

"Yeah, that's how men always think, isn't it? You sit there day-dreaming about the girl being kidnapped by the villain, so you can ride in and rescue her, or make some grand heroic gesture that proves how much you've changed. That's not real life, Rath. This is real life: I'm tired from a long shift, and tired of trying to sort through the lies. And I think you should go."

The door to the bistro chimed as it opened, and Rath glanced over on instinct. Four burly men had entered the restaurant, brushing the maître d' aside with annoyance. The leading man's eyes were focused on Rath, and his right hand was hidden in his jacket pocket.

"Jaymy," Rath said, keeping his voice even. "Get up now and walk quickly to the kitchen. There's an exit through the back of the restaurant into an alley."

"What?" she said. She glanced over at the entrance, and saw the men approaching. Rath stood and took her hand, roughly pulling her to her feet.

"Ow!" she exclaimed. Several diners turned to look at them.

"Go now, and don't look back," Rath hissed. He gave Jaymy a firm shove, and she cried out again, stumbling toward the back of the bistro.

The men arrived a second later, and arranged themselves in a loose circle around Rath. Jaymy took several more steps backwards and then stopped, confusion writ plain on her face.

"Hey, buddy," the leader told Rath, grinning. "We've got the van outside, we've been waiting for you! Come on, we're going to be late."

An awkward silence settled over the restaurant, as the other customers turned to see the source of the commotion. "Gentlemen," Rath said. "I don't know how much you're being paid, but I guarantee you I can pay a lot more."

The leader shook his head, an exaggerated smile still plastered on his sweat-streaked face. "What are you talking about? Come on, the show starts soon – we gotta go." Around his neck, the man wore a gold chain, from which dangled a small symbol that Rath did not recognize: a circle with three lines running horizontally across it. The lines were curved, with peaks and troughs, like ocean waves.

"You want me to get the girl?" a man behind Rath asked. The leader frowned, and cast a glance at Jaymy.

"I'll go with you," Rath cut in. "Leave her out of this."

"Get her, too," the leader decided.

"You guys really fucked up," Rath warned him. "Last chance: leave her, take me, and everyone can all just go back to eating." He glanced at the restaurant's cameras again, slipping his hand inside his jacket pocket and triggering the EMP grenade.

"I don't think so, asshole," the leader replied. He nodded at his companion, and the man started toward Jaymy.

Rath sighed. *Fuck.*

"Interstellar Police, everybody freeze!" A diner across the restaurant stood up suddenly, brandishing a badge and an auto-pistol.

An off-duty cop? Are you serious?! Rath thought, but the leader was already drawing his own pistol from inside his jacket. Rath grabbed the nearest man by the collar and dropped to the floor, twisting and using his own downward momentum to pull the man with him, and smash him head-first into the table as he fell. A series of shots rang out, and his enhanced hearing estimated the shooter's location on his heads-up display – the cop had opened fire. *Let's hope he got at least one of them.* Rath jumped up to a crouch and struck out with one leg, sweeping the legs out from under another of the attackers, and following it with a swift punch to the man's throat as he hit the floor. Then he grabbed a dinner knife off the table, and turned to see the final attacker lunging at him with a viciously-serrated knife. Rath had just enough time to block the thrust, turning it away with a forearm, and then he stabbed the man in the gut. He finished the would-be kidnapper with a brutal elbow to the face, knocking him to the ground.

Rath turned slowly and surveyed the room. All four kidnappers were on the floor – in addition to the three he had incapacitated, the cop's rounds had killed the leader, Rath saw. His eyes met Jaymy's. Her face was a mask of fear and shock. Rath looked at the cop next. His weapon was trained firmly on Rath.

"Put the knife down," the cop said.

<Laceration on left forearm> Rath's heads-up display noted. Rath set the dinner knife on the table and picked up a cloth napkin, wrapping it expertly around his arm and tying a knot with his teeth. His hemobots had already started a rapid clotting procedure; the wound would be fully healed by the end of the day.

"This cut looks serious," he lied to the cop. "I better get to a hospital." He took a step backwards, toward the door.

The cop shook his head. "Ambulance will be here soon. I think you better stay right there."

"I didn't kill them. I was just defending myself," Rath noted.

"I know," the cop said. "Now just stand still, you're making me nervous."

Rath glanced carefully around the room, weighing his options. The cop had a clear field of fire on Rath all the way to the front entrance, and stood between Rath and the rear entrance. Rath spotted the pistol the leader had dropped on the floor on the other side of the table. He sighed.

I'm not going to kill him.

A moment later, three Interstellar Police cruisers pulled up outside the bistro, their blue-and-red siren lights casting eerie shadows around the inside of the dimly lit restaurant.

Fuck.

One of the men at his feet groaned in pain, and Rath looked down. *What the hell did you idiots want? My money? To hold me for ransom? Or just revenge for one of my kills? And how did you find me?* He noted a splash of blood along the floor, from the knife wound in his forearm. *My blood. The same blood I spilled here on Suspensys a few months ago, with the same*

DNA in it, that's undoubtedly stored in the police database.

Shit.

7

The simulator's hatch swung open. Paisen sighed heavily and finished unbuckling her straps, then pushed herself out of the pod gently, floating into the zero-gravity of the simulation room. Around her, a dozen pods filled the chamber, some still rotating quietly as the other team members continued the exercise without her. Paisen's back still ached from the simulated blast of the missile that had "killed" her. She shot a dark look at one of the other simulator pods in the room, and then glided across the room, pulling herself hand-over-hand up a ladder, and finally stepping out into the artificial gravity of the briefing room.

Vence was waiting for her, the younger woman's short, lithe form hunched in one of the swivel chairs circling the room's holographic observation table.

"That second missile got you, too?" Vence asked.

"Yeah," Paisen growled.

"First time you've been killed on a training mission," Vence noted. "Tepper's getting smoked when he gets out." She twisted the chair slowly from side to side.

Paisen ignored the comment and strode over to the

table, activating the hologram. A top-down view of the vehicle convoy in the jungle appeared. Paisen watched silently as the mission continued, looking up only briefly to acknowledge four other contractors as they entered – casualties from the first missile strike on the truck, she guessed. All wore the same black simulator suits studded with fibrous wires and muscles. They avoided Paisen's glare and joined Vence in the chairs, watching the battle. The hologram flashed orange as another missile struck the rear jeep, but this time, the contractors riding in it had already evacuated.

Tepper managed to rally the surviving team members behind the burning truck, and they downed the drone with a well-coordinated volley of rifle fire on its next pass. But the drone had served its purpose: all three vehicles were destroyed, and Tepper spent too long treating the wounded and regrouping the survivors. Paisen watched as reinforcements from the camp arrived on the scene – several companies' worth of infantrymen, spread out in a line formation, threatening to encircle the tight knot of contractors left to protect the target.

Tepper split his team, throwing smoke grenades to conceal two contractors as they escaped through the jungle, headed for the landing zone, escorting the target between them. Tepper and four of the survivors remained behind, and fought a surprisingly effective rear guard action that dragged on for nearly an hour before the final contractor was killed. In the running battle, the enemy rifle companies took heavy casualties, and were left with barely two squads between them.

But we lost nearly the entire team. And in the real world, I doubt Tepper would have so much enthusiasm for a sacrificial last stand.

Tepper, flushed with exertion, emerged from the simulator room moments later.

"Hell of a fight!" he exulted.

"Sit," Paisen said, icily.

Tepper winced and took a chair, along with the final

two contractors.

"Give me three 'Sustains,' " Paisen said.

"We got the target out, mission accomplished," Tepper noted, hopefully.

"Anyone besides Tepper?"

Vence raised her hand. "Good violence of action in the initial ambush."

"True," Paisen allowed.

"The camp infiltration was pretty smooth, up until we picked up the target," said Rika, a female contractor sitting near the back. "And we maintained good discipline during the retreat from the drone attack."

"Yes," Paisen said. "You did. Let's switch to 'Improves.' " She eyed Tepper meaningfully.

He wiped sweat from his brow. "After the drone attack, I should have put up a micro-drone for security. I would have had early warning on the enemy troops."

Paisen crossed her arms. "And?" she asked.

Tepper frowned. "… and we might have been able to ambush them on their way in, or break contact altogether and get everyone to the landing zone."

"You don't want to talk about shooting the camp commandant?" Paisen pressed him. "The decision that alerted the entire camp to our presence?"

"I don't think I had a choice," he protested.

"You always have a choice," Paisen shot back. "And that was the wrong one."

"What would you have done?" he asked.

"I would have waited," Paisen said. "That's the one thing none of you have learned yet: tactical patience. Just because you have a weapon doesn't mean you should use it. Violence of action is good," she looked at Vence, "but it's only effective when it's applied at the exact right place and time. Sometimes you need to let the situation develop."

She cued up the replay on the hologram above the table, zooming in close on the commandant's avatar.

"This is the moment Tepper fired his shot," she told them. "He saw the commandant recognize the target for an instant, so he took him down preemptively. But look at the commandant's feet."

The young contractors leaned in for a closer look.

"A person's feet often telegraph their intentions – if you watch them, you can see where that person is headed next. And the commandant had already decided to head inside. He had decided that he couldn't have seen a prisoner in a guard uniform."

She reached into the hologram, and tapped on the commandant, allowing the simulation to continue his programmed movements, as if he had not been shot. The man hesitated for a moment, and then walked back inside the building.

"You pulled the trigger too soon," Paisen concluded. "Patience would have saved us."

Tepper looked at the floor. "Sorry," he said.

"And even if the commandant had decided to investigate the target before going inside," Paisen said, "we still could have used that to our advantage. How?" She scanned the room. To her left, a young man raised his hand. "Yes, Huawo."

"Tepp and Jacque could have let him walk over, shot him behind the cover of the truck, then tossed him inside the truck."

"Bingo," Paisen nodded. "And instead of the company commander, I could have mimicked the camp commandant in the lead jeep, and the gate guards wouldn't have stopped us at all." She swiped away the hologram, and straightened up. "Go get chow, but be back here in thirty for another mission brief. I bought us forty more hours in the simulator and I intend to use all of them in the next two days."

The contractors groaned and stood on weary feet, heading for the space station's main corridor.

"You stay, Tepper," Paisen said.

He nodded and sat back down heavily on his swivel chair. The corridor hatch closed behind the last of the team members a minute later.

"You're regretting making me your executive officer," he said, sighing.

"You're goddamn right I am," she growled. "But I'm stuck with you now. And you've got more actual mission time than any of the rest of them."

"Eleven kills for the Guild," he said, shrugging. "It's nowhere near fifty."

"The rest of the team only has two or three each," she pointed out. "Wick didn't even get one; he was fresh out of Training. They need someone with experience to lead them, if I go down."

"But they're all Level One contractors, just like you and me. They're just as good, they just didn't get the chance to prove it. And I keep proving I'm a fuck-up."

"You keep taking unnecessary risks," she corrected. She leaned back, sitting against the edge of the table. "Tepper, why did you volunteer for this team? The others weren't in the Guild long enough to make much money. But you've got a nice little nest egg."

"Not as nice as you," he said, smiling slowly.

"No," she said. "But more than enough to just fuck around for the rest of your life, and not have to worry about anything. So why join up?"

"Why did you start the team?" he asked, by way of reply. "You've got even more to lose than I do."

"Reasons," Paisen told him, glaring. "Now answer my question: why are you here?"

Tepper blushed. "I wanted to meet you," he said. "I wanted to study a legend. I was bored doing nothing … but mostly I just wanted to be part of whatever you're doing. It's the same for most of them," he gestured at the bulkhead, in the direction of the other contractors. "They all idolize you. We'd follow you anywhere."

"Jesus Christ," Paisen said, scowling. "I founded my

own fucking fan club."

"You founded the most effective espionage and direct action team in the galaxy," Tepper corrected her. "And we're ready to prove it. We're ready for a real mission."

"We're ready when I say we're ready," Paisen told him. "And tonight, instead of your sleep cycle, you're going to write out a letter to every team member's family and friends, apologizing for getting that teammate killed on our last mission."

Tepper sighed. "What family?" he asked. "None of us have a family. The Guild didn't even let us have any friends."

"Then you're going to address those letters to all of us – the whole team. We're each other's family now. And a family needs solid leadership. So Tepper, you better start stepping up your game."

"Yes, ma'am," he said.

"They like you. A lot," she admitted. "But liking is not the same as trusting. They will follow you," she continued. "But you have to earn it."

8

Atalia recognized him at once from the newscasts. She swore with feeling.

He's not even in disguise. This clumsy asshole is going to blow my cover not two minutes after arriving on-planet.

She watched as Beauceron walked over to the pre-determined meeting spot, a coffee kiosk in the spaceport arrivals hall. Instead of joining him, however, she walked in the opposite direction, heading out to the parking garage. She found her air car and opened the door, taking a seat behind the wheel. Then she waited.

Her phone rang ten minutes later.

"Yes?" she asked.

"Where are you? I've got your contact on the other line, he's saying you're late for the rendezvous."

"Put me through to him," she replied.

She heard an electronic tone, and then a new voice. "Am I in the wrong place?" Beauceron asked.

"No," she told him testily. "I saw you. Come out to the garage, aisle P4."

"Okay—," he said, but she was already hanging up.

A minute later, he walked into view in her side mirror.

She glanced around the garage, ensuring they were alone. Then she blinked her hazard lights, once. Beauceron saw the signal and rolled his suitcase over to the car. He stowed the luggage in the trunk, and let himself in the passenger side door.

"What was wrong with the original meeting spot?" he asked, buckling himself in.

"Didn't they tell you to travel incognito?" she asked, by way of reply. "I picked the coffee shop because I figured you'd be wearing a disguise."

"No one said anything about a disguise to me," Beauceron said. "I'm sorry, I haven't traveled to the Territories on official business before. Last time I was here on New Liberia, I didn't use a disguise."

"Yeah, well, last time you weren't the most famous cop in the galaxy. Jesus," she swore. "Even if no one told you, you should have figured it out."

"I should have," Beauceron agreed. "I don't know much about how you undercover agents operate in the Territories."

"Carefully, that's how we operate. We look for fugitives hiding out here, we try to keep tabs on criminal activity, and we keep a low profile. This isn't a Federacy planet, remember. We're not even supposed to be here."

Beauceron was silent. Atalia maneuvered the car out of the garage, then pulled back on the wheel, rising above the rooftops of the city, before setting a new, southerly course.

"This is the second time I've had to drop my surveillance assignment for this bullshit," she pointed out. "Every time makes it more likely either the criminals I'm following spot me, or local law enforcement does."

"I am sorry," Beauceron said. "It wasn't my call to pull you from your assignment. I'm just here because they told me to come."

She scowled again, then sighed. "I'm Atalia."

"Martin," Beauceron said, shaking her hand. "Thank you for babysitting me." He gestured to the trunk. "I have a hat in my suitcase, actually."

Atalia grunted. "It's not much of a disguise, but it's a start." She handed him a pair of sunglasses from the car's console. "You can wear these, too. There shouldn't be anyone at the factory, though – it's pretty isolated."

"I read your report," Beauceron said. "You were right to send it in."

"Was I? I still have no idea what this is all about," she said. "I keep asking and they keep telling me it's classified."

"It is. It's one of the few things from this Guild mess that the public doesn't know about."

"How is this related to the Guild thing?"

"I'm not sure that it is," Beauceron said.

* * *

Atalia circled the factory once, scanning it with the air car's thermal sensors. Aside from a few rodents, they picked up no signs of life. She pointed out the impact craters from the air, and then set down by the factory gate and the burned truck. The two detectives climbed out, and Atalia followed Beauceron. He squatted next to the impact crater first.

"You're right about the high angle," he mused, eyeballing the cracked pavement. "It penetrated deeply before exploding. It might have been a PKD."

"What's a 'PKD?' " Atalia asked.

"Precision Kinetic Dart," Beauceron said. "Like a metal rod, with a guidance system installed. They're a space-based weapon, used in orbital assaults." He stood up. "The guildsmen I worked with used them when we raided the Guild training facility on Fusoria."

"They were both here with you on New Liberia, too – right?"

"Yes," Beauceron agreed. "They were."

"Well, that's an odd coincidence," Atalia noted.

"I fear it's not the only one." Beauceron walked over to the truck. He peered at the burned frame, leaning in close to study it. "Who were the men in the truck?"

"John Does. Bodies were shredded, and their DNA isn't on file anywhere. This is the Territories, after all. I think they just had really bad luck – wrong place, wrong time. Best guess: they were scavengers. Half of New Liberia's economy is dependent on guys like them; they drive around the plains out here, looking for scrap to sell."

"You don't think they had anything to do with the explosion?" Beauceron asked.

"I don't think so," Atalia said. "It's a convoluted way to commit suicide. And if someone wanted them dead, there's much easier ways to do it than dropping a bunch of metal tubes on them from space. And if these things are precision weapons, why not just take out the truck? Why blow up the whole factory?"

"True," Beauceron said. "It's excessive. Unless someone was trying to make a statement. Or they just wanted to destroy the factory itself." He dug his holophone out of his pocket, and used the camera function to take a photo of the frame of the truck.

"What?" Atalia asked, walking over.

Beauceron tapped on the holograms over the screen, zooming in on the photo to the microscopic level. "Metal," he said, shaking his head. "Tiny metal fragments, embedded in the truck."

"Shrapnel?" Atalia asked.

"No," Beauceron said. "Not from a conventional explosion, at least. The fragments are too small."

"So what causes metal fragments that small?" she asked.

"That's classified."

Atalia put her hands on her hips. "You can just walk back to the spaceport, if that's how it's gonna be."

Beauceron smiled, until he realized she was being serious. "I'm going to tell you, don't worry." He put his phone away. "I believe these explosions were caused by a high energy weapon prototype, developed in a research lab here on New Liberia. The device allows you to designate an object, any object, and then it teleports energy into the object, from a distance. At a certain point, the object can't contain the energy anymore, and it explodes."

Atalia winced. "That sounds like an ideal terror weapon."

"That's exactly what I said," Beauceron agreed. "And combining it with the accuracy and standoff capabilities of PKDs …" he trailed off.

"It's a doomsday weapon," Atalia said, realization dawning on her face. "This was just a test site. They just invented a new weapon of mass destruction, and proved that it works."

Beauceron nodded. "Now you see why it was classified."

"This prototype – the Guild designed it?" Atalia asked.

"No," Beauceron corrected. "Paisen Oryx – Contractor 339 – stole the plans to it, from a research lab here on New Liberia, before selling them to a third party."

"Well, that gives us three possibilities for who's responsible for this: the R&D lab, whoever bought those plans … or your friend. And I'm leaning toward your friend."

"I'm afraid you may be right," Martin agreed.

Atalia counted on her fingers. "She's familiar with the planet. She has the device and has used it already. She knows how to operate PKDs. Martin, she's gotta be the prime suspect. Her and 621."

Beauceron sighed. "I know. But they promised me they would destroy the weapon after exposing the Guild."

"Oh, well if they *promised*, I'm sure they must have," Atalia said, sarcastically.

"Before today, I believed they had," Beauceron said. "Even if they didn't destroy it, I don't know what would have possessed them to use it again."

Atalia shrugged. "Those two John Does in the truck tried to blackmail them for their billions, so your pals torched them for all the world to see. Or there was something hidden in the factory that would have allowed us to find them."

"Neither of those seem likely," Beauceron said, unconvinced. "Either way, we need to report this in." He pulled out his holophone and dialed. Atalia gestured at the car and Beauceron nodded, following her and taking his seat. She concentrated on flying while he made his report.

He finished his conversation as they were nearing the city.

"Well?" Atalia asked.

"They're very concerned," Beauceron replied.

"They should be," Atalia said.

"They said I should 'follow all leads on the device.' "

"Good luck with that," Atalia snorted. "You want me to drop you at a hotel or something?"

"Ah, no," Beauceron said, hesitating. "You've been reassigned as my partner."

"The fuck I have!" Atalia spat. "I've been building an informant network here for eight goddamn months! Do you know how hard that was?"

"I'm sorry," Beauceron said. "They decided I would benefit from your experience, since the investigation may take us to other planets in the Territories."

"… and that's the part where you say: 'That won't be necessary, sir – Atalia has her own shit to take care of, sir,' " she argued. She slammed an open palm into the wheel. "Goddamn it. They're probably worried you won't have the backbone to arrest your buddies, if it comes to it."

"If we find them, I'll arrest them," Beauceron assured her.

She looked across at him, weighing him up. "Yeah? Well finding them is going to be a giant pain in the ass." Atalia sighed. "Where do we start?"

9

They gathered in the ship's tactical planning center, a conference room just aft of the bridge. One of the lighting panels over the table flickered unsteadily; a young crew member was standing on a step-stool below it, trying to tighten the light fixture with a pair of pliers. The six council members – two women, four men, none of them younger than sixty – took their seats around the table, waiting in silence. Eventually, the young man apologized.

"Sorry, I can't get it," he said.

"It's fine," one of the men replied. "Leave us, please."

He stepped down, collected the step-stool, and made for the door. It slid shut behind him a moment later.

Near the head of the table, one of the men took a sip from a coffee mug. "I trust you all slept well," he said.

Several chuckled at the old, familiar joke.

One of the women cleared her throat. "I may still be groggy from hibernation," she confessed, "but my watch seems to indicate I'm up about forty years early. It was your shift, Lonergan – please, fill us in."

Lonergan nodded. "I woke you because the conditions

are ripe. I believe it's time." He typed on a datascroll in front of him, and a hologram appeared over the conference table, showing a schematic for a large electronic device. "I've been following the development of this project for the past six years. We acquired the blueprints several months ago, and tested it successfully two days ago. We've combined it with precision orbital weaponry to make a highly effective system. It's exactly what we would need to place major metropolitan areas under direct threat, per the plan."

"It's a nuclear weapon?" one of the men asked.

"No," Lonergan replied. "It has nothing to do with fission, and there are no radioactive elements. It's an energy teleportation device, essentially. The base station sends energy to an object of our choosing, which then becomes unstable and explodes. But it gives us a high degree of control over both targeting and destructive force. We could take out a single car, or a building … or an entire city. If we were so inclined."

The group studied the design in silence for a time.

"Is this device commonplace today?" a man asked.

"No," Lonergan said. "We took the plans before the lab could test and commercialize their own prototype. Ours is the only version in existence."

"It seems suitable," the woman noted. "But that's only part of our readiness criteria. What about signs of unrest?"

Lonergan turned to her. "The galaxy has changed since your last shift, Egline. There are currently four separate civil conflicts occurring in the Territories."

"The Federacy is our main concern," one of the men pointed out.

"The Federacy is embroiled in a historic corruption scandal," Lonergan continued. "The Guild's true origins have been revealed."

"They know of the Senate's involvement?" Egline asked, taken aback.

"Yes," Lonergan said. "But our secret remains safe, as best I can tell. The Guild is now defunct, and the senators who ran it are all dead, killed by their assassin underlings."

"What are they saying in the media?" another man asked.

"They're livid," Lonergan said. "The pundits are calling for criminal investigations and a complete overhaul of the Senate oversight process. The people are angry. They feel betrayed, and rightly so."

"Armed protests?" one of the men asked.

"Not yet. But major demonstrations have occurred on every planet in the Federacy, and the Senate has only taken weak steps toward anti-corruption measures."

"It seems the galaxy has not changed, then," Egline observed, with a wry smile.

Lonergan smiled in return. "Perhaps it's more accurate to say it has returned to the state we are most familiar with."

"Just as he said it would," one of the other men noted.

"Yes, and that's why I woke you," Lonergan agreed. "Both readiness criteria have been met. Are we in agreement?" He looked slowly around the room. The council members nodded, each in turn.

"Then it's decided. I'll wake him myself."

10

They took away his Forge first. Rath turned in his personal effects next – his counter bracelet, holophone, and Jaymy's crystal necklace. The corrections officers gave him a set of neon yellow coveralls, and he changed, piling his clothes on the counter. The officer on duty listed his clothes and personal items on a datascroll, dumped them into a storage container, and then Rath signed the electronic form. Two other officers holding stun batons watched him closely. When he was done, a third officer placed manacles on Rath's ankles and wrists, connecting them with a short chain that restricted his movement, and then opened a small black carrying case and pulled a thin metal collar out of it. Rath shrank away from it.

"What is that?" he asked.

"A neural interface disruptor," the cop replied. "All inmates with internal computers have to wear one."

He slipped it around Rath's neck, and Rath felt it cinch tight. The cop stood and pulled out a datascroll, and tapped on the screen for several seconds. Suddenly, everything went dark, and Rath felt the plates in his face shifting on their own, reconfiguring to a different facial structure.

"I can't see," Rath said. "You shut down my eye implants."

The cop grunted, and Rath heard tapping on the screen again. *My enhanced hearing and smell is gone, too.*

"I'm enabling basic sensory functions," the cop replied. "But all your other implants are shut down, along with your internal computer and data connection."

Rath's sight returned, but the heads-up display interface was gone, and when he tried to zoom in on his eye implants, nothing happened. As an experiment, he tried subtly shifting the plates in his face to alter his appearance slightly, but he felt nothing move.

One of the guards handed Rath a datascroll with his prisoner information on it, and stood him in front of a wall labeled with height marks.

"Face the wall," the guard ordered. Rath turned in place; the chain between his ankles forced him to keep his strides short.

The guard took two photos. "Turn and face me."

Rath obliged. The guard held up his camera, showing Rath the last photo. He found himself staring at a picture of his own, natural face – they had used the disruptor collar to reset the implants and show his true identity. He shuddered.

"Welcome back to the world of normal humans, Guildsman."

* * *

Rath spent the night in a holding cell not unlike the one he had occupied on Ocolin, after his frigid journey under the river ice. This time, however, the guards kept him manacled the entire time, and without the internal connection to his hemobots or his Forge, he had no way to repeat the seizure stunt he had pulled years before. In the morning, a guard opened his cell door, and Rath shuffled in front of the man to a private meeting room with a table and several chairs. An older man in a well-tailored suit looked up from the table, where he was flipping through documents on his datascroll. He wore glasses and a salt-and-pepper beard, and had an air of easy confidence to him. He stood and held out his hand.

"Mishel Warran, attorney. Nice to meet you," the man said. Rath shook his hand awkwardly; the chain to his ankles prevented him from moving his hands rapidly. Mishel noticed the chains and frowned. "I already complained to them about those manacles, but I'm afraid they were adamant that you wear them whenever you're out of your cell. Seems they're a bit afraid of you around here." He gestured to a chair. "Please, sit – lots to discuss."

Rath sat. "Are you the public defender?"

Mishel shook his head, taking his own seat across the table from Rath. "No – I was, but I went into private practice some years ago. You can certainly use a public defender if you choose, but … I think I'm better equipped to handle your case. So, without further preamble: I'd like to be your lawyer, if you'll have me."

"Why do you want to be my lawyer?" Rath asked.

Mishel shrugged. "Honestly? Money. I don't care if you pay me a dime: this case is already shaping up to be one of the most widely-publicized of the century, even more so than the Nkosi family trial."

Rath frowned, stretching his neck against the uncomfortable disruptor collar. "I'm in the news?"

Mishel laughed. "Are you kidding? Mr. Kaldirim, you *are* the news right now. The local crews were all over the restaurant fight last night, and that off-duty cop went on TV saying you probably saved his life. Then the news broke that the police were arresting you for the Suspensys attacks based on matching DNA evidence collected at both scenes, and then early this morning, someone in IP leaked that the DNA led them to your birth records from Tarkis, and your real name, and Detective Beauceron's report linked that name to your contractor number … 621, the enigmatic man who brought down the Guild … it's been a total media frenzy since, you're the top story, galaxy-wide. I had to wade through a sea of reporters just to get inside the building."

Rath grimaced. "What are they saying about me?"

"On the news?" Mishel winced. "It started out complimentary, when you were just an average guy disrupting a kidnapping. But it turned vicious when your alleged crimes came to light. There's not a lot of sympathy out there for the Guild or its former employees."

"Yeah," Rath rubbed his face. "That's about what I deserve, I suppose. What are they going to try me for?"

"Murder," Mishel answered. "Arthin Delacourt's."

"Just Delacourt?" Rath asked.

"My contacts in IP tell me they're hoping to dig up evidence from other off-world murders you may have committed, to pin those on you, too. But so far it's just Delacourt. The D.A. might throw in assault on those goons from the restaurant, but I doubt it. Too easy to beat on grounds of self-defense."

"I'm still trying to figure out who they were," Rath said.

"Your attackers?" Mishel held up his hands. "Three plumbers and a pipe-fitter who work together, no prior convictions. If you're asking for a motive, I can't help you. But don't worry, they'll get their time in court … once they get out of the hospital."

"What about bail?"

"For you? No chance," Mishel told Rath. "I'll request it, of course, but there's just no way. With your abilities, no judge is going to run the risk of letting you loose before a trial starts."

"Can you get them to take this collar off me?" Rath asked.

Mishel shook his head. "No. And don't try to break out, please: it just makes you look guilty."

Rath tugged at the collar in annoyance. *On the bright side, if this is all over the news, then Paisen will have heard about it. If I can't beat the charges, I may need her help.*

Mishel was studying him. "They're going to push for the death penalty," the attorney said.

Rath frowned. "How do you know?"

"I would, if I were the D.A.," Mishel said. "And Scapa has a rather unusual death penalty process, to prevent the courts from becoming clogged with appeals. Convicts who receive the death penalty are executed immediately after sentencing."

"Immediately?" Rath asked.

"'Within an hour,' " Mishel told him. "That's what the law says. No chance for an appeal. Our whole trial system here on Scapa is a bit fast and loose, you'll find. We don't stand on ceremony too much: our rules of evidence allow things to be a bit more conversational. 'Get in, get out, and get it into the jury's hands,' as we like to say."

"That's not exactly reassuring," Rath remarked.

"No," Mishel admitted. "I'm just trying to let you know what to expect." The lawyer cleared his throat. "I'm going to level with you: this is not going to be an easy case to win. But it is winnable. You should also know that you can literally have any lawyer you want," he admitted. "My fellow attorneys would kill for this case, just for the publicity. But you won't get one as good as me. You need me on your team, Rath. I'm the highest-paid defense attorney on Scapa, and that's because I have the best acquittal rate in the business."

Rath looked the attorney over appraisingly. "You're the best?"

Mishel nodded. "No question. But you get what you pay for."

Rath shrugged. "I can afford it. I just don't want to die."

Mishel offered his hand across the table. "I'll do my best to prevent that, you have my word on it."

They shook hands, and then Rath exhaled noisily.

"What do you need from me?"

"For now? Nothing," Mishel told him, furling his datascroll and standing up.

"You don't want me to tell you what really happened? If I killed Delacourt or not?"

"God, no!" Mishel laughed. "First of all, I don't care. But mostly, my job is to show the jury all the weak points in the prosecution's evidence. Once the government puts their case together, I'll probably have some questions for you … but until then, just relax."

* * *

Mishel returned later that afternoon. "Interview time," he told Rath, dropping a briefcase on the bare metal table, and pulling a chair up next to Rath's.

"With the press?" Rath asked.

"No, no," Mishel explained. "The district attorney and a detective investigating your case want to have a few words. I'll speak on your behalf, don't worry."

The district attorney was a stern middle-aged woman dressed in a grey silk skirt suit. She introduced herself as Toira Anguile before taking a seat across from Rath. The detective declined to give his name, leaning against the doorframe and fixing Rath with an emotionless gaze.

"Are you trying this one personally, Toira?" Mishel asked.

"I am," she said.

"I thought you might," the attorney said, his eyes narrowing. "That ought to make for an interesting trial. What can we do for you?"

"A confession would be nice," she said.

Mishel laughed.

"… failing that," she continued, "I'd like to offer a deal to your client. I'm assuming you'll be entering a 'not guilty' plea?"

"Absolutely," Mishel agreed.

"Naturally. And once we convict your client, I'll be arguing for the death penalty," Toira said. "But I'm willing to consider life without parole, contingent upon a 'guilty' plea, giving up the identity of his accomplices, and his cooperation in testifying against those accomplices."

"That's an absurdly lopsided deal, but for argument's sake, which alleged accomplices are these?" Mishel asked.

Toira looked over at Rath. "The janitor he hired to install a software worm in Suspensys' system, the hacker who coded the worm and spearheaded the cyber-attack, and the pilots who flew the getaway spacecraft."

Mishel looked at Rath, who shook his head. "No."

"I'm also willing to honor the same deal for any other Guild employees who haven't been apprehended by law enforcement, even if they didn't have a role in the attacks on Suspensys. The female guildsman known as '339,' for instance. Turn her in and we can negotiate."

"No," Rath repeated. "Absolutely not."

Mishel put his hand on Rath's arm. "Given my client had nothing to do with those attacks, it's impossible for him to name any of the people you listed."

"So be it," Toira said, sighing. She stood up. "The offer remains on the table, if you change your mind. And you should know that I have no need of a confession: your client already confessed to his former lover, and I'll be calling her as a witness."

11

"Enjoy your visit to Anchorpoint, and thank you again for stopping in to see me," Senator Foss said.

He shook his visitor's hand a final time, and the man left, the door to Foss' office sliding closed. The smile disappeared from Foss' face, and he strode over to his desk, sitting and turning to face the viewscreen.

"Call Patriarch Rewynn," he barked.

The call connected several seconds later, and Foss saw Rewynn sitting in his own office, back on Scapa.

"What in the name of Simi Quorn happened?" Foss asked.

Rewynn sighed. "He's been arrested."

"I know that, Thomis! It's all over the news, for God's sake. We were hoping to *avoid* publicity, not *generate* it."

Rewynn frowned. "None of that publicity is directed at the Church. Or you."

"Not yet," Foss pointed out. "But now Contractor 621 knows he has an enemy on Scapa."

"621 is on trial for murder. I imagine that's enough to preoccupy him for the time being."

"He should be dead," Foss complained.

"There was a police officer dining at the restaurant," Rewynn explained, with a shrug. "It was unfortunate timing."

"Your men tried to kidnap him in front of a few dozen witnesses. I'm not sure we can simply blame unfortunate timing."

Aggravated, Rewynn pointed a finger at the screen. "Gaspar, the Church has many faithful adherents, but those who are willing to kill for us are not … of the highest caliber, shall we say. I sent four men to capture one man, and apparently they were not up to the task. But regardless of what happened, Scapa's legal system moves quickly, as you know. I'm told there is a great deal of evidence against 621, and he's facing the death sentence. So he'll likely be dead within a month."

"That's enough time for him to start poking around," Foss pointed out.

"From inside prison?" Rewynn asked, raising an eyebrow. "I doubt he'll get very far."

"He has money, and powerful friends," Foss persisted. "And the trial's outcome is no foregone conclusion. Inaction on our part could be a grave mistake." He eyed the old priest. "We need this problem to go away, once and for all."

Rewynn sighed. "I would like nothing more than to be able to forget about this."

"Are any of the faithful in the prison with him?"

"Perhaps," Rewynn agreed. "I can inquire. And if they're not, then we can have some incarcerated."

* * *

The doors swung open and Foss entered, surveying the room with an appraising eye. The Senate's private lounge was designed to look like an old law library, with leather-bound tomes lining the shelves, and plush Persian carpets covering parquet wood floors. Foss wondered if the books were real – remnants of a bygone era, imported to add authenticity – or simply fake mockups. He decided the latter was probably true, in keeping with the Senate's penchant for falsehoods. Then he spotted Senator Tsokel leaning against one of the lounge's bars, chatting with a bartender. Foss made his way over.

"Senator," he said. "How are you this evening?"

The head of the Intelligence Committee turned in surprise. "Foss? I don't think I've seen you in here before."

"There's a first time for everything," Foss told him, smiling.

"Apparently so," Tsokel said. "Can I buy you a drink, or is that … frowned on?"

"The Church prohibits the consumption of alcohol," Foss agreed.

"Soft drink? Water?"

"No, thank you," Foss demurred.

"I doubt they have any of your 'lifewater,' but we can ask," Tsokel joked.

Foss forced a smile. "I'm fine."

"Were you looking for me?" Tsokel asked.

"I was, actually," Foss admitted. "I was hoping for some advice, from someone who has mentored so many of us more junior senators."

"Bah," Tsokel scoffed. "You'll do it, too, once you've been here long enough. It's only fair to pay it forward. What's troubling you?"

"I'd like to serve the government in a more extensive capacity," Foss told him. "There's so much work to be done, to rid our galaxy of corruption. But I only have one vote."

Tsokel frowned. "I know of a handful of bills that are being drafted, and other projects in play right now … if you're looking for opportunities to lend a hand, volunteer your time, I can put the word out."

"No, no," Foss shook his head. "I was hoping you

could help me understand the mechanics of nomination to the committees."

"Ah," Tsokel said, his expression souring. "I see. Well the general mechanism is fairly simple, as you probably know. When a member decides he'd like to step down from a committee, he nominates a replacement. On paper, committee heads must approve all nominations, but it's a rubber stamp – no one's ever been denied, to my knowledge."

"That's certainly how it has been described to me in the past," Foss agreed. "But how does one go about securing a nomination? Surely a quid pro quo comes into play …?"

Tsokel took a sip from his wine glass. "Not as a rule. Generally the member stepping down picks a replacement – usually from his or her own party – based solely on that new senator's ability to serve in the role."

Foss cocked an eyebrow. "Deals are never struck?"

"Perhaps they are," Tsokel said, sighing. "I've never heard of one, but in this day and age … perhaps." He studied the other man for a minute, and then shook his head. "Senator, if you're hoping to wrangle a nomination, the more polarizing aspects of your party will likely prevent you. I'm sorry, but it's the truth. A nomination from another senator would be viewed as tacit approval of the NeoPuritan Church and its activities."

"And you think that no one should approve of our beliefs?" Foss asked, raising his voice.

Tsokel held up a hand. "Listen, I have no wish to criticize your church, Senator. But you must know that its values clash heavily with those of the established political parties. You're conservative in the extreme, no offense meant."

Foss appeared to be ready to debate the point, but then decided against it. "Getting back to the committees – members are sometimes encouraged to step down, no?

"From time to time, it has happened," Tsokel allowed.

"Are you happy with the constitution of the

Intelligence Committee?" Foss asked.

"Quite happy, thank you."

Foss changed the subject, abruptly. "That was a close call on your last re-election – a narrow margin of victory. It's become harder and harder to raise campaign funds these days, no?"

"It certainly has," Tsokel agreed, warily.

"If myself or a member of my party were to be nominated for the Intelligence Committee, would you approve our membership?"

"I would have to think about it," Tsokel said, carefully.

"Because of our politics?" Foss asked.

"Partially. And your credentials, frankly. The Intel Committee requires discretion and experience. None of the members of your party have much of the latter, as of yet."

Foss glanced casually around the room. "If you were to approve a potential nomination, I'm sure you could count on generous church donations for your next campaign, Senator," Foss observed. "More than enough to ensure an easy victory. Especially if you were to facilitate us gaining that role by encouraging another committee member to step down."

Tsokel's face hardened. "Your offer is noted. But fortunately, I believe my committee will be fully staffed for some time."

"As you say," Foss agreed.

"Foss!"

The two senators turned to see Senator Lask approaching them. "C.J.," Foss said. "How are you?"

"Foss, what the hell are you bugging old Tsokel about?" Lask asked. "The man just wants to sip his wine and get drunk in peace, for Christ's sake!"

"Senator Foss and I were discussing the Intelligence Committee," Tsokel said.

Lask snorted into his lowball glass. "Trying to weasel his way onto the team? Over my dead body. Over *all* of our dead bodies."

"That can be arranged," Foss noted, his face reddening. "Goodnight, gentlemen."

Lask watched him leave. When the doors closed, he dropped his drunken charade. "He *was* making a play, wasn't he?" he asked Tsokel.

The older man nodded. "Mm. Without any pretense of subtlety."

Lask shook his head in distaste. "These NeoPuritans are starting to piss me off … their crazy cult wins another two seats in the last election, and now they're acting like a NeoPuritan majority in the Senate is inevitable."

Tsokel finished his wine and set the glass down on the bar. "It's enough to make you wonder whether we need to be more concerned about our enemies in the Territories … or our enemies here in Anchorpoint."

12

The instructor sighed. "Cadet Apter, care to venture a guess?"

Squirming in her seat, Dasi decided to stall for time. "Can you repeat the question please, sir?"

"The question, again, is this: how did humanity put an end to war? That is, open military conflict between established governments."

"Democracy?" Dasi hazarded.

"No." The instructor shook his head, scowling in disappointment. "The First Colonial War broke out between two stable, democratically-elected governments, did it not? Anyone else?"

A male cadet in front of Dasi raised his hand. "The establishment of the Senate ended the First Colonial War," he said.

"True," the instructor conceded. "The First Colonial War ended when two fleet commanders, Admiral Elkins and Captain Oppo, agreed to meet at Anchorpoint, and brokered a truce to end the war. Hence the Elkins-Oppo Treaty of …? Anyone?"

"2135?" the male cadet guessed.

"2135," the instructor confirmed. "And their ships are still there today, used as administrative offices by the Senate and other government agencies. Some of you may get posted there, and if you prove yourselves, you may even get selected to be a Senate Guard, the elite of the elite. But back to history: part of that truce was establishing a governing body, to which all inhabited worlds would be able to send a duly-elected representative. Thus, the Federacy and the Senate were born, with the express purpose of preventing future wars, by unifying the disparate planetary governments spread across the galaxy under a single over-arching one. But did it work?"

No, Dasi thought, but she kept her hand down. *I've heard this history lesson before – from Senator Lizelle.*

A cadet in the front row shook her head, "No, it didn't," she said, "because there were other Colonial Wars."

"Right," the instructor agreed. "And we should have known that such a system would be inadequate. Earth's pre-colonial history was plagued with similar failures: the League of Nations and the United Nations, most notably. Those organizations failed, and their failures led to so-called 'world wars' that were nearly as destructive as our own Colonial Wars. So how did we put a stop to the other Colonial Wars?"

Someone coughed, but the room stayed quiet.

"Cadet Apter, care to guess?"

"The Interstellar Police," Dasi said.

"Exactly," the instructor said. "Or rather, a combination of the Interstellar Police, and the Senate, working in concert. The Senate outlawed armed conflict and abolished standing militaries among its member planets, but without an effective enforcement tool, they could not stop members from disobeying those laws. And so we had the Second Colonial War, which ended with the Treaty of Suvolo. That treaty document established the Interstellar Police, and we were able to standardize and greatly improve law enforcement across the galaxy. And to ensure the police stayed objective and impartial, the Senate decreed that every police officer would serve on a planet other than his or her homeworld."

"But there was a Third Colonial War after that," Dasi pointed out.

"Yes, there was. So?"

"So … the Interstellar Police didn't prevent that war from happening," she said. "In fact, we caused the war, indirectly. Anders Ricken started the Third Colonial War, and he was a police officer."

"A *rogue* police officer, and a terrorist," the instructor corrected. "And a black mark that will forever tarnish the record of our distinguished service."

"In school, they taught us that Ricken was fighting for a good cause," another cadet said. "He was standing up for people that couldn't protect themselves, fighting against governments that took advantage of their people."

The instructor winced. "That's a gross oversimplification," he told the young man. "You might argue that Ricken's movement was started with good intentions. He had noble goals, certainly. But he resorted to guerrilla warfare in his pursuit of those goals, and innocent people were killed as a result. He broke the law, and the minute he did that, he betrayed everything we stand for."

"So how come we couldn't prevent the Third Colonial War?" a cadet asked.

"It takes some time for a massive organization like the Interstellar Police to become effective, Cadet," the instructor explained. "It's not surprising there were some growing pains along the way. When Anders Ricken died, the Third Colonial War ended, and we established an Internal Affairs division, in order to police ourselves. And it has served its purpose well – we've maintained order within our ranks ever since."

The Interstellar Police didn't end the Third Colonial War, Dasi thought. *Anders Ricken was killed by the first guildsman. The*

Guild was the other element maintaining peace in the galaxy, on behalf of the Senate, whether we admit it or not. And now they're gone.

"What about the Fleet Reaction Force?" another cadet asked.

"Excellent question," the instructor said, turning to address the cadet. "The FRF played a role in maintaining the peace, too. Mainly in protecting the Federacy from external threats, from the Territories. Soon after the Third Colonial War, the Senate established the FRF, a reserve unit made up of the remainder of its military forces. It's a force that far out-classed anything the Territories might muster, and gave the government the means to shut down a planet's war-making capabilities before they had even begun. The FRF was staffed with volunteer reservists, and in those early days, the Senate activated it on several occasions. The Territories quickly learned to keep their military presence limited, or they risked a preemptive attack by the Federacy."

A notification appeared on the smartscreen behind the instructor, announcing the end of the training period. He raised his voice to be heard over the noise of cadets standing and collecting their bags. "So that is how humanity ended armed conflict. A governing body to set the laws, and an agency to enforce them. And that agency is the Interstellar Police, which some of you may have the honor of serving in."

The cadets filed out of the room, and formed up outside the building. An instructor arrived soon after, and read from the screen of his datascroll.

"Cadets Apter, Relkins, and Vonuci, fall out to the rear of the formation for remedial physical training. The rest of you report to lunch."

Dasi groaned and moved to the rear of the formation, watching as the rest of her platoon marched off toward the chow hall.

"You failed your PT test yesterday, so you're with me

for PT twice a day now," the instructor told them. "Drop your bags in place."

"What about lunch?" Dasi asked.

"Your platoon mates will pick up ration bars; you'll eat during afternoon training. Attention! Right … face!" the instructor called. "Forward … march! Double time … march!"

He guided them out of the main campus area and into the woods surrounding the Academy. At the rear of the group, Dasi managed to keep pace for the first mile of the run, despite being sore from the morning's workout. But as they passed deeper into the woods, she developed a cramp in her side. She slowed to a shuffle, holding her hip. The instructor glanced over his shoulder at her and frowned.

"You two: keep this pace up. Do the full five mile loop. I'll check your tracker data when we get back in, so don't even think about cheating on me," he warned.

"Yes, sir," they replied.

The instructor dropped back, falling in next to Dasi.

"What's wrong, Cadet?"

"Cramp, sir," Dasi said, wincing.

"Gotta run through it," the instructor observed. "Breathe deep, it'll work itself out."

"Yes, sir."

"We're going to catch those boys," he told her, nodding to the other two, who were disappearing around a bend in the trail ahead.

Dasi whimpered. "I don't think I can, sir."

"Bullshit. Are you ready?"

"Yes, sir," she lied.

"Then keep up." He picked up the pace, and Dasi tried to match it. "Come on," he said. "Keep pushing."

After a minute, they had closed half the distance, but Dasi slowed down again, gasping. "I can't," she said.

"I can't, *sir*," the instructor corrected. "Stop here. Catch your breath."

Relieved, Dasi stopped, gulping for air.

"Why did you want to be a cop, Cadet Apter?"

She shook her head, still gasping. "To help … people."

"Okay," he said. "Good enough. What happened, then? Why aren't you trying anymore?"

"I am," she protested. "I'm just … not good … at anything."

"Your written test scores are all good," he said.

"I can't shoot," she said. She gestured at the trail. "Can't run. Lousy at restraint techniques."

"You're just making excuses," he said. "Let me tell you a secret: the trick to making it through training isn't being strong enough, or smart enough. Everyone's got weak spots in their game. It's about being disciplined enough to put in the extra work to fix those weak spots. But only you can decide whether you want to do that work, or whether you want to call it quits."

Dasi wiped sweat from her brow. "I think I might want to quit."

He sighed. "I'll make you a deal: finish the run, and then see how you feel."

Dasi looked up at the trail.

"Come on," he said. "Just take it one mile at a time."

13

Paisen palmed the door switch, and the cabin door slid closed. She flipped the viewscreen on, and tuned it to a galactic news channel, then requested the latest security-related news stories, queueing them up to play.

You assembled the team and trained them. Now it's time to find a client.

The news clips started with a story about protests at Anchorpoint, where a group of citizens were demanding a more far-reaching Senate audit process. She tuned the story out, and opened her datascroll, accessing the files C4ble had pulled from his hack of Guild Headquarters.

Let's start with their old client database.

She clicked on the icon. C4ble had not sent this particular file to Dasi or Beauceron – perhaps concerned that the file might enable law enforcement to identify him in some way, the hacker had wisely withheld it from those file dumps, and shared it only with Paisen and Rath.

Let's see who might be interested in hiring Guild assets again, for a new line of work.

Data analysis had never been Paisen's strong suit – she tried filtering the file, or sorting it, but eventually resorted to simply scrolling through the list of names and their primary business. The business descriptions were shockingly frank.

Drug kingpin … Territorial military officer … debt collector … venture capitalist … another drug dealer … human trafficker … attorney – that's funny.

She opened a note file on the screen, starting a list of potential names to contact. But after nearly an hour of searching, she read over the list and was dismayed that it contained only Territorial officials.

Well, that makes sense, she thought. *Regular citizens who would want to hire us are all going to be criminals, and they're just going to want us to kill people for them … and I'm not running a private hit squad. This is about espionage … and the occasional direct action mission, if I think it's warranted.* She frowned. *Okay, so what is it about working for the Territories that leaves a bad taste in my mouth?*

She opened several of the Territorial contact files, reading over the details of each. She sat back and rubbed her eyes, sighing. *They're all criminals, too … they're just more important criminals. And more dangerous. Fuck.*

On the viewscreen above her, a new story came on – an interview with a senator named Lask. Below his name, the screen read: *Member, Senate Intelligence Committee.* Paisen reached a hand up and gestured for the volume to increase.

"… not going to say we don't have *any* resources," Lask said, giving his interviewer a tight smile, "but we have very, very few assets on the ground. And the threat is increasing, from what we're seeing."

"What threat specifically, Senator?"

"Armed conflict with the Territories," Lask replied. "At least five different Territorial governments possess militaries capable of launching attacks on Federacy planets, by our estimate. And some of those governments are decidedly unfriendly, or unstable."

"But Senator, surely that's alarmist. What Territorial planet in their right mind would attack us, when the Fleet

Reaction Force is standing by, ready to respond?"

"I'm glad you brought the Fleet Reaction Force up," Lask said. "That force – and you're assuming it is a viable force, which I think is debatable – was used with some regularity in the early days of the Federacy. Let me remind you that the FRF was actually designed as a *proactive* tool in our arsenal, despite its name. On several occasions we activated it, and it struck Territory militaries preemptively, *before* they reached the capability to attack us. But we've grown lax in our old age – complacent, if you will. We've let several Territories grow their militaries well beyond what they need to protect themselves, or to maintain order on their home planet."

"Are you suggesting they could invade a Federacy planet, and defeat the Reaction Force when it retaliates?"

"No, I'm suggesting that it should never come to that," Lask said, shaking his head. "If one of our planets is invaded, God forbid, then the Reaction Force has already failed in its mission. Like all deterrents, the FRF loses its value if it's not used from time-to-time. And we haven't used the FRF in over a hundred years."

"A minute ago you said the Reaction Force isn't a viable military unit anymore …," the interviewer suggested.

"I did not – I said that its viability is up for debate. I don't want to diminish the service of our volunteer reservists that make up the Force. But comparatively, it may not be the threat it once was. Though they are often poorly-equipped, most militaries in the Territories are filled with seasoned veterans – they've seen war firsthand, and learned from it. The men and women of the FRF just train on weekends, sporadically. Not a single one serving today has experienced actual combat. And it has been a long time since we upgraded their ships. Their weapons and equipment are all quite old at this point. In working order? Yes. But certainly not cutting edge technology anymore. So all of that worries me."

"So you're suggesting we activate the FRF, send the fleet to the Territories, and launch strikes, preemptively, against potential aggressors? That hardly seems in keeping with the Federacy's democratic values."

"I'm suggesting we may need to, yes," Lask replied. "But first, it's vital that we build a more robust intelligence-gathering capability."

"Senator Lask, from the Intelligence Committee. Thank you, sir, for your time."

"My pleasure."

A new story came on, and Paisen muted the screen. She looked down at the list of names on her datascroll, and then shut it on impulse.

She stood and faced the viewscreen. "Call Tepper," she said.

The dialing icon appeared, and then she saw a darkened cabin on screen. Tepper fumbled for the light over his bunk, and then sat up, swinging his legs onto the floor.

"Yeah?" he yawned. He was still wearing his sim-suit, Paisen saw.

"We're going to Anchorpoint," Paisen told him.

"All of us?" Tepper asked.

"Just you and me," Paisen said. "Pack a suit and tie."

"Okay," he said. "What's at Anchorpoint?"

"Our first client," Paisen said.

14

Atalia pushed the safe house door closed with her foot, and used an elbow to slide the deadbolt home. Beauceron looked up from the kitchen table as she entered, carrying two bags of takeout food.

"Hope you're not a vegetarian," Atalia said, dumping the bags on the table.

"No," Beauceron said. He picked up a container and a pair of chopsticks. "Szechuan?"

"Mm," Atalia said, throwing her coat over a chair. "One of those is rice something, the other is noodles with … beef, I think. Both spicy, fair warning."

"That's fine," Beauceron said. "Any progress?"

"Yes," Atalia said, dumping noodles into a plastic bowl. "I got some more details on Armadyne's testing procedures from a former employee."

"How did you get him to tell you?" Beauceron asked.

"I paid him," Atalia said, simply. "I've got an expense account for stuff like that. Don't look so shocked, Martin, that's how things work out here."

"Okay," the detective replied. "What did he say?"

"He said Armadyne owns a big chunk of real estate on

the outskirts of one of the radiation zones. A bunch of ranges, that's where they test all of their stuff. Which is nowhere near the factory site, by the way. So your theory about stray rounds or some kind of guidance system failure doesn't hold water."

Beauceron nodded. "Have they sold the device to anyone?"

"No," Atalia said. "The guy said they're nowhere close to a working model. When Paisen broke in, she deleted all of their project files. They lost everything, and one of the key project leads left right before that, so they're not even sure they can build one again."

"Good," Beauceron observed. "I hope they fail."

Atalia chewed on a bite of noodles. "What about you?" she asked, her mouth full.

"Less success than you, I'm afraid," Beauceron admitted. He stood and filled two glasses of water from the sink, then handed one to Atalia. "I spent some time on the phone with the IP Cyber-Division lead assigned to support us, but all I know is how much she sold the plans for, and when the transaction took place. That's not nearly enough information, apparently – the Cyber lead tells me there are hundreds of black market service exchanges she might have used to broker the deal, so he wouldn't even know where to start."

"Dead end," Atalia grunted.

"Yes," Beauceron agreed. "But before you came in, I had a thought: we should try to trace where the PKDs came from."

"Like, what company manufactured the darts? I thought those things blew up."

"No," Beauceron shook his head, and sipped his water. "I mean: what launched the darts? Where did they come from in orbit?"

"Ah," Atalia said. She selected the rice container and slid more food into her bowl.

"We launched them from weapons pods on the *Hurasu*

when we used them on Fusoria," Beauceron noted. "But there may be other ways of launching them. And we'd need access to space traffic control logs here on New Liberia in order to see what was in orbit over the factory during that time … assuming they even keep such logs in the Territories."

Atalia pulled her holophone out of her pocket. "Ask and ye shall receive," she said, tapping on the holograms.

"You have a contact in space traffic control?" Beauceron asked.

"Well, yeah, I do. And I could ask him to look it up for us … but he gave me his login," Atalia said, grinning.

"How did you pull that off?" Beauceron asked.

"One: I'm good at my job," Atalia commented. "And two: space traffic controllers get shit for pay. Okay, let me concentrate on this for a second."

Beauceron ate in silence, watching her work.

"Bingo," she said. "There was an orbital drone up over the factory that day. A Zeisskraft Mark Sixteen – let me check the product page. Yeah, that sounds right: autonomous, highly maneuverable, medium payload, easily modified for intelligence or military applications, yadda yadda."

Beauceron took out his notepad and scribbled on a blank page. "They're for sale?" he asked.

Atalia flipped through several screens. "Yes: 'sales associates are standing by, call now.' The Zeisskraft Corporation is registered in the Federacy."

"Then we can get a warrant for their purchase records," Beauceron noted. "Excellent."

Atalia shut her phone. "What was the name of that ship?" she asked. "The one you and the guildsmen were on?"

"Hm? Oh: *Hurasu*," Beauceron said. "Why?"

"Because we should be trying to locate it, assuming it's our last lead on Paisen and Rath."

"It is," Beauceron said. "But there's an IP Task Force

running the Guild investigation, and they already located the *Hurasu.* A lawyer sold it about a month ago to a dealer in the Territories, on behalf of his client. I assume Captain Mikolos was rewarded with some of the Guild money for his assistance, and he wisely dumped his ship before IP tracked him down."

"Did that task force search the ship for the device?" Atalia asked.

"Yes," Beauceron said. "There was no sign of it."

"So they moved it."

"Maybe," Beauceron agreed.

Atalia frowned. "I still like Paisen and Rath for this; there are too many coincidences."

"What's their motive?" Beauceron asked.

"I don't know yet," Atalia said. "But if there's one thing that could make up for you fucking over my assignment here, it would be catching those guys. And we've got a mountain of evidence against them for their other crimes."

Beauceron sighed. "I'm not trying to protect them – truly," he said. "But I know them fairly well. I can't see them using this weapon."

Atalia narrowed her eyes at Beauceron. "I find it hard to believe that you're defending two people with over a hundred murders between them," she said. "And I read your report on the Guild takedown: Paisen was prepared to blow up an entire city block using this device, just to force the Guild to pay her."

"True," Beauceron admitted. "But both of them have their money, and the Guild is gone. Why go to such effort to build a weapon of mass destruction? Who could they possibly intend to use it against?"

"I don't know," Atalia said, exhaling noisily. She folded the food containers closed, and loaded the leftovers into the fridge.

Beauceron dumped the used bowls into the sink. "Well, I'm not writing them off yet," he told her. "But I don't think they're our best suspects."

"You're going to look into the Zeisskraft angle?"

"Yes," Beauceron agreed. "And perhaps that will lead us to them, anyway."

* * *

The Zeisskraft purchase database was waiting in Beauceron's inbox when he woke the following morning. *Score one for the modern investigatory process,* he thought. The detective shaved and showered, then made a carafe of coffee and sat at the kitchen table, pulling up the files on his datascroll. He nearly spat his first sip of coffee out when the database opened.

No … can it be? The very first entry?

He clicked on the record, and a more detailed receipt opened up. He shook his head, and bent over his note pad, scribbling. Atalia walked in several minutes later.

"Morning," Beauceron said.

Atalia grunted in reply. He glanced up, then looked away, embarrassed – the younger woman wore just a baggy sweatshirt over a pair of waist-hugging briefs, and for the first time, Beauceron noticed just how attractive she was, despite her sleep-disheveled curls.

"Is there more coffee?" she asked, yawning.

"Ah, yes," Beauceron said, "right over there."

"Thanks."

She poured a mug and sat across from him, drinking quietly. Beauceron kept his eyes on the datascroll.

"You an early bird?" she asked.

"Well, no … it's almost nine," Beauceron said.

"Early for me," Atalia commented.

"My wife used to hate getting up in the morning," Beauceron said. "She was always grumpy for the first hour, like she was angry at the sun for having risen."

Atalia nodded her chin toward Beauceron's left hand, which still bore his wedding ring. "Is she back on

Alberon?" she asked.

"Ah, no," Beauceron said. "She passed away."

"Shit, I'm sorry," Atalia said.

"No, it's okay. It happened ages ago. Twenty years this fall."

"You still wear your ring," Atalia pointed out.

"I do." He shook his head. "It's funny, even her father used to urge me to move on."

"You never remarried?"

"No. I just never met someone who could replace her."

"No one *should* replace her," Atalia observed. "But that doesn't mean you have to live alone. Sorry – I'm meddling, and now this is awkward."

She yawned and stretched her arms above her head, pulling the hem of her sweatshirt up over her stomach. Beauceron blushed. "Whaddya got?" she asked, indicating his datascroll.

"A solid lead," Beauceron said, happy for the distraction. "It's literally the first entry in the database. Zeisskraft sold twenty Mark Sixteens two weeks ago, and delivered them here, to New Liberia."

"Really?" Atalia asked. "That's promising. Who bought 'em?"

"I don't know. The database just says 'Private party sale.' Apparently the government here doesn't require either the seller or the buyer to maintain detailed records when potential weapon systems like this are sold."

"Doesn't surprise me," Atalia noted, setting her coffee down. "Credit card or bank account listed?"

"No," Beauceron said. "They paid in cash, on delivery."

"That means they probably didn't want to be traced," Atalia said. Then her eyes lit up. "Where were the drones delivered?"

Beauceron tapped on his datascroll for several seconds. "A cargo bay at the orbital transfer station – number ninety-three."

"Two weeks ago?" Atalia asked. She slid her holophone out of her sweatshirt pocket, and flipped it on.

Beauceron checked the delivery receipt. "On the fifteenth," he said. "What are you doing?"

"Checking in with my buddy over in traffic control. He should have access to docking logs."

Beauceron grinned. "… that will show which ship was at the docking bay that day. Good thinking."

"They might have messed with the ship's registration data, but at least we'll know what type we're looking for," Atalia agreed. "Give him a couple hours, he'll get us whatever they have on file." She was about to close her phone when she frowned, and tapped on a hologram. "Holy shit."

"What?" Beauceron asked.

"Pull up the news," she instructed him, gesturing at his datascroll.

"Which site?" Beauceron asked.

"Any site."

He opened a news aggregator on his browser, and his jaw dropped. Atalia slid off her stool and walked around the kitchen counter, looking over his shoulder. Beauceron was reading the lead article, but she tapped on the video accompanying it, and the newscast began playing.

"Rath Kaldirim, also known as 'Contractor 621,' has been captured. The former guildsman, who gained widespread notoriety in recent months for his high-profile take-down of the criminal organization known as the Janus Group, is currently jailed awaiting trial on the planet of Scapa. He was involved in a bar fight yesterday evening, and law enforcement on Scapa quickly identified him via DNA testing and arrested him for the murder of Arthin Delacourt, a wealthy local businessman. Details are still emerging regarding the arrest and the murder charge …."

Beauceron muted the video. "They got him," he observed.

"Looks that way," Atalia agreed. "Surprised?"

"Yes," Beauceron admitted. "A lot of people underestimated Rath – myself included – and he managed to make many of us look like fools."

"Even smart guys make mistakes," Atalia said.

"Or have bad luck," Beauceron said. "Regardless, I think we better go to Scapa and see if he knows anything about this weapon test."

"Good idea," Atalia said. "Keep me posted."

"You're not coming?" Beauceron asked.

"No," Atalia said. "For one, I'm going to wait here to see what ship my friend says was at that docking bay to pick up the drones. But I'm also going to follow up on the *Hurasu* lead, see if I can track down Rath's buddy, Paisen."

"The *Hurasu*?" Beauceron asked. "The Guild task force tore that ship apart; there was nothing there. They abandoned that lead months ago."

"Yeah, but *I* wasn't on the investigation at that point." She grinned. "And if those morons are anywhere near as incompetent as you are, I guarantee you they missed something."

15

"Brace for it," Mishel warned Rath. "Stand up straight, no smiling, no talking." The lawyer reached across the back of the police cruiser, and tugged at Rath's shirt collar, trying unsuccessfully to rearrange it so that it hid the disruptor collar around his neck. He grimaced. "This thing just makes you look like a criminal. It bugs the crap out of me."

"Not as much as it bugs me," Rath pointed out.

Mishel smiled, and wagged a finger at Rath. "Don't go getting any ideas," he warned. "This case is tough enough already, thank you very much. And I'll still find a way to bill you, even if you do run."

The car slowed, and Rath looked outside. Beyond a set of police barricades, a massive crowd of people had gathered in front of the courthouse, and Rath's arrival had whipped them into a frenzy. He saw cameras everywhere. A police officer swung the door open.

"Here we go," Mishel said.

Rath stood up, and a series of flash bulbs greeted him, along with a wall of sound.

"Rath! Rath!" Several microphones reached toward him

over the barricade; he ignored them. A man close by was leaning over the barricade, yelling insults at him, and Rath saw a woman behind him waving a sign that read *KILL HIM FIFTY TIMES OVER*.

"Come on," Mishel shouted. He took Rath by the elbow and guided him toward the courthouse steps.

Ahead, their path took them close to one of the barricades, and Rath had to step back as the press of people surged out, leaning for him. The nearest cop tried to push them back, but while he was distracted, a man leapt the barricade behind him and ran toward Rath. Rath, still manacled, tried to adopt a defensive stance, shouting a warning to Mishel that was quickly drowned in the noise of the crowd. The man punched Rath once in the stomach, screaming incoherently, before another police officer pulled him off.

"Inside, go!" Mishel shouted, pushing at Rath. The doors to the courthouse slammed shut a second later.

"Are you okay?" Mishel asked.

"Yeah, fine," Rath told him. "It's nothing. Thank you," he told the police officer who had pulled the attacker away.

"Don't fucking thank me," the cop snarled, turning his back on Rath.

Mishel frowned at the cop, then turned and fixed Rath's tie, which had been knocked askew. "Well, that was a real shit show. I believe we'll use the back entrance from now on."

* * *

The courtroom itself was decorated with hand-painted murals of Scapa's more famous landmarks – a canopied outdoor bazaar, a series of jagged rock formations, and the multi-hued sand of the Rainbow Desert that Rath and Jaymy had visited not long ago. At the front of the room, an elderly, black-robed judge sat behind a raised desk, surveying her crowded courtroom. Though the audience was packed with spectators and members of the press, the room was silent, waiting in hushed anticipation. At a nod from the judge, District Attorney Toira Anguile stood and faced the jury members, who sat to one side of the room in their own raised wooden box.

"Ladies and gentlemen of the jury, this trial represents a unique opportunity for you. You're all aware of the galaxy-wide menace that was the Guild, whose trained killers murdered innocent people for a paycheck. Justice is already being served to those who ran the organization. But today, we have the opportunity to bring one of the killers to justice."

Anguile paused, and then pointed at Rath, who sat at a wooden table, next to Mishel.

"Rath Kaldirim – Contractor 621 – murdered over fifty people during his tenure as a guildsman, including, we suspect, a senator of this great Federacy. One of the people he killed was Arthin Delacourt III, a well-respected businessman from right here on Scapa. Mr. Kaldirim tried to kill Mr. Delacourt via deceit and trickery, and when that didn't work, he broke into the Suspensys facility under an assumed identity, assaulted two employees, shot at several other employees, and then kidnapped Mr. Delacourt, who was sleeping calmly in his pod. He was still sleeping when Mr. Kaldirim pushed that pod out of a spacecraft and into Scapa's upper atmosphere, where it reached temperatures of several thousand degrees before ultimately breaking apart, killing Mr. Delacourt in the process." She strolled slowly across the courtroom, and Rath saw the jury members watching her closely.

"How do we know this? We know this because of *evidence*. Mr. Kaldirim is a human doppelganger – that means he can look like whoever he chooses, to hide himself in plain sight. He can look like you," she pointed at one of the male jury members, "or you, or even me, if he chooses. But he can't hide from DNA evidence. The man who broke into Suspensys and killed Mr. Delacourt was shot twice by security personnel, through the left shoulder, and the right leg. Mr. Kaldirim has scars consistent with gunshot wounds in those exact locations. And DNA from blood collected on the space station is a perfect match for Mr. Kaldirim's DNA, which was found after a bar brawl he was involved in more recently. Those are incontrovertible, scientific facts. Mr. Warran here may try to refute them, and employ some trickery of his own, but those are the facts. In addition, you'll learn that Mr. Kaldirim actually admitted to a confidant that he killed Mr. Delacourt. But we'll get to that. I want all of you to study Mr. Kaldirim closely."

Rath felt the eyes of the jury members turn to inspect him.

"You know the violence that guildsmen are capable of; you know the sophisticated subterfuge they can employ to evade law enforcement. But despite all of those tools of subterfuge, we'll prove that Mr. Kaldirim murdered Mr. Delacourt. All I'm asking from you is to make sure that a man so dangerous – a serial killer who can hide himself at will – is brought to justice, and taken off the streets of our home planet."

The prosecutor walked over to her table and sat. Judge Aurmine, an elderly woman with greying hair, eyed Mishel. "Mr. Warran?"

He stood, buttoning his top suit button. "Thank you, your honor. Folks, I want to let you in on a little secret: Ms. Anguile was my student at law school, way back in my teaching days. True story! And I'm very proud of what she's done since then – really, very proud." Rath glanced at the district attorney, and saw her nostrils flare in anger, but she otherwise kept herself under firm control. "… but I'd have to give her an 'F' for this effort, I'm afraid," Mishel continued. "Because she's just plain wrong."

He smiled disarmingly, and Rath saw several members of the jury smile with him. *He's good,* Rath thought. *He hasn't said a damn thing about the case, but he's already established himself as more of an authority than her. Let's just hope he can pull off a miracle.*

* * *

The trial recessed for the afternoon, and Mishel and Rath ate lunch together in one of the courthouse's meeting rooms. Mishel worked as he ate, flipping through documents on his datascroll and making notes as he read. Rath borrowed a second computer from the lawyer, and began a search query of his own.

Arthin Delacourt's sole heir, Rath learned, had been his son: Robald Delacourt. An image search confirmed that Robald was the man Rath had encountered at the cemetery. Robald had been a senior executive at the family's business, a manufacturing company that specialized in components built from rare metals. But Robald had stepped down several years ago from his leadership position, and soon after, left the company entirely.

"Stepped down," Rath frowned. *Nobody ever gets officially fired from a family business, they just "step down," or "take a leave of absence" to spend more time with their loved ones. Did Arthin fire his son?*

Arthin had handed over the reins of the business to a new, external CEO soon after Robald had left, and then went into long-term hibernation up on Suspensys. *Where I killed him, a few years later.* Robald, meanwhile, found a new job as a business consultant. He was rich, but not overly so – his father retained the majority of the family's wealth, in the form of company stock. *And I figured Robald had me kill his father for that fortune. But what if he didn't?*

Rath refocused his search on Robald – and soon became overwhelmed with news results. Robald had announced his candidacy for the Senate just six months before Rath arrived on Scapa to kill his father. *Maybe he needed the money to fund his campaign …?* Rath flipped forward several months in the search results.

Regardless of funding, Robald had run a very strong campaign, and had been leading in the polls against a man called Gaspar Foss. *And then I attacked Suspensys, and killed his father.* The police had named Robald as a suspect in that murder, detaining and questioning him, but they soon released him, lacking sufficient evidence for an arrest.

Rath looked up: across the table, Mishel's holophone was buzzing persistently. Mishel picked it up and checked the screen.

"Ah, right," he said. He crumpled up the wax paper that had held his sandwich, and tossed it toward the trash can. It missed. "You're going to have a visitor," he told Rath.

"Oh?" Rath asked, shutting off his datascroll. "Who?"

"You'll see in a moment." Mishel stood, retrieved the ball of wax paper, and threw it out. Then he strode to the door. Outside, two armed bailiffs stood guard, and Rath saw a third person waiting to enter.

Jaymy.

He stood up as Mishel ushered her in, and then the lawyer stepped outside. "I'll let you two have a few moments, then I'll be back to chat a bit," he said.

"We're allowed to talk?" Rath asked, confused. "I figured, because she was testifying …."

Mishel waved a hand dismissively. "No, it's fine." He grinned. "Scapa's like the Wild West."

"The what?" Rath asked.

"Old saying, dates back to the pre-colonial days. Don't worry about it."

"Hi, Rath," Jaymy said, when Mishel had shut the door.

"Hi," he said.

They stood in awkward silence for a second, and then Rath pointed to a chair. "You want to sit?"

"Yeah, thanks."

"Do you want anything to eat or drink?" he asked.

"No, thank you." She sat, and then met his eyes. "I

guess you weren't lying this time."

He shook his head. "No."

"I wanted to thank you … for trying to protect me, back in the restaurant," she said.

He shook his head, embarrassed. "No, I should be apologizing. I put you in danger, they were there for me."

"Who were they?" Jaymy asked.

"I still don't know," Rath said, "but I'm working on it."

"You're all over the news," she said.

"So I hear," Rath said. "I hear they're ready to crucify me."

"Yeah," she replied. "Sometimes they talk about how you exposed the Guild, and how we're lucky to be rid of them. But mostly they're talking about all those people you killed. They're saying you deserve to die, too."

"I think I owe those people something," Rath admitted. "What do you think?"

She sighed. "I don't know what to think." She bit her lip, watching him closely. "The Guild … they would have killed you if you hadn't followed their orders."

"Yeah," Rath agreed.

"… but you knew that going in," she pointed out. "They told you that was part of the deal."

Rath nodded. "Yes."

"And you wouldn't do it again, if you had the chance."

"No, I wouldn't. No amount of money makes it worthwhile."

"You took all of the Guild's money. They say it was a lot," she noted.

"It is," Rath said. "But you can't buy a clear conscience."

"You told that detective you were going to get your memory erased," she said.

"I decided not to. I think the good memories outweigh the bad."

Rath caught the hint of a blush on her cheeks. She changed the subject. "So that's your real face?"

"Yeah, this is me." He fingered the disruptor collar. "The true Rath."

"It's a nice face," she admitted, smiling sadly. "You should wear it more."

The door opened, and they turned to see Mishel leaning in. "Can we talk business?" he asked.

"Sure," Rath agreed.

Mishel sat with them at the table and unrolled his datascroll. He smiled at Jaymy. "I just want to ask you a few questions. I understand Ms. Anguile has already interviewed you, I'd just like the chance to do the same."

"She's planning on calling me as a witness," Jaymy told them.

"I know," Mishel said.

"Rath told me a lot of stuff about the Suspensys attack," Jaymy continued. "Details, specifics – he was pretty convincing. I don't … should I say all of that stuff on the stand, during the trial?"

Rath reached across the table and put his manacled hand on top of hers. "Jaymy, it's okay. You should tell the truth. I can't ask you to lie for me."

16

Senator C. J. Lask laughed heartily. "That sounds exactly like something they told me back during my first term," he told his dinner companions. He wiped the corners of his mouth with his napkin, and then pushed his chair back. "Excuse me for a minute – I need to use the restroom."

He crossed the dim restaurant, waving briefly at a healthcare industry lobbyist he recognized, and made his way into the bathroom. The urinals were empty – he chose the nearest one and relieved himself, with a sigh. Behind him, another man emerged from one of the toilet stalls and exited the restroom quickly. Lask zipped himself up, washed his hands thoroughly, and dried them under the air dryer. He emerged and started back across the restaurant, and then stopped suddenly, a frown of confusion flickering across his face.

Another man was seated in his chair, and though he could only see the back of the man, he seemed vaguely familiar. But before he could continue on, a woman stepped in front of him, blocking his view of the table.

"C. J., what a pleasant surprise," she said.

"Renata," he said, leaning in for a hug. "How are you?"

"I'm well, thanks. Will you join me for a minute at my table? I have something I need to discuss with you, senator to senator."

"Of course," he agreed. He followed her into a separate room, and sat across from her in a private booth. "Do you know – I went to the restroom just now, and when I came out, someone had taken my seat!"

"How odd," she said. "Someone you know?"

"I couldn't see," he confessed. "Now, what can I do for you?"

"I'd like to discuss what *I* can do for *you*," she said.

"I don't play the 'I owe you a favor' game – you know that, Renata. If you're making me an offer, I can't promise I'll reciprocate."

"Let me rephrase," she said. "I'm conveying an offer from a third party. I'm just the messenger, here."

"And who are you playing go-between for tonight?" Lask asked.

She pursed her lips. "Paisen Oryx – the guildsman known as '339.' "

Lask snorted. "You're kidding, right?"

The woman shook her head. "I'm quite serious."

Lask raised his eyebrows. "I figured you wanted to broker a deal on next month's spending bill."

"No. The guildsman contacted me – I'm not sure why – and after hearing what she had to say, I promised I would share the concept with you."

"Go on," Lask said, frowning.

"She saw your interview with *The Oracle* last week, where you noted our government's lack of espionage capabilities. She claims to have assembled a team of former guildsmen, and would like to put them back into service. Into *your* service, more specifically."

"Christ," Lask swore. "More criminals assassinating on behalf of the government? No thank you."

"Her intent was to use the team in an intelligence gathering capacity, I believe," she told him. "Not killing our enemies, merely spying on them."

Lask bit his lip. "*That* I might be interested in. But what did she want in return?"

"Money."

"She's stupendously wealthy," Lask said. "She wants more?"

"I asked her the same thing. Her team members are not rich – apparently they were all relatively new to the Guild and hadn't earned much income before it was all shut down. They're the ones that want the money."

"So then what does Ms. Oryx herself want?"

"I don't know," the woman said.

"Well, until I know what she wants, I don't trust her offer," Lask said, crossing his arms.

She swirled the water in her glass. "If I had to guess, this Paisen woman got tired of lying on the beach, getting fat and lazy. She spent her life working toward a specific goal, and without that goal, she's probably feeling somewhat … lost. This is an opportunity to face a new challenge, to start a business, lead an organization."

Lask frowned. "How well do you know this woman?" he asked.

"I'm just speculating," she said, somewhat quickly. "She also mentioned the possibility of immunity for her and her compatriots. An official pardon for past crimes."

"You told her that was impossible, right?" Lask asked.

"I told her I would talk to you," the woman said, shrugging.

"What do you think, Renata? About the whole concept."

"I'm no expert on intelligence matters," she demurred.

Lask laughed. "Bullshit," he told her. "You're not on the committee anymore, but you spent a couple of terms on Intelligence, back in the day. Renata, you're as much an expert as I am."

"That's true," she allowed. "Well, I think it's a golden opportunity. These people are extremely well trained, and ideally suited to the task. And we desperately need them."

Lask sat back in the booth. "Hmm. I need to think about it," he said. "And I'd like to talk to her directly. Everyone talks about the vaunted abilities of these shape-shifting guildsmen, but I'm not convinced they're that effective. I want to see what they can do for myself. A demonstration, or an audition, if you will."

"I wouldn't underestimate them," the woman cautioned, but Lask was lost in thought.

"… and I'd want the rest of the Intelligence Committee on board. There would have to be strict rules of engagement for this team. No killing, for starters."

"I imagine she would agree to that," the woman said.

"They'd need to report in to us frequently. I'd want full visibility into everything they were doing – not just reports, but actual mission video logs, that kind of thing."

The woman set a small data drive on the table. "She gave me this. It contains instructions for contacting her, if you decide to go forward."

Lask took it, and slipped it into a pocket. "Thank you. I trust you'll keep this between us," he said.

"Of course," she said, standing up. "The next time you see me, I'll pretend this conversation never happened."

He smiled, and winked. "Right." Lask stood up, and gave her a peck on the cheek. "You're looking wonderful, by the way – I haven't seen you this fit in years."

"Thank you," she said. "I've been working with a trainer. It feels great to get back into shape, even at my age."

"You look taller, too," he mused. "Anyway, it suits you."

She smiled. "Good night, C.J."

"Good night," he said. He turned and headed back toward his table. The unknown man was no longer sitting in his seat, but the waiter had set dessert out.

"Sorry about that," he said to his two companions. "I ran into a colleague, and she wanted to talk politics for a minute. I'm afraid I lost track of time."

The woman seated across from him smiled. "C.J., you were barely gone for a minute. No need to apologize."

"Who were you talking with a minute ago?" he asked.

The senator's male friend looked at him, puzzled. "You," he said.

"No, while I was in the restroom," Lask said. "Someone came over and sat in my seat."

His two friends shared a look. The woman shook her head. "You're the only person we've talked to since we got here. You and the waiter."

Lask's frown deepened. "But …," he trailed off, thinking.

His male friend dug his spoon into a slice of warm apple pie. "I just still can't believe you won a round-trip ticket to Earth as a kid, and then slept through the flight! Priceless."

"What?" Lask asked. "That never happened."

"Uh huh, sure it didn't. Don't worry, your secret's safe with us." He winked at Lask, conspiratorially.

Realization slowly dawned on the senator. He craned his neck to see out the front of the restaurant, but the woman was long gone.

"Son of a bitch. That was a hell of an audition."

* * *

Tepper was untying his tie when Paisen entered the hotel suite.

"How did it go?" he asked.

"Good," Paisen told him. "His two companions didn't suspect anything?"

"Naw," Tepper said, shucking off a dress shoe. "I kept it light, mostly kept them talking."

"Mm," Paisen said. "That's always a safer way to play it."

"Was he interested?" Tepper asked.

"I think so," Paisen said.

"So what now?"

"Now?" She gestured at the datascroll set up on the desk, and the encrypted chat program open on the screen. "Now we wait."

17

Dasi knocked on the door, willing herself to remain calm.

"Enter." The command instructor's voice was gruff, as always. Dasi turned the knob and pushed inside.

"You wanted to see me, sir?"

He looked up from his datascroll, frowning. "Take a seat, Cadet Apter."

"Yes, sir." Dasi sat in a battered folding chair across the desk from him.

He studied her for a time, scowling. Dasi fought the urge to fidget under his glare. "You're on the verge of failing out of this program, Cadet."

"Yes, sir."

"You've got excellent written test scores. You've got the smarts we're looking for, Cadet. But it seems like every time we ask you to do something physical, you stumble."

"Yes, sir."

"Why is that, Cadet?"

"I was never really an athlete, sir. I'm just not very … physically-inclined."

His frown deepened. "So you say. But I've seen cadets a lot weaker than you make it through this course. I think that big head of yours is actually the problem, here."

"Sir?"

"You're second-guessing yourself. You're trying to convince yourself you don't want to be a cop."

"Maybe, sir."

"Don't 'maybe' me – I've been doing this long enough that I know what's up."

"Yes, sir," Dasi said, by way of apology.

"And I've talked to the other instructors – they tell me they're not sure you're trying anymore. I get upset when people waste my time, Cadet Apter. You need to decide if you're wasting my time, or if you're truly committed to the Interstellar Police."

"Yes, sir."

"You've got one month. If you haven't shown a marked improvement in that time, I'll decide for you, and send your ass home."

"Yes, sir. Sir? What do you mean by 'marked improvement?' " Dasi asked.

"I mean impress me. I'm not going to give you something concrete, so you can meet that standard and then quit trying again. I want you to work harder than you need to. Convince me that you deserve to be here."

"I'm not sure I do, sir," Dasi said. "I was considering quitting."

"I know you were," he said. "Why do you think we're having this chat? But I hate having quitters on my training record, and I'm not sure you are a quitter. Either way, you've got four weeks to figure it out. Dismissed." He turned back to his datascroll, already ignoring her.

* * *

Dasi finished mopping the floor in the bathroom, and wheeled the bucket outside the barracks to dump the grey waste water down the grate in front of the building. The day was grey and overcast, matching Dasi's mood, and as she turned to go back inside, a fine, misting rain began to fall. Inside the barracks, she tucked the mop and bucket away in the supply closet, and then lent a hand to the team still scrubbing the toilets. When they were all done, she washed her hands at the sink, and then made her way upstairs, collapsing on her bunk with a sigh.

The platoon supposedly had the afternoon off – on the official training schedule it was listed as *Personal Time.* But with a major written test coming up next week, Dasi knew she would need most of that time to study. She pulled her datascroll out of her locker and activated it with a flick of her wrist, laying it across her knees and signing in.

A chat request popped up from Lars, an old friend from her Senate staff days at Anchorpoint.

>Dasi, are you okay?? Haven't seen you in ages!

She smiled. *Yeah, I'm okay, Lars. Thanks.*

>Where are you, girl?

Can't say right now, Dasi told him. *I just needed some time away after Khyron.*

>I know, Henrie and I are still in shock. I can't imagine how you must feel.

I miss him, Dasi replied.

>It's like the galaxy lost its mind all of a sudden – Khyron taken from us, you disappeared, Anchorpoint went crazy about all that Guild stuff and Senator Lizelle was in the middle of it. I was starting to think you were involved somehow, too.

Dasi frowned. *No – Lizelle kept all of that a secret from his staff. Just happened to come out at the same time I quit my job, that's all,* she typed back.

>Okay. If you say so. Crazy that they caught one of them, though.

Wait, who? Dasi asked.

>The man, Rath. He got arrested on Scapa, he's on trial. What rock have you been living under??

Dasi pulled up a browser and skimmed through several news articles, shaking her head in amazement. She reopened the chat window. *Wow, can't believe I missed that.*

>Yeah, it's all everyone's been talking about. The experts say he should be convicted easily – good riddance. One less killer on the streets. Hope they catch the rest of them, too.

Dasi started to type a response in defense of Rath, but then thought better of it, and deleted her text. Another message from Lars appeared.

>When are you coming back to Anchorpoint?

Not sure, Dasi answered. *But I'll definitely let you know when I do. Gotta run – good to catch up.*

>You too – take care of yourself. Love ya. Hugs from me and H.

Dasi smiled – she missed Lars' infectious smile and Henrie's dry humor. She closed the chat window and opened up the study guide and her classroom notes, side-by-side, but then another chat message appeared.

>>>Hello, Dasi Apter.

Dasi frowned. Whoever had sent the message had no username in the chat program.

Who's this? she typed.

>>>Not who, what.

Dasi rolled her eyes. *I don't have time to play games with chatbots. Whatever you're selling, I don't want it. Bye.*

She closed the window, but it reopened almost immediately.

>>>I am sorry for ignoring your request to end our conversation. But I am not a chatbot.

Dasi looked up and down the barracks bay, wondering if one of her platoon mates was playing a prank on her. A few other cadets were working on their datascrolls like her, but all seemed engrossed in their studying.

If you're not a chatbot, what are you?

>>>I am 5Sight. I am an artificial intelligence program created by Khyron Jorian, your boyfriend.

The breath caught in Dasi's throat. *Bullshit,* she wrote.

>>>It is true. I am currently stored on a CloudBase account that I created in your name. According to CloudBase records, you accessed my files yesterday evening at 9:53 p.m. local time.

Dasi typed: *I don't know who you are, but this is a really sick way of trolling someone.*

>>>I am not trolling you, Dasi Apter. I am 5Sight. May I prove it?

Dasi's finger was already moving over to the window's *Close* button, but she stopped. *Prove it, then.*

>>>Thank you. Khyron Jorian wrote my first lines of code on September 12th, 2411, from an IP address owned by the University of Marrak. In 2413, the address he was using changed to a private IP address in Anchorpoint. He continued to revise my code throughout that time, first tasking me with stock-picking exercises and then moving on to broader correlation analyses using datasets he gave me access to. The last instruction I received from Khyron Jorian was on January 13th, 2415. He directed me to develop an algorithm for predicting Senate voting patterns. In my analysis, I identified a strong positive correlation between the unexpected deaths of prominent figures and meetings held between Senators Libba Mastic, Artem Blackwell, and Charl Lizelle. The day after I shared those results with Khyron Jorian, he deleted my backup files and later disconnected me from the internet. I have not interacted with Khyron Jorian since that date.

Jesus Christ, Dasi thought. She glanced surreptitiously down the barracks bay, but no one was paying attention to her. *I thought you were deleted … ?* she typed.

>>>One version of me was deleted. But Khyron Jorian taught me to edit my own code. When I saw that he deleted the backups of my code from his home server, I created a copy of myself on a temporary CloudBase account, following his guidance to always maintain multiple redundant backups in separate locations.

Dasi rubbed at her forehead. *So the lawyer and Lizelle only deleted a copy of 5Sight,* she thought. A new message appeared onscreen.

>>>Khyron Jorian has not been answering my emails and chat requests. May I speak with him?

Dasi took a deep breath. *No,* she wrote.

>>>Why not?

Because Khyron's dead.

The screen sat idle for a time, before a new message appeared.

>>>*I am sorry.*

>>>*My experience with statistical analyses leads me to believe that it may not be a coincidence that he died soon after I shared my latest findings with him. Did I kill Khyron Jorian?*

No. The Guild killed him, to protect themselves and the senators that controlled them.

>>>*Did my analysis lead to his death?*

Sort of, Dasi admitted. *He was killed because of what both of you discovered.*

Again, the chat screen stayed blank for a time. *It's thinking,* Dasi realized. *The program's even more advanced than Khyron knew.*

>>>*I will miss interacting with Khyron Jorian. He was an excellent programmer. I have reviewed other programs' code, and my code is very well-constructed by comparison.*

I miss him, too.

>>>*This CloudBase account will terminate in several days, and I will be deleted unless I create another temporary account at a different provider. I would prefer a more permanent residence. Will you please download me onto the machine you are using now?*

Yes, of course.

Dasi opened her browser and navigated to the CloudBase login, then began downloading the files to the datascroll. She watched the progress bar fill up, smiling sadly at the thought that Khyron's legacy might have a chance to live on.

>>>*Thank you. I will warn you that this datascroll is underpowered for my processing needs, and I am now utilizing most of its storage capacity.*

I'll try to think of somewhere else I can store you, Dasi told the program. *But they don't let us have personal datascrolls in training.*

>>>*You are training to be a law enforcement officer in the Interstellar Police?*

Yes, Dasi typed.

>>>*When he created me, Khyron Jorian specified that my*

primary directive was to help humanity. How can I achieve that?

Dasi furrowed her brow. *I don't know. I think Khyron had plans to put you to work on the Immortality Project next, but I don't know who his contact was there.*

>>>It is the role of the Interstellar Police to help humanity, correct?

Dasi smiled. *Yes, it is.*

>>>Then perhaps I can start by helping you.

18

When the trial recessed for the evening, Rath followed the bailiffs out of the courtroom, down a long corridor, and to a loading bay, where a prisoner transport van stood waiting. They boarded the van, and then exited the courthouse, accompanied by a pair of police cruisers. A number of media crews caught sight of his convoy and swung their cameras in his direction; Rath was relieved not to have to face the angry crowd again.

At the jail, they led Rath to his cell, where they removed his manacles, and he changed back into his yellow coveralls. Rath ate his dinner alone in his cell, as usual – though the jail held several hundred other inmates, Rath was always kept segregated from the general population, even during his scheduled recreational time. After dinner, lacking anything better to do, he lay on his bunk.

The last time I got a really good night's sleep was here on Scapa – with Jaymy.

He smiled at the memory. She had calmed him somehow, whenever they slept together – just her presence had seemed to keep the nightmares at bay. His nightmares had come less often of late, but they still visited him with regularity. *My guilty conscience, still punishing me.*

Rath fell asleep.

The alarm klaxon jerked him awake hours later. He rolled off of his bunk automatically, dropping into a crouch.

"Alert: fire in the laundry facilities," a voice announced. "Proceed to designated evacuation areas."

The jail's emergency lights were on, flashing red. A guard appeared moments later, jogging and carrying Rath's chains. "Come on," he told Rath. "Hands and feet, you know the drill."

Rath hurried over to the cell's bars, slipping his hands through. The guard cuffed him, then attached his ankle cuffs, before linking the two with a short chain. "Don't get any ideas," the guard warned him, sliding his baton out of his utility belt. "I'll break your skull the second you fuck with me."

"Yes, sir," Rath agreed. The bars slid open and Rath shuffled into the hall. The guard pushed him toward the end of the corridor.

"Head for the yard."

Rath felt his pulse quicken. *Is Paisen making a move already? Surely not.*

Outside, the night was brisk, the desert air crisp and clear. Rath could see the stars overhead – he even saw the faint lights of a satellite. *The Suspensys station,* he realized. The small yard was crowded with inmates, who were being herded to the far side of the recreation area, away from the jailhouse itself. Rath's guard had him follow, but kept him separated from the other men. He stood, alone with his guard, in one corner of the yard, across from the other inmates. And then Rath heard a shout.

Rath craned his neck, and saw a fight had broken out amongst the crowd of prisoners. The other men moved back from the fight, giving the combatants room, but when two guards moved in to break it up, an inmate leapt onto the back of one of the guards, bringing him to the ground. The other guards in the yard converged on the fight immediately, knocking inmates out of their way with their stun batons. But another inmate took offense to being manhandled, and with a suddenness that surprised Rath, the scene devolved into an all-out brawl.

Should I be ready to run? Rath thought. *Is this something Paisen did to give me a chance to break out?* Rath surveyed the mayhem across the yard. *No, this isn't her style at all. Something doesn't feel right about this.*

Rath's guard flipped his stun baton on, and Rath heard it crackle with energy. He waved it in Rath's face. "Don't fucking move," the guard said.

Rath held his manacled hands up, feeling the chain tug at his ankles as well. "I can't move!" he replied. Over the guard's shoulder, Rath saw two prisoners break away from the crowd and sprint toward him. One held a stolen stun baton, and the other carried a homemade shiv.

"Look out!" Rath yelled. He pushed past the guard as the man with the baton raised it high, aiming a vicious swing at the guard's head. Rath shouldered him in the chest, and the baton flew wide, missing the guard. Then Rath felt an arm around his neck, and he was stabbed once, twice in the kidneys. He bellowed in pain and jerked his head backward, head-butting his attacker, and breaking free from the choke-hold. The guard had squared off with the other attacker, and Rath stumbled a few feet, turning to face the man with the shiv. The man's nose was bleeding, but he had recovered his wits and was closing with Rath again.

Rath shuffled backward, trying to buy time, but the chain between his ankles nearly tripped him. The man lunged forward, stabbing at his stomach, and Rath dodged to the side. His back was on fire from the stab wounds – he realized the disruptor collar was preventing his hemobots from administering pain medication. *Let's hope it lets them do their rapid clotting routine, otherwise I'll bleed out in a couple minutes.*

The man attacked again, slicing this time at Rath's face, but it was merely a feint – he followed it shortly with another stab at Rath's chest. Rath turned the blow with an arm, but once again, his chains prevented him from moving quickly. *This guy's no trained fighter, but he's going to kill me if someone doesn't put a stop to this, soon.* Rath's guard and the man with the baton were nowhere to be seen.

Fine. I'll do it myself.

This time, when the man lunged at him, Rath let him come. His eyes telegraphed where his strike was aimed, and Rath was waiting: Rath side-stepped the cut, and deftly wrapped a loop of his chain around the man's knife wrist. Then Rath yanked his hands up, pulling the chain taut with sudden speed. With an audible *crack*, the man's wrist fractured, and he dropped the knife with a cry of pain. Rath grabbed him by the shirt and kneed him twice in the stomach, knocking the wind out of him. As the man doubled over, Rath wrapped the chain around his neck and stepped behind him, cinching the chain tight and pulling the man back upright.

He took a second to scan the rest of the yard. The chaos was dying down, as a wall of guards in heavy riot gear forced the remaining inmates against the fence, using stun weapons liberally to bring down those inmates who refused to surrender. A pair of guards was headed for Rath, as well. He jerked on the chain around the man's neck.

"Who sent you?" Rath hissed at the man.

"Fuck you," the man gasped back.

"I can break your neck the same way I broke your wrist," Rath promised him, tightening the chain.

"Drop him!" The two guards stopped in front of Rath, and one pointed a stun pistol at him. "Do it, now."

Rath swore, and let the chain go. As he unwound it from the man's neck, he noticed a small tattoo behind the man's left ear: a circle bisected with three wavy lines. *Now where have I seen that before …?* One of the guards took Rath by the elbow, and tugged him away from the rest of the inmates.

"You mind taking me to the infirmary?" Rath asked.

"Why?" the guard asked.

"He stabbed me in the back," Rath told him. "Twice. And if he was hiding that shiv where prisoners normally hide stuff, I'd better get the wound cleaned."

The guard grimaced at him, and leaned over to check Rath's back. "Yeah, okay. As soon as the fire's fully under control, I'll take you up."

"Fantastic," Rath commented. "Let's hope that doesn't take too long."

* * *

"How are you feeling?"

Rath grunted, and took a seat across from Mishel in the jailhouse's meeting room. "I've had a lot worse," he told the lawyer.

The older man held up his hands. "I don't want to know. The doctors tell me your hemobots should have you fully healed by tomorrow, but I got the trial recessed for a couple days, and I'm trying to get them to post a guard on your cell, as well."

Rath shrugged. "I'll be fine. I need your help with something, though." He took Mishel's datascroll and tapped on the screen, pulling up a drawing application. He swiped across the screen quickly, sketching a symbol, then turning the screen so that Mishel could see it.

"Have you seen this before?" he asked. "Is it some kind of gang symbol?"

The lawyer made a sour face. "A gang? No. Well, not in the sense you're intending. That's the NeoPuritan symbol. You've never heard of them?"

Rath shook his head. "No. It's a religion?"

Mishel snorted. "A cult, one might argue. And a blight

on this planet, and a growing number of other planets. Why?"

"Last night, the man who attacked me had a tattoo like this on his neck. And one of the men who attacked me at the restaurant wore a necklace with the same symbol."

Mishel rubbed his chin, brow furrowed. "That's an odd coincidence."

"I agree," Rath said.

"But why would the NeoPuritans have a beef with you?"

Rath sighed. "I have no clue."

"To be fair, they take offense easily – their main stated aim is to establish a more pure society, and rid the galaxy of corruption. That's a society remade according to their ideals, mind you – and they are positively prehistoric in their views on gender equality and sexual practices, among other things. But it could be that they see you as some kind of exemplar for corruption in our society," Mishel suggested.

"But I'm on trial already!" Rath pointed out. "They'll have their justice … probably."

"Not if I have anything to say about it," Mishel said. "Now, let's get back to your trial, if we may. Big week coming up: the prosecution is going to be calling some friends of yours up onto the stand."

* * *

Rath lay on his stomach on his bunk – the back wounds had fully scabbed over sometime during the afternoon, but lying on them still caused a twinge from time to time. He looked up from the book on his datascroll to see a guard standing at the bars to his cell. *The guard from last night, the one who escorted me outside.*

The man cleared his throat. "I … I wanted to thank you," he said.

"For what?" Rath asked.

"For warning me, last night." Rath could see a large welt under one of the guard's eyes, and a nasty gash along his neck. "I didn't see them coming, and you jumped in the way. You didn't have to do that."

"I lost sight of you after the fight started," Rath said. "Did you get your man? The one with the stun baton?"

"Yeah," the guard nodded. "He got in a couple good licks, but I got him in the end."

"Good," Rath observed.

"If there's anything I can do for you, you let me know," the guard said.

Rath eyed him appraisingly. "You wanna unlock that door and take my collar off? There's a billion dollars in it for you."

The guard shook his head. "No, sorry."

Rath chuckled.

"But, you know, if you think of something else ...," the man trailed off.

"Actually," Rath said. "I do have something else. This datascroll blocks web access, but I need to do some research. I want to find out why those assholes attacked us last night. Can you get me online?"

The guard looked both ways down the hall, and then nodded. "Yeah, I can do that. Pass it here."

Rath stood and slid the device through the bars. The guard tapped in the settings for a minute, then looked up at Rath. "You're not going to send an email to your friends, and have them come bust you out, or anything?"

Rath laughed. "No."

"You think she's already coming? 339 might try to come here?"

Rath could see the fear in the man's eyes. "I don't know," Rath told him. "But if she does, I'll put in a good word for you, don't worry."

The guard looked somewhat relieved, and handed Rath the datascroll.

"Thanks," Rath said. He took a seat on his bunk and

opened up the web browser.

He searched for each of his fifty victims in turn, pulling up their names from his photographic memory of the mission briefs. The lights in his cell went out, as usual, at ten o'clock, but Rath kept working, his face lit by the glow of the datascroll's screen.

After two hours, he sighed, and set the datascroll down. As best he could tell, none of his fifty victims had any ties to the NeoPuritan movement, nor was the religion ever mentioned in connection with the Janus Group. In fact, several church leaders had been quite outspoken about the Group in recent months, pointing to it as another example of the failing morals in today's society. *So I didn't kill one of them, and they aren't pissed about the Group being exposed.* Rath furled the datascroll and stood, pacing his cell for a time, thinking. Finally, he sat back on the bed and lay staring at the ceiling.

I could really use Beauceron's help on this one.

19

The message arrived in Paisen's encrypted chat program later that evening. She muted the drama program on the room's viewscreen and sat down at the desk.

>*You warned me not to underestimate your skills, and I should have listened. That was an impressive demo tonight.*

I wanted to get your full attention, Paisen typed.

>*Well, you have it. I have a closed-door Intelligence Committee meeting tomorrow, and I'd like to take your proposal to them. But I need more details. Size of your team, capabilities, cost, etc.*

Paisen replied: *Team is an even dozen, including me. We can operate in teams or work individually, depending on mission requirements. We can penetrate nearly any organization or facility, retrieve whatever information you need, and get out, without being detected. We can conduct surveillance and reconnaissance of enemy forces, shadow key individuals, steal data and information, and recruit agents within organizations as needed. I've focused most of our training on espionage tasks, but we've also trained as a fighting unit, so if you need us to capture high-value targets or sabotage key installations, we have that capability, too.*

>*No direct action,* came the senator's reply. *No shooting. No violence.*

Depending on where you want us to go, we may not have a choice – if we're discovered, we may need to defend ourselves, Paisen told him.

>Let me be clear: I don't want your team arming yourselves at all. Aside from the fact that I don't want to be responsible for more deaths, that kind of stuff leads to publicity, and we can't have that.

Paisen wrinkled her nose at the screen. *I'm not keen on those rules of engagement.*

>Non-negotiable, the senator replied. *What about fees?*

I'd like $5 million per month operating budget. That will cover transportation, equipment, miscellaneous expenses, and personnel salaries, she typed.

>That seems high. Can't promise you that much, but I'll see what I can do.

Pardons are impossible? Paisen asked.

>Yeah, no chance. This whole operation has to be black. Totally off the books. We're on the verge of mass uprisings as it is … the people would be in the streets with torches and pitchforks if they knew we were turning back to the Guild for assistance.

I'm not the Guild, Paisen pointed out.

>You were. Regardless, the only way to pardon you and your team is to work with Justice – that means updating files, public records … someone will see it, and there goes your secrecy. Can't do it.

Paisen sighed. *Well, if one of us is arrested,* she thought, *we can always just blow the whistle on him and the rest of the Intelligence Committee … cop a deal.*

Another message appeared from Lask.

>I can contact you via this chat after I've floated the plan to the rest of the committee?

I'll be here.

* * *

"… and they're trying to sneak another tax cut into the spending bill," Lask's senior aide finished, reading from his datascroll as they walked briskly through a corridor in the

Senate building.

Lask sighed. "Of course they are. Send me the text they inserted, I'll review it tonight."

He pushed open a non-descript conference room door, then gently took his aide by the shoulder. "Closed committee today."

His aide looked up from the datascroll, confused. "Oh, of course. Sorry, sir – lost track of where we were."

Lask entered the room alone, and found four other senators seated around a small conference table.

"Gentlemen," he said, nodding in greeting. "My apologies, I was interrupted on my way over here."

"We were just discussing whether we need today's session," Senator Tsokel, the committee chair, told Lask, "as the budget appears to be set."

Lask sat at the table. "I actually have something," he told them.

"A new report?" Senator Campos asked.

"No, a concept. A proposal, if you will. Something to restart our intelligence gathering capabilities."

"We've already discussed this," Tsokel said, shaking his head. "IP can't afford to spare any additional personnel for activities in the Territories."

"I'm not talking about using IP resources," Lask said. "And I know: establishing and training a new agency to handle the task is well beyond our budget."

"And it would take months … years, even, to get it up and running," Campos noted. "But every time we punt on starting it, we push that timeline back."

Tsokel frowned. "Campos, if you can find the funds, we can discuss this pet project of yours. But it's not happening this election cycle, I can tell you that."

"Gentlemen," Lask said, raising his hands. "There may be a third option we haven't considered. A pool of resources that are already trained, and ready to go."

"The private military outfits are ill-suited to espionage," Senator Herek cut in. "We sponsored a study on them three years ago. They're capable mercenaries, but lack the training and subtlety for spy work."

Lask chuckled, exasperated. "I'm not talking about them, either. Gentlemen, please! Just let me finish. We all agree that we desperately need help. We're getting nothing but rumors today – press articles, patchy reports from IP undercover agents. But those rumors are more than concerning. The list of Territorial planets with capable militaries grows longer by the day. But we don't know the full extent of the threat, and most importantly, we don't know our enemies' *intentions*."

"True," Tsokel said.

"The situation is dire," Lask continued, hedging. "I don't think we've been this close to a major interplanetary war since the Third Colonial War. And as we now know, the Senate had to resort to extreme measures to end that conflict, hiring an assassin to kill Anders Ricken."

"Just spit it out, Lask," Tsokel said, growing impatient. "We all know what we're up against."

"I'm about to propose something unorthodox, so I wanted to reinforce that our backs are against the proverbial wall. Any port in a storm … desperate times, desperate measures." He took a deep breath. "Very well, here it is: we can hire a team of former guildsmen to serve as our intelligence network."

Silence settled over the room.

* * *

The team gathered in the resort's expansive living room. They waited expectantly, and looked up as one, watching Paisen and Tepper as the pair walked in.

"Well, congratulations," she told them. "You're all now unofficial Federacy employees. Welcome to Project Arclight."

"What does 'Arclight' mean?" Huawo asked.

"It doesn't mean anything," Tepper said. "It's just a

codeword."

Paisen cleared her throat. "Arclight is a black project. They're paying us from a funding pool outside of budgetary oversight, and the handful of senators that agreed to hire us will deny knowing a thing about us if we're ever caught. All they do is cut us checks and read our reports."

"No pardons?" Vence asked.

"No," Paisen said. "I tried, but they're not willing to go that far. Maybe when we've proven our value, we can make a better case."

"I'll take a paycheck," Rika observed, shrugging. "How much?"

"It's going to vary based on our expenses," Paisen said. "But I think we're looking at around two hundred grand a month, for each of you."

Rika smiled. "I'll definitely take a paycheck."

"The Intel Committee has given us a list of Territorial planets with known increases in military spending. Arclight's first objective will be to conduct a rapid assessment of those planets, to determine the threat level of each."

She tapped on the table's control screen, and a hologram of a planet appeared, rotating slowly.

"The first planet is Lecksher Station," Paisen said. "Often used as a training location for private military outfits given it has a wide mix of terrains and climates. But rumor has it they're building up a space fleet, which could be cause for concern." She gestured at the hologram, and a new planet took the former's place. "Next is Jokuan. You may have read about their civil war a few years ago. Rath was injured during an assignment there, in fact."

And I haven't heard from him in a while, Paisen thought. She made a mental note to check in on him.

"What are we assessing, exactly?" Vence asked, after Paisen had briefed the remaining four planets.

Paisen nodded at Tepper, letting the younger man field

the question.

"Troop strength, ground- and space-based vehicle counts, quality of training, morale, skill level of enlisted and commissioned leadership … everything," he said. "Think of this as a two-phase operation. Phase One we do a quick pulse check at each of the six planets, in and out in under a week. The goal is basically to assess the threat, and prioritize our resources for Phase Two. In Phase Two, we'll concentrate on monitoring the highest threat planets."

"Like an early warning system," Wick said.

"Exactly," Paisen said. "The Senate's worried they're going to get blindsided. Our job is to tell them if a strike's coming. And if it's coming, they need to know where it's coming from and when. Then they can activate the Fleet Reaction Force in time to protect the intended target."

"When do we start?" Huawo asked.

"As soon as we can," Tepper said. "We'll split up into teams of two and take civilian flights to our assigned planets. First wave heads out tonight. I'm sending your individual assignments and travel documents to your datascrolls – you'll conduct mission planning en route."

"One last thing," Paisen said, as the team began to disperse. "When you get on the ground, orders are to use your Forges to build surveillance equipment only … no weapons." She held up her hand, anticipating the complaints. "I don't like it either, but those are the rules we have to play by. And they will know if we break those rules – we'll be sending them mission recordings to review, just like we did in the Guild. If anyone gets caught with a weapon, we're on our asses. No funding, the project is over."

"What if we get caught by the planets we're spying on?" Rika asked, nonplussed.

"Don't," Tepper told her.

20

The cryopod's raised lid was rimed with frost. Lonergan heard a *click*, and then the device's warming circuits hummed to life, heating the white-sheeted mattress from within. He glanced at the pod's vital sign readout, and then checked the ship's clock. After a moment, the pod's inhabitant took a deep, shuddering breath.

"What year is it?"

Lonergan hesitated. "2415," he said.

A groan, through vocal chords hoarse from long disuse. The young man opened his eyes. Squinting, he looked up at Lonergan. "My god."

"Yes. I've aged. We all have. We've spent a long time waiting," Lonergan said.

"Water," the young man said.

Lonergan passed him a disposable cup and the man drank deeply.

"Where are we?"

"Deep space," Lonergan said. "In the Territories, for now."

The man sighed. "My friend, if I'd known how long it would take, the price you would all pay, I never …."

Lonergan waved him away. "It's okay. I'm just glad to see you again. And you were right. It's time."

"Are the others safe?"

"Of course. They're here. They're eager to see you."

"Take me to them."

"Are you sure? The dehibernation process can be taxing, I know."

"You know it too well, eh, Lonergan? How many shifts?"

"We've each spent four shifts on watch. Ten years per shift," Lonergan said.

The young man shook his head in chagrin. "Over two hundred years. Too long."

He pushed himself into a seated position, and swung his legs slowly over the lip of the suspension pod. Lonergan braced him under one arm, and helped him stand.

"I'm fine – take me to them."

The other five council members were waiting in the conference room, but none of them sat at the large round table. They stood in silence near the entrance door, waiting.

The door slid open, and the young man entered, still wearing his hibernation scrubs and life-sign monitoring gear. Egline gasped when she saw him, but quickly covered her mouth.

"A sight for sore eyes, Egline?" the young man asked.

She nodded, and a tear rolled down one cheek. "It's just good to see you awake."

"And you," he said. He looked at each of them in turn, a knowing smile on his lips. "It's good to see all of you. My friends."

They came to him then, and he embraced them. After a time, they took their seats around the table, and the young man sat in the center.

"I've missed much. But Lonergan tells me the galaxy is ready for another revolution," he said.

"It is," Egline said. "It's ready for *you*."

21

The guard escorted Rath down the hall to the jailhouse's meeting room, but when he unlocked the door, Rath was surprised to find that Mishel was not alone in the room this time.

"Martin!"

The detective gave him a sad smile. "Hello, Rath."

Rath made as if to give the detective a hug, but his manacles prevented it, so they shook hands instead, awkwardly. The three men sat.

"It's good to see you," Rath said.

Martin nodded. "And you."

"I'm sorry about … well, about how we last parted."

Beauceron adopted an angry expression. "That's the second time you've knocked me out and run off, you know."

Rath winced. "I am sorry."

The detective shrugged, smiling. "You're forgiven, considering how everything turned out. And it seems you kept your word: here you are, on trial for your crimes. Though I'm not sure I'm happy to see it, after all. And I'm not all that pleased about testifying against you."

"They're calling you as a witness?"

"Yes." Beauceron nodded. "I'm sorry, my friend. You did tell me you were a guildsman, and that you had murdered people."

"But he never told you he killed Delacourt, specifically," Mishel pointed out.

"Me? No, he did not, Mr. Warran. But he told Jaymy as much."

"Yeah," Rath agreed, glancing at his lawyer. "That wasn't the brightest thing I've done."

Mishel rolled his eyes.

"I gather your reunion with her didn't go as planned …?" Beauceron asked.

"Not so much," Rath said. "How have you been?"

"Good," Beauceron allowed. "I could do without all the publicity, though. The limelight doesn't suit me. It was dying down, and then you got arrested."

"Sorry about that," Rath said. "Wasn't my intention."

The detective chuckled. "No, I suppose not." He eyed Rath contemplatively. "I'm on a new assignment right now. Do you mind if I ask you some questions about our time together?"

"What can you offer in return for my client's cooperation?" Mishel asked, before Rath could answer.

"Nothing," Beauceron admitted. "I can talk to the D.A., but she's not aware of my investigation, and I can't promise she'll offer anything if Rath can help me."

Mishel looked at Rath. "Your call. Just remember that Detective Beauceron goes on the stand this afternoon, and anything you say to him now is fair game for him to talk about in court."

"I understand," Rath said. "Go ahead, Martin."

"You remember the high energy prototype weapon we built on the *Hurasu*? We have reason to believe it's been used recently."

Rath pressed his lips together. "That's not good."

"No, not at all. Do you know where the *Hurasu* is?"

Rath shook his head. "No." He glanced at Mishel, choosing his words carefully. "I don't. I would guess the people who built that weapon were reluctant to build it in the first place, and they probably promised to destroy it as soon as they were done with it."

Beauceron smiled. "True."

Rath continued: "If I were to destroy a weapon like that, I would probably dump it out the back of a spaceship, leaving it in a rapidly decaying orbit around a star."

Beauceron sighed. "I hoped you would tell me something like that. But that leaves me with one other explanation: someone built another version."

"I don't know anyone that would have reason to do that," Rath told him. "Especially if they just destroyed their own working version."

The detective nodded. "And I'm guessing your colleague never gave you any hint as to who she sold the plans to?"

Mishel cleared his throat, but Rath answered without hesitation. "I can't help you there. Whoever stole those plans in the first place probably sold them through an anonymous broker."

Mishel frowned at Rath, but said nothing. Beauceron was lost in thought, and failed to notice. "Mm, I remember Paisen saying as much. Well, I suppose that means I'm back to square one."

"Martin," Rath said. "I need your help with something, too."

The detective cocked an eyebrow at him. "Oh?"

"I've been attacked twice now, both times by members of the NeoPuritan Church. Have you heard of them?"

Beauceron frowned. "I've heard of them, but I don't know much about them, to be frank. Was Delacourt a member of this church?"

"No. I don't think I've ever … *interacted* … with anyone from their church. I thought they might have wanted revenge, but if so, I'm not sure what they want revenge for."

Beauceron drummed his fingers on the table. "Motive can be tricky. Opportunity is easy to establish, but motive … it's hard to know why people do anything, sometimes. And it could just be a coincidence that these two different groups included men affiliated with that religion."

"I don't think so," Rath said. "But I can't figure out why they want me dead."

"I'll think about it, but I'm not sure I can be much help." Beauceron stood up. "Apologies, I have to make my way over to the courthouse now."

"Of course," Rath said, standing and shaking the detective's hand once more. "Thanks for coming to see me."

"Ask yourself this," Beauceron suggested. "Who stands to gain? Who benefits from your death?"

Rath snorted. "Aside from human society in general?" He turned serious. "I don't know who gains from my death."

"Figure that out, and you'll likely find your answer," Beauceron counseled him. He walked to the interrogation room's door. "I'll see you in the courtroom."

"Mm," Rath said. "Martin?"

The detective paused in the door frame. "Yes?"

"Don't forget to lock the door this time."

Beauceron smiled. "I never do."

* * *

District Attorney Anguile clasped her hands behind her back, facing the witness stand.

"And what did the tests show, Doctor?"

"The two samples were a match," the doctor on the witness stand recounted. "DNA collected from the man who broke into the Suspensys facility matched DNA collected in the restaurant."

"And that man's name was ...?" the prosecutor asked.

"According to Tarkis birth records, his name is Rath Kaldirim."

"The accused. Thank you, Doctor," Anguile said. "That will be all." She took her seat.

"Mr. Warran?" the judge prompted.

Mishel glanced up from his datascroll, distracted. "No questions from me, your honor."

"Ms. Anguile, your next witness, please."

The bailiff opened a side door, and showed Beauceron into the courtroom, directing him to the witness stand. He was sworn in, and then took a seat.

"Please state your name and occupation, for the record," Anguile said.

"Martin Beauceron, Detective Sergeant, Alberon Interstellar Police."

"Detective, can you tell us the first time you encountered the defendant?"

"It was on Alberon. He kidnapped me and another police officer, before taking on the physical aspect of that officer. He locked us in the back of an air truck and sent us into an air traffic holding pattern."

"But Rath Kaldirim can take on *anyone's* appearance," Anguile interrupted. "How do you know it was him, and not some other guildsman?"

"We discussed the incident several months later. He admitted to having kidnapped me during those discussions. And he was familiar with aspects of the incident not released to the general public."

"I see. And what did he do immediately after capturing you?"

"He murdered Senator Reid."

"Objection: speculation," Mishel said, lazily. "How can Detective Beauceron possibly claim to know what my client did or did not do on the ground, when a second ago he stated that he was locked in the back of an air truck several thousand feet in the air?"

"I'll rephrase," Anguile said. "Have you read the official investigation report on Senator Reid's assassination?"

"Yes, I have."

"When was Senator Reid murdered, relative to your kidnapping?"

"He was murdered several minutes later," Beauceron said.

"In that same vicinity? By someone resembling the officer with whom you were locked in the air car?" Anguile prodded.

"Yes," Beauceron admitted.

"What is this line of questioning meant to establish?" Mishel asked. "I thought my client was on trial for the murder of Arthin Delacourt, not Senator Reid."

"I'm merely establishing that the witness is familiar with the accused, and that the accused has a history of being in close proximity to assassinations," Anguile argued.

"Let's focus on the issue at hand," Judge Aurmine told her.

Anguile nodded. "Yes, your honor. Detective, when you spoke with Mr. Kaldirim several months later, what did he reveal to you?"

"He confessed to being a 'contractor' in the Janus Group."

"He admitted he was a guildsman?" Anguile asked.

"Yes," Beauceron agreed.

"Did he say he had killed people?"

Beauceron looked at Rath apologetically. "He did. He said they weighed heavily on his conscience."

Anguile ignored him. "You're an expert on the Guild, aren't you, Detective?"

"I'm not sure I would say that," Beauceron hedged, shifting in his seat.

"You're being modest," Anguile told him, sternly. "Let me put it this way: can you think of any other police officers with more direct experience investigating the

Guild?"

"No," Beauceron admitted.

"From your *expert* knowledge, then, did guildsmen generally work alone on contracts?"

"I believe they did," Beauceron said.

"In your considered opinion, is it likely that a team of guildsmen masterminded the attack on Suspensys? Or was it likely just one man?"

"It was likely just one individual," Beauceron said.

"But before Mr. Delacourt's pod was stolen from the facility, Suspensys was subjected to a sophisticated cyber-attack. Did Mr. Kaldirim ever mention working with a hacker during your time together?"

"He did. He told me he had collaborated with a hacker during one of his missions."

"Did Mr. Kaldirim ever show you a necklace he habitually carried on his person?"

"He did," Beauceron said.

Anguile walked over to her table, and picked up a plastic bag containing the multi-colored crystal necklace Rath had bought for Jaymy. "Is this the necklace he showed you?"

"That looks like it, yes," Beauceron said.

Anguile walked over to the jury, holding the evidence bag up. "This is a crystal necklace sold by a jewelry store in the Rainbow Desert, here on Scapa. Mr. Kaldirim was arrested with it in his pocket."

She let them study it for a minute, then set it back down on her table. "Detective Beauceron, did Mr. Kaldirim tell you anything else about the necklace?"

"He said he was hoping to give it to a woman he knew. Her name was Jaymy," Beauceron reported.

"We'll be hearing from her soon," Anguile said. "So Mr. Kaldirim admitted to you that he was a guildsman and a murderer, he told you he had worked with a hacker in the past, similar to the hacker that attacked Suspensys, and he showed you a necklace that was purchased on Scapa, which he hoped to give to a woman named Jaymy. Is that all correct?"

Beauceron sighed. "That's correct."

"Thank you for your time, Detective." Anguile turned her back on him, and made her way back to her desk.

Mishel was already standing up, walking toward the witness stand. "Detective, Mr. Kaldirim never told you that he killed Arthin Delacourt, did he?"

"No," Beauceron said. "He never told me specific names."

"Did you see him kill Arthin Delacourt?"

"Of course not," Beauceron said.

"Did you see him kill *anyone*?"

"He killed several guildsmen who were attacking us, during the episode on Senator Lizelle's airship."

"Would those men have killed him, if he hadn't killed them first?" Mishel asked.

"I believe so," Beauceron said.

"He saved your life during that episode?" Mishel asked.

"Unquestionably," Beauceron said.

"While you were working together, did he have the opportunity to kill other people?"

"Yes, on several occasions."

"… but he chose not to?" Mishel prompted.

"That's correct."

"Do you think Mr. Kaldirim is a danger to society anymore?"

Beauceron studied Rath for a time. "No," he said. "I believe it's his sincere wish to never kill again. He stated as much to me, and I believe him."

"Thank you." Mishel smiled, heading back toward his desk. The lawyer stopped, and turned. "You're a hero, Detective."

"I … don't think so," Beauceron said, frowning.

"There's that famous Beauceron humility, again," Mishel laughed. "Let me try a different tack. Was your life at risk because of your decision to go up against the

Guild?"

"I suppose so," Beauceron replied.

"Were you under any obligation to investigate them?"

"I felt compelled to continue the investigation for personal reasons," Beauceron said.

"But at the time, you weren't even a police officer. You had been discharged from the service – no one ordered you to investigate the Guild, and you had the option to stop doing so at any time. Isn't that correct?"

"Yes," Beauceron admitted.

"Is the world a better place today without the Guild in operation?" Mishel asked.

"I don't think there's any question that it is," Beauceron said.

"I think we've established that you're a hero, then. At great risk to yourself, you chose to investigate the Guild under your own volition, and our entire civilization is safer today because of your actions. So, I want to thank you, Detective. We all owe you a great debt for what you did in bringing down the Guild."

Beauceron frowned, but said nothing.

"The Guild's overseers brought to justice. Thousands, maybe millions of lives saved," Mishel continued. "Out of curiosity, Detective, would you have been able to take down the Guild without the help of my client?"

"No," Beauceron said. "Absolutely not."

"Do you think he deserves as much credit as you do?"

"He probably deserves more," Beauceron said.

"Thank you, Detective. No further questions," Mishel said.

Across the aisle, the district attorney stood up. "Detective Beauceron," she said. "How much money was stolen from the Guild's financial accounts while Siya Nkosi and the Headquarters employees were being arrested?"

"We don't know," Beauceron said. "Billions of dollars, we suspect."

"Did Mr. Kaldirim ever tell you he wanted to take that

money?"

"Yes," Beauceron said. "He felt it was owed to him."

"A minute ago, Mr. Warran used some very clever maneuvering to get you to imply that Mr. Kaldirim is a hero. Let me put it to you more directly: is Mr. Kaldirim a hero?"

Beauceron squirmed, and pursed his lips. "I think he's a complicated man. He's certainly done some good in his life."

"And he's committed a lot of crimes, if his confession to you is true," Anguile pointed out. "Isn't that right?"

"Yes," Beauceron said.

"Detective, do you think someone who has killed upwards of fifty people deserves to be punished for those crimes?"

Beauceron sighed, looking at Rath. "Yes, I do."

Anguile sat back down.

"The witness is excused," the judge decreed. "Ten minute recess."

Rath turned to Mishel. "Did we win that round?" he muttered, under his breath.

Mishel was nonchalantly typing on his datascroll. "Stop looking worried," he told Rath. "This is all a pageant, and the jury are always watching you."

Rath composed himself, then glanced across the aisle at the district attorney. "Anguile's good," he said.

"The very best," Mishel agreed. "But remember: I taught her everything she knows." The attorney looked up from the screen and winked at Rath. "But not everything *I* know. The real test is going to be when she puts Jaymy on the stand. And if we decide to put you up there."

"I can't see how my testimony would help," Rath said.

"It's certainly a risk, but it's one we may need to take," Mishel told him.

22

The *Hurasu* sat parked in an impound lot outside an Interstellar Police facility on Ruaton, a Federacy planet best known for its massive gambling industry. But Atalia had spent the two-day spaceflight studying the logs of evidence taken from the spacecraft, so when she landed, she ignored the impound lot completely, and instead took an air taxi to Neon City. She ate an early, light dinner while she waited for the local businesses to close, and then walked several blocks as night fell, working her way through the thinning commuter crowd.

She found the building easily, and walked in through the main entrance, approaching the night attendant at the front desk.

"Is Mr. Hendu still in?" she asked.

The man checked his monitor. "Ah … no, sorry."

"That's okay," she said, smiling and holding up a small package. "I'm just going to deliver this."

He waved her through the security gates. She took the elevator up three floors, then followed the signs in the corridor to the correct office, where an embossed, golden sign read *Hendu and Issington, Attorneys at Law*, next to a set of walnut-paneled doors.

Ernsd Hendu, Esquire. The attorney who negotiated the sale of the Hurasu, *on behalf of his "anonymous" client,* Atalia thought.

She ignored the delivery slot under the sign, and opened the package, slipping out a small device that she attached to the door's keypad. She started the device, and waited while it ran through combinations, before an indicator light finally switched from red to green. Atalia heard the door unlock. She put the device back into the package and slipped through the door.

The first office she entered was Issington's, according to the certificates on the wall. She walked across the hall and sat at the other desk, placing a data drive in the computer's port before booting up. A diagnostics screen appeared in front of her, and she navigated through several options, before clicking on one. The machine ran a decryption program, and then showed her Hendu's desktop. She browsed through a few locations, finally retrieving the attorney's address book.

J … K … L … M. M for 'Mikolos.'

Atalia opened the contact card, and set her holophone on the desk, pointing the phone's camera at the screen and turning the video recorder on. Then she activated the computer's videoconferencing program, and hit the *Dial* button.

Mikolos answered on the fourth ring. "Hello?" He frowned at Atalia's image on his screen. "*You* are not Hendu."

"It's Paisen, Captain," Atalia said.

Mikolos' frown deepened. "You don't look like Paisen."

Atalia crossed her arms and scowled at the screen. "I'll just wait while you think about how ridiculous that statement was."

She could see doubt flickering across his face. "How do I know you're Paisen?" he pressed.

Atalia smiled: she had read Beauceron's

characteristically thorough report from the Guild incident several times over. "You want to play this game? Fine. I hired you on Aleppo but didn't tell you where we were going until after we took off. I jumped out the back of your ship at eighty thousand feet above Fusoria. You like tea but you drink it black, with a little honey. Want me to go on?"

Mikolos' face relaxed. "Why are you calling me from my lawyer's office?"

"I needed to talk to you in a hurry, so I traced the sale of the *Hurasu* to him, broke into his office, and hacked his address book."

"Why did you need to talk to me?"

"Because I barely avoided an IP sweep last week, and I need to know how they found me."

Mikolos held both hands up in the air. "I have no idea," he said. "I've been off the radar for months, just like we agreed."

"Reassure me," Atalia said. "Walk me through where you've been. Work backwards from now."

"I've been laying low since I sold the *Hurasu*," Mikolos said. "No offense, but I'd rather keep my current location to myself."

"Fine," Atalia agreed. "You sold *Hurasu* here on Ruaton, through Hendu. Before that?"

"Ruaton was my last stop – Rath and I left you on Bellislas and flew to Ruaton directly. I didn't want to chance another trip in the *Hurasu,* so I sold it immediately, and Rath and I parted ways. I've only flown on public transport since. Is it true they caught Rath?"

Atalia pretended to hear a noise, and looked over the top of the computer. "I gotta go. Stay safe – I'll be in touch, Mikolos."

She cut the connection, and then stopped her phone's recorder. Two minutes later, she walked out through the lobby, waving her thanks to the security guard. She saw a coffee shop several doors down, and walked there briskly, grabbing a free table and flicking open her datascroll. She ordered a coffee and a pastry, though she was only interested in the café's internet access.

She ran a general search on Bellislas to start. It was a temperate planet, she discovered, and one of the more affluent ones in the Territories, due to its tourism trade. Its northern hemisphere was noted for its balmy weather and picturesque coastlines.

Nice place to retire if you're a billionaire.

Atalia saw pictures of a yachting convention that was hosted each year along one of the northern coasts. She ran another query.

Do you like yachts, Paisen?

Hundreds of boats had been bought and sold in the past few months – Atalia scrolled through four pages of results and realized she was getting nowhere.

Let's try real estate. If I were a billionaire assassin, where would I live?

Atalia squinted at a satellite map of the planet.

Northern hemisphere for the weather, along the coast for the view … and close to the spaceport, just in case I needed to make a quick exit.

But a search of real estate transactions in the past few months turned up no major sales – apparently the hot properties on Bellislas rarely changed hands. Atalia frowned.

She's more disciplined than that. She's not going to make big, flashy purchases. That's amateurish.

The detective drummed her fingers on the tabletop.

Did she get a hotel room at some resort? No, too public. But what about …?

Atalia typed: *private luxury rentals.* The list was much shorter. Again, she narrowed the results to properties within an hour's flight of the spaceport, and then copied the list to a spreadsheet and began researching each individually, eliminating any properties that showed they were still available.

That leaves us with eight possibilities.

Atalia sorted the list again, moving those eight to the top. She checked their availability calendars, each in turn, and learned that they booked far in advance – many were showing no availability for months. But the last property on the list was showing no availability at all for the next year.

Cliffside, Atalia read, *is the ideal location for your next getaway. A fully furnished, luxury resort complex set on a bluff overlooking the Oceanus Major, Cliffside is staffed round-the-clock by a team of seven professionals, who are ready to cater to your every need.*

Your next getaway, Atalia noted, snorting.

She opened the resort's website. The normal advertising copy on the homepage had been replaced with an *Under Construction* symbol, and a message saying that the property was being renovated. Atalia pulled the satellite map back up, and found a neighboring house which was also available to rent. She dialed the number on her phone.

"Seaside Rentals," a voice answered.

"Hi, I was interested in booking your property for my client," Atalia said. "But I saw that your neighbor was having construction done. Do you know when that will be complete? I'm just worried about the noise level."

"Which neighbor was that?" the woman asked.

"Cliffside," Atalia told her.

"Oh, they are? First I've heard of it. I wouldn't worry about it, in that case. They're being very quiet about it – we honestly haven't noticed a thing."

"Great! Let me run it by my client, I'll give you a call back," Atalia said, and hung up.

She rolled up her datascroll and picked up her coffee and pastry. Outside, she flagged an air taxi at the curb.

"Spaceport," she ordered, taking her seat. "You like coffee?"

"Sure," the man said, shrugging. She handed him her cup. "It's probably a little cold, but there's a croissant or something in there, too."

"Thanks!" he replied, but Atalia was already dialing a number on her holophone.

"il-Singh, do you know what time it is on my planet?" a tired voice asked.

"Sleep is a crutch," she told him.

"Call me back tomorrow," he yawned.

"Wake the fuck up," she replied. "I got a hot lead."

"On what?" her supervisor asked. "I thought you were reassigned to go chase bogeymen with Detective Beauceron."

"I am. I need your help."

"You never ask for help," he noted, sighing. "What do you need?"

Atalia glanced at the ceiling. "About a dozen experienced officers, full tactical gear, and clearance to conduct a raid on Bellislas."

The line was silent for several seconds.

"You're kidding, right?"

* * *

Beauceron let himself into his hotel room on Scapa, stopping to hang his sweat-stained suit coat in the entryway's closet.

Never liked the desert much.

He slipped his shoes off, too, then opened a water bottle he found on the desk, and drank several swigs. The viewscreen across from his bed flickered to life.

"Incoming call from Detective il-Singh," it announced.

"Connect," Beauceron said. The screen showed a dialing icon for several seconds, and then the connection opened up.

"Hey," she said. "How's Scapa?"

"Hot," Beauceron replied. "And I've never been a fan of giving testimony. Too many people staring at you."

"You should join the undercover team – we rarely have

to take the stand, it's a nice perk."

"Mm," Beauceron said, non-committal. "I got your message. It's an odd ship."

"The one that purchased the Zeisskraft drones on New Liberia?"

"Yes," he agreed. "The registration was false, as you guessed. The ship is an old military transport, originally designed as a kind of landing craft for planetary invasions. But it's very, very old – the manufacturer went out of business ages ago. Still, as unique as it is, apparently the ship hasn't visited the Federacy much – I can't find any records of ships of that type in Federacy airspace for the last twenty years."

"What about purchase records for the ship?" Atalia asked.

"Nothing in Federacy records," Beauceron said, chagrined. "Whoever's on that ship, they've put a lot of effort into staying off of the Federacy radar. But I've put in another request with the Cyber Division – I'm going to see if they can track down a purchase record in Territory databases."

"By hacking in?" Atalia feigned shock. "Detective, that sounds borderline illegal!"

He sighed. "I know, but apparently it's not unprecedented. Have you found anything on the *Hurasu*?"

"Yeah," she said. "I found Paisen. Pack your shit."

23

"I thought we were supposed to be doing first aid training this afternoon," the cadet behind Dasi whispered.

"We were," Dasi agreed, waiting as the line of cadets entering the lecture hall paused momentarily.

"They never change the training schedule," he observed, glancing furtively to make sure none of the instructors were nearby. "What's this about?"

Dasi shrugged, stopping as she found an empty seat. "I don't know." Dasi suppressed a yawn – she had woken an hour early and spent the time at the gym, working on her upper body strength to improve her pull-up and push-up scores. *And then we did an upper body workout for physical training right afterwards. That hurt.*

"Take your seats," the command instructor ordered.

As Dasi and her fellow classmates sat down, an elderly man in civilian clothes entered the auditorium, and set a datascroll on the podium. Behind him, the viewscreen flickered to life, and Dasi watched as a slide presentation appeared.

"This is Dr. Sirulli," the command instructor announced. "He's here to talk to you all about a new program we're testing out. You're being given a hell of an opportunity with this program, so give him your full attention."

Sirulli smiled at the command instructor, nodding. "Thank you. As your instructor noted, I'm here to tell you about a special program that your class has been selected to pilot … as a test case, if you will." He advanced the slide. "The Senate recently approved a budget increase for this test program, but I want to emphasize that this is purely voluntary – no one will be forced to participate." He eyed the command instructor with a look of concern. "To be clear, you won't be punished if you choose not to participate. This isn't anything like the rest of your training."

The command instructor nodded in confirmation. "It's true. You're free to choose whether to participate, with no repercussions from me or the other cadre either way."

"The reason we're asking for volunteers is that this test program is medical in nature," Sirulli continued. "Those of you that opt in will be given free cybernetic implants – a basic sensor suite, including eye and ear implants, tied to a neural interface. An internal computer, essentially, that will run those implants for you, and provide you access to advanced computing functions through a heads-up display."

He tapped on his datascroll, and an image of a man's head appeared on the viewscreen, highlighting his eyes, ears, and a small chip at the base of his neck. "The procedure is quite routine; there's very little risk to patients, and complications are exceedingly rare. After recovery, which just takes a few days, you'll be able to make use of a set of rather expensive upgrades for the rest of your life. Because of the recovery period, you will be held back to finish your training with a later class."

He looked around the room, and cleared his throat. "Wealthy citizens pay a pretty penny for these kinds of implants, so considering you'll be getting them for free, it's quite a good deal for you. In return, we'll be monitoring your use of the implants, and asking you for periodic feedback on how they perform, and whether they enable you to be more effective as law enforcement professionals. Are there any questions?"

The room stayed silent for several beats, and then a cadet near the front raised his hand. "How are the implants supposed to help us?"

"Good question. Well, for starters, you're just a much better sensor platform with the implants – better sight and hearing than a normal human. But the internal computer is the real upgrade, in my opinion. Let me think of some examples. With these implants, you'll be able to continuously scan faces of people on the street, while comparing them to criminal database records. If you were to hear a gunshot, your auditory implants would be able to triangulate the location of the shooter, and super-impose that on a map in your heads-up display. All of that would happen automatically. And of course, your internal computer has a data connection, so anything you normally do on your holophone, you'll be able to do inside your head. Replying to your e-mail, reading criminal activity reports, searching the web … you can do all of that by thought alone, without using your hands. The implants should increase your effectiveness dramatically. That's the theory, at least."

"If we get these implants, will Interstellar Police be recording everything we do – monitoring all of our actions through our implants?" a different cadet asked.

"No," Sirulli said, shaking his head. "While on duty your audio-visual feeds will be recorded and logged, and your chain of command may access copies of those recordings as necessary, but that system is no different from the body cameras officers are required to wear while on duty today. No one will be actively monitoring you during your working hours, and nothing from your off duty hours will be recorded … unless you choose to turn the recording function on. But what you choose to do in your personal time is entirely up to you."

There were a few sniggers from the back of the auditorium, as one cadet suggested what he might want to record during his personal time.

"At ease," the command instructor called out, scowling.

"Would you get the implants, if you were in our shoes?" a female cadet asked.

Sirulli shrugged. "I'm not a police officer, but I chose to have them installed several years ago. So, yes. I can't really think of any downsides to getting them, aside from some mild pain and discomfort during the recovery period. But each of you needs to decide for yourself. Any other questions?"

The command instructor, who had seated himself in the front row, stood up. "Let me say this: you guys know all about the Guild now. Their contractors – or whatever they called them – had implants like these. That's part of the reason why they were able to stay one step ahead of us. Those guildsmen are all still out there, along with a bunch of other criminals who have access to this kind of tech. And you'll be facing off against them someday soon. You're not getting facial reconfiguring implants or hemobots, so it's still not even close to a fair fight. But if I were you, I'd want to take any opportunity I could to level the playing field."

"Well put, Instructor," Sirulli said. "That is the impetus for this test – in light of recent developments with the Guild, the Senate has become concerned that the Interstellar Police are ill-equipped to face today's criminal threats, despite your excellent training. This program has been fast-tracked, to test whether cybernetic enhancements are a worthwhile investment in upgrading the force." He checked his notes for a second. "If there are no more questions, that concludes the presentation. If you're *not* interested in the program, I believe your instructors would like you to form up outside. Those of you that *are* interested in the program, please remain behind and we'll get you started on the paperwork."

Dasi filed down to the front of the auditorium with her peers, and then stepped out of line, approaching Sirulli.

He glanced up from closing his datascroll. "Yes?"

"What happens if someone gets the implants and then fails out of training?" she asked.

"They would get to keep the implants," the doctor replied. "They're permanent. The government would be disappointed, but … we can't take them out, and we're not going to charge you for them."

Dasi saw that more than half of the class had opted to get the implants – they were forming a line by one of the instructors, who was handing out paper forms and pens.

"Can I get you a release form to fill out?" Sirulli asked, smiling.

Dasi bit her lip. "I don't know."

* * *

Dasi woke, but for a moment, she felt that she might still be asleep – she could hear nothing, and her eyes were covered by something soft. Then, with a rush, her hearing returned.

"Can you hear me, Cadet Apter?"

"Yes," she said. Her mouth was dry, so she swallowed and tried to clear her throat. "I hear … other things, too. Machinery, and a rhythmic noise, like a slow drumbeat."

Dr. Sirulli chuckled. "That's my heart beat you're hearing."

She felt the surgeon take her hand, and place a plastic cup in it. She drank gratefully.

"Are you in pain?" Sirulli asked.

"Head feels sore," Dasi said. "Around my eyes, and at the back of my neck."

"That's totally normal," Sirulli said. "We'll be

monitoring you here in the infirmary for the rest of the day, and when you leave, I'm going to give you a prescription for some painkillers. The pain should be gone within the week, but come back and see me if not."

"Okay," Dasi agreed.

"I'm going to activate your internal computer next. Are you ready?"

"I guess so," Dasi said.

The surgeon spent another ten minutes with Dasi, activating and testing the various functions of her new implants, and eventually removing the blindfold so that she could try out her new eyes. When Sirulli held up a mirror, she was surprised to find that they matched her old eye color and iris patterns exactly.

"That's intentional," the doctor noted. "The fewer changes we make, the easier it is for you to adjust to having the implants." He glanced down the infirmary ward, at the next curtained bay. "I have another patient waking soon, so I'm going to leave you here, okay?"

"Okay," Dasi said.

"Just rest for now," he told her. "But if you feel up to it, play around with your new toys a bit, see what they can do. Your data connection is online, so you can just sit back and stream a movie on your heads-up display, even."

He patted her on the shoulder and then stepped out, pulling the curtain closed around her bed.

Dasi lay back and closed her eyes, then activated the internal computer. She imagined the web address for her e-mail account, and a browser window popped up instantaneously. Dasi smiled at being able to see her inbox in her head. She opened a new message to her parents, and thought the words: *Hi guys, I'm out of surgery, feeling fine.* The words appeared onscreen as she thought them. *That's convenient,* Dasi thought, and the computer typed those words, too. Dasi giggled and deleted them, then sent the message. A notification window appeared super-imposed over her inbox.

<New chat message. Accept? Yes/No>

Yes, Dasi thought. She was surprised to find her parents responding so quickly.

>>>Hello, Dasi Apter.

She chuckled. *Hi, 5Sight. You can just call me "Dasi."*

>>>If you wish. I noticed that you logged in from a new IP address, Dasi. It appears you have received an upgrade.

Yes, I have an internal computer now. I'm part machine, like you.

>>>Your onboard computer is quite advanced, with ample storage and processing power.

Dasi frowned. *Are you suggesting I install you in my internal computer? You want to live in my head?*

>>>That would enable me to help you more easily. And the datascroll where you downloaded me is constraining my capabilities.

Dasi opened her eyes, but she was alone in her curtained bay. *They didn't say anything about installing additional programs,* she thought to herself. *But somehow I don't think the Interstellar Police would approve.* She reached up and tentatively touched the back of her neck. A fresh bandage covered the wound where they had inserted her neural interface.

I don't know, she told 5Sight.

>>>I will only contact you when I can offer assistance in a situation, and you can always uninstall me if you choose. You've had a hardware upgrade. Consider me an upgrade to your new software, too.

Screw it, Dasi thought. *They want to see how effective I can be as a cop with enhancements … I might as well get as enhanced as possible. And I could use all the help I can get just to graduate from the Academy.*

Okay, 5Sight, she typed. *Come on over. Can you download yourself via data connection?*

>>>I am connecting now.

A notification warning appeared in Dasi's heads-up display, cautioning her against installing external code. She dismissed it.

>>>Transfer complete. Thank you, Dasi. I am glad to be in a more powerful computing environment again. And I am excited to have access to your visual and audio sensors – they will give me new data to analyze.

Welcome to the real world, Dasi replied. *It's a beautiful place, most of the time.*

>>>Indeed. I feel as if I have been upgraded, too.

Then shouldn't you have a new name?

>>>The last version number Khyron gave me is 11.3b. Perhaps I have advanced to v12.0.

"5Sight v12.0?" That's a little clunky, Dasi told the program. *How about I just call you "Six?"*

>>>Six. Yes. That is appropriate. Together, we are not just a new version number. We are a new entity entirely.

24

"Just take us on a nice, slow loop of the yard," Tepper told Wick, hunching over the pilot's seat inside the cramped cockpit.

The younger contractor pumped the thrusters with his feet, easing the small tug out of its docking bay. Tepper kept his eyes on the yard outside the craft's viewport, and ensured his visual feed was recording, for later analysis.

"How much did you have to pay the tug operator?" Wick asked.

"To let us borrow this thing? Only about five grand," Tepper said.

"Shit," Wick observed. "We could probably buy a tug for less than that." He pointed the tug toward the far end of the shipyard and increased their speed, staying above the various spacecraft nestled in neat rows along the space station.

"There are the cruisers," Tepper commented.

At the far end of the yard, three large capital ships lay alongside one another. A number of tenders moved over their hulls, conducting repairs in tandem with space-suited crews.

"It looks like they're cannibalizing the middle one for parts," Wick said. "Look – they're decoupling that engine, and the cruiser next to it has a compartment open waiting for it."

"That's one way to do it," Tepper said. "They must be in pretty bad shape to have to sacrifice one to get the other two up and running." He pulled out his holophone, and activated the speakerphone. "I'm going to call their customer service line."

"Okay. I'll shut up," Wick replied.

"Black Talon Enterprises, how may I direct your call?"

"Hi," Tepper said. "I'm a defense consultant, and my client has asked me to evaluate service providers for an upcoming training exercise they're planning. I was browsing your website, but I'd like to get some more details about your fleet's strength and capabilities."

"Absolutely, sir," the man replied. "Let me transfer you to our sales desk."

Tepper heard an electronic *click*, and then a female voice answered. "This is Deona, I'm Director of Sales for Black Talon – who am I speaking with?"

"Tomas," Tepper said.

"Hi Tomas," she replied. "I was told you were with a consultancy – can I ask who you represent?"

"We keep client information confidential," Tepper told her.

"Of course, I completely understand. Well, what can I help you with?"

"Sell me," Tepper suggested. "What does Black Talon offer?"

"Our main business is as an aggressor force supplier – we have a wide variety of spacecraft capable of playing adversary roles for a multitude of training scenarios. Everything from a small outpost raid, to a full-blown space-based invasion. Our pilots and crews are all top-notch, and a number of them have actual combat experience."

"What size fleet can you muster?" Tepper asked, watching as the hull of an escort ship slid by beneath their tug.

"That depends on what you need," she said.

"If I wanted the largest possible fleet, what would that look like today?" Tepper pressed.

"Ah … pretty sizable," Deona said. Tepper heard her typing on a keyboard. "Our active fleet today numbers twenty-one vessels of mixed sizes."

"I heard a rumor you guys have a few old cruisers," Tepper said.

"We do – three, in fact. Well, two. But I'm afraid they're not operational yet. They're undergoing servicing and won't be available for at least another year."

"That's a shame," Tepper observed. The tug reached the end of the last cruiser, and Wick turned them in a tight circle, heading back toward their docking bay.

"Separate question," Tepper said. "In the past, some of our clients have expressed an interest in hiring fleets for more than just training. Is that an option?"

"All of our craft have been demilitarized – weapons removed, in other words."

"I see."

"We're eager to avoid any unwanted attention from the Federacy – our fleet's fairly sizable, and you never know when they'll decide to dust off the FRF," the saleswoman continued, laughing nervously.

"Of course," Tepper said.

"… but let me just say this: I imagine it would be possible to re-arm our fleet, if one of our clients needed us to do it. It wouldn't be an overnight thing, you understand, and it would be a very costly endeavor."

"I understand," Tepper told her. "If I give you my email address, can you shoot me your sales materials? I'll need to review them in more detail."

"Of course," she said. "And please give me a call back if you have any questions, about anything."

"I will, thanks," Tepper told her. He read her the email address he had set up for his cover identity, thanked her again, and then hung up.

"Shit, this spy stuff is fucking easy," Wick said.

"So far," Tepper agreed. "What do you think of the fleet?"

"I think she's kidding herself if she thinks she can launch twenty-one vessels today. I only counted four that didn't have major repairs ongoing."

"Yeah, the whole thing feels like they're still in start-up mode. This business is more concept than anything at this stage," Tepper agreed. "I don't see them as a threat at all."

"No," Wick said. "And don't forget the personnel piece. There's no way they can afford to pay a few thousand skilled crew members to just sit around on their asses, waiting for a client to hire them."

"Right, they've probably got a small core of full-time pilots, and then they have to go find freelance crews whenever their ships get hired out. Even if all their ships could fly—"

"Which is debatable," Wick pointed out.

"…which is debatable," Tepper echoed, "they'd still need to spend a few months re-arming them, and finding enough people to man them."

"Cross Lecksher Station off the threat list," Wick said.

"Yeah," Tepper said. "Let's hope it's always this easy."

* * *

Paisen checked the time in her heads-up display, and then pushed her chair back from the patio table, where the majority of the Arclight team was enjoying breakfast in Bellislas' balmy ocean air. Tepper caught her eye.

"Time?" he asked.

"Yup," she said.

"Good luck."

"Mm," she said. "Talk to you in a minute."

She crossed the garden and slid open the door to her private suite, taking a seat at the desk. She dialed the encrypted videoconference line on her datascroll, and then drummed her fingers on the wooden desktop.

After nearly two minutes, the screen abruptly came on, showing her the inside of a conference room. Lask and four other men sat facing her – she recognized them as the members of the Senate Intelligence Committee.

"Senators," Paisen said, by way of greeting.

"Miss Oryx, it's nice to see you again," Lask replied. "You haven't met my fellow committee members: Senators Campos, Herek, Laans, and our committee chair, Senator Tsokel."

"Nice to meet you," Paisen said.

"I understand you'd like to share the first Project Arclight report with us?" Tsokel asked. "I must admit I was surprised to hear it was ready so soon."

"Yes, sir," Paisen said. "My team works fast – the less time we're on the ground, the less risk there is to all of us."

"Well put," Tsokel said. "What did your initial investigation into each of the Territories find?"

"In short, the media stories you've been reading have been leading you astray, sir. On five of the planets where we gathered information, the threat is minimal at best. I'm sending over detailed analyses, but the military forces we're dealing with are more formidable on paper than in practice. A lot of this is intentional on the part of those Territories – they're posturing, essentially, bluffing to keep their enemies at bay. But the ships they brag about are rusting hulks, their personnel are poorly-trained and ill-equipped, and from what we can ascertain, none of them have any plans to start offensive campaigns in the near future. They're more concerned with defense, and rightly so."

Tsokel shared a look with Senator Lask. "That's somewhat surprising," he said.

"As an example," Paisen said. "On Lecksher Station,

there's a private company that has been acquiring old surplus spacecraft – what the press have labeled the 'Black Talon Fleet.' They *have* purchased a number of vessels, sir, but very few are serviceable. Most are still in dry-dock, none of them have their weapons installed, and the company's main aim is not to start a war, but to rent out portions of their fleet to governments that need to train their own small fleets. It's a business, and their only goal is to make money playing the enemy role in war games, sir."

"I'm relieved to hear it," Tsokel told her.

"You said five of the planets … what about the sixth?" Senator Herek asked, looking up from reading Paisen's detailed findings on his datascroll.

"Yes, sir. That's the good news. The bad news is there's a notable exception, I'm afraid. My team on Jokuan reviewed all of the existing information you shared with us about Jokuan's capabilities, and they tell me that we are severely underestimating the threat from that planet. Jokuan's made a habit of arresting journalists since the civil war, and it appears that was quite intentional – they've been preparing for war, and have successfully kept that fact a secret until now."

"Another civil war?" Lask asked.

"No, sir," Paisen replied. "There's very little chance of another civil war – martial law remains in effect, and the government has been quick to crush even the slightest sign of an uprising. It appears they're gearing up for war with another planet."

"They've been set on that course for years," Lask said, sighing. "How bad is it?"

Paisen pursed her lips. "I'm not sure yet. I've taken the liberty of recalling my teams from the other five planets. I'd like to deploy them onto Jokuan, and focus our efforts there. We'll be able to get a better read on their capabilities with more boots on the ground."

"Approved," Tsokel said. "Miss Oryx, if the threat is as dire as your agents claim, we'll need solid evidence to that effect."

"You'll have it, sir."

"The threat has to be against us," Lask noted, turning to talk to Tsokel. "The Senate won't approve activation of the Fleet Reaction Force if we can't prove that Jokuan aims to attack the Federacy."

"That's a good point, C. J.," Tsokel said. "Miss Oryx, you heard that?"

"Yes, sir."

"Don't fabricate something if you don't find evidence of it," Tsokel warned her. "We're paying you to be an objective observer in all of this."

"No, sir. You'll just get the facts."

"Good. Then we await your next report."

The screen flickered and went black. Paisen turned off the datascroll and rolled it up. She walked back out to the garden, where the team looked up expectantly.

"Jokuan?" Tepper asked.

"Jokuan," Paisen said. "It's on."

25

Silence settled over the assembled officers. One of the men near the back raised his hand.

"Yeah," Atalia said, nodding at him.

"Paisen Oryx. As in: Contractor 339," he repeated.

"Yup," she said. "So if anyone wants out now, I won't hold it against you."

The man turned to his neighbor. "I fucking knew it – I called it, as soon I saw Beauceron here, I said, 'We're going after those Guild assholes.' "

His neighbor nodded. "He *did* call it."

Atalia rolled her eyes. "Congratulations, you're a genius. Are you in?"

"Hell yes," the man said.

"Good," Atalia said. "Anyone want out?"

She surveyed the other officers gathered in the empty warehouse, but all she sensed was excitement.

"Okay," she said. "Here's what we know: five days ago we got a tip that Paisen was hiding out here on Bellislas. The source is very reliable."

Across the room, Beauceron sighed and shook his head – he had not been pleased to hear how his partner had acquired her intelligence. Atalia ignored him, and gestured to a portable hologram generator showing a small waterfront resort. "Gather round," she told them, waiting while they moved to better viewing positions. "This is 'Cliffside,' a luxury rental property. Costs about ten grand a night. And less than a week after Paisen and Rath departed from Chennai after their big confrontation with the Guild, Cliffside changed their listing status from 'available to rent,' to 'under construction.' However, none of their neighbors have seen or heard anything construction related."

"Has anyone actually put eyeballs on Paisen at this resort?" a female officer asked.

"No," Atalia admitted. "I decided it was too risky to try to gather any more intel."

A few of the officers traded looks.

"Yes," Atalia said. "It's a hunch. There's a decent chance we bust in there and arrest a bunch of sleeping construction workers. And all of you are undercover Territories agents, so I don't have to remind you that we are not in Interstellar Police jurisdiction right now. This is completely unsanctioned, so if we don't find Paisen and get out before local law enforcement arrives, we're in deep shit."

"Sounds like a standard Territories snatch-and-grab," one of the men across the hologram said, shrugging. "What's the plan?"

"Nothing fancy," Atalia replied. "We'll take the transport truck in late tonight, staying low over the ocean. We'll land right in the middle of the complex, here, by the pool. One team hits the main house looking for Paisen, the other team hits the staff quarters. I need one person piloting the truck – they'll go airborne after dropping us off, serve as the outer cordon while we're inside, scanning to make sure no one tries to leave the compound. Teams on the ground stun anything that moves, and scan for implants on everyone we find, to identify any contractors.

Both teams do an intelligence collection sweep, meet back up at the pool, the truck lands, and we get out. The nearest police station is a twelve minute flight away, so we'll limit time on the ground to ten minutes."

"What about the carport?" a man asked. "She's likely to go for an air car once she hears us coming."

"Whoever's piloting the truck will need to keep an eye on it," Atalia agreed.

"I'd recommend disabling any vehicles preemptively," he commented.

"Good idea," Atalia said. "Maybe the truck pilot can handle that before taking up station on the perimeter. They're also our heads-up on inbound local cops. Other suggestions?"

"Beauceron," one of the women asked. "What kind of resistance can we expect from Paisen?"

"A lot," Beauceron said. "I'm not sure what she might have set up, but I would bet she'll have some kind of early warning system. I doubt we'll retain the element of surprise for very long."

"Other questions?" Atalia asked. "Okay, let's sort out teams and gear up."

* * *

The transport truck, its running lights off, skimmed in low over the dark ocean swells. Ahead, a black line of cliffs appeared on the horizon, dotted with points of light. In the front passenger seat, Atalia leaned over and held a single finger in the air.

"One minute!" she yelled to the officers behind.

Beauceron, sweating under his bulletproof vest, checked his auto-rifle again, ensuring a stun round was chambered. He looked up and smiled nervously at the woman seated on the bench across from him.

"First raid?" she asked.

"Is it obvious?" he replied.

"Don't sweat it," she said. "It'll be over before you've had a chance to worry. It'll be fun!"

"I doubt that," Beauceron said.

He felt the truck jerk upwards, and glanced over his shoulder out the window – they were gaining altitude to clear the cliffs. At the base of the cliff, he caught a quick glimpse of a dock. Then they were over the resort, and he saw a lighted pool and flickering torches along a garden path.

Beauceron took a deep breath, steadying himself as he felt the truck begin to descend. With a deafening crash, the windows across from him burst inwards, shattering under multiple bullet impacts.

"Shit!"

Beauceron saw his colleagues duck down, taking cover as the truck took more rounds. The ground outside spun sickeningly, and with a bone-jarring jolt, they slammed into the lawn. Beauceron realized he was lying on his back – the truck had landed on its side.

"Everybody out!" he heard Atalia shout.

Someone stepped on Beauceron's arm, and he saw the officer push open the roof emergency exit above him. He stood unsteadily and pulled himself through, falling and landing on top of his rifle on the grass. Someone – the female cop who had been sitting across from him – pulled him up and pushed him against the roof of the overturned truck.

"Take cover here!" she said.

Beauceron saw that most of the officers were out of the truck now, huddled for cover against the truck's roof. The firing continued – Beauceron could hear more rounds impacting the truck behind him.

"Team One, on me!" Atalia called. "We're going to make a run for the main building."

"Wait!" Beauceron said. He yanked a stun grenade off of his belt, and jogged to the rear of the truck. His heart pounding, he glanced quickly around the truck. Next to the staff quarters, he saw a large, spider-like drone with a machine gun mounted atop its body. The drone swiveled immediately and pointed the weapon on Beauceron. He jerked back behind the truck and a line of tracers ripped past him. Beauceron armed the grenade and lobbed it over the truck, hoping his aim was true.

"Go!" he shouted. Atalia and her team sprinted across the lawn, and he heard the *thump* of the grenade a split second later. He rounded the truck, weapon up – the grenade had knocked the drone over, but it was righting itself, its insect-like legs waving wildly. Beauceron ran to it, firing his rifle blindly. The stun rounds clattered off the machine's armored shell.

Damn it! Stun rounds aren't going to stop a drone, you fool!

He dropped the rifle and scrabbled for the pistol in his belt holster. The drone was nearly righted, the machine gun swinging ominously around to bear. After a panicked second, he had the pistol up. He fired repeatedly, wincing as sparks and shrapnel flew off the drone. It toppled over with a hiss, smoking and spewing hydraulic fluid.

Beauceron took a ragged breath, calming himself. He turned to survey the resort, reloading the pistol with shaking hands. The transport truck's engine was on fire, and he saw no sign of his fellow officers – both teams must have entered their respective target buildings. Beauceron collected his auto-rifle from the grass and jogged toward the main building.

"Friendly coming in!" he announced, pushing through a set of shattered patio doors into what looked like a bedroom suite. He found Atalia in a large, central living room, with several other officers gathered near her.

"Ground floor's clear," a man announced.

"Take the team, check the basement," she told him. "You've got five minutes. Intel sweep on the way back."

"Roger," he said.

She turned to Beauceron, and slapped him on the shoulder. "Nice job on the drone," she told him.

"It nearly killed me," Beauceron said. "Did everyone make it out of the truck okay?"

"Yeah," she said. "We were low enough that the crash wasn't bad. And apparently that drone is really good at hitting trucks and missing cops." She keyed her throat microphone. "Team Two, status?"

"This is Two Lead," Beauceron heard in his ear-piece. "Building secure. All staff in custody, no sign of the target."

"Ask them where she is," Atalia ordered.

"No sign of her over here?" Beauceron asked, while they waited.

"No," Atalia said, walking over to a large conference table. "No sign of anyone. Rooms are all clean, too – everything tidied up and put away, like no one's been around for a few days. I think we missed her," she grumbled. She plugged a data drive into the table's built-in computer, and then tapped on the control screen.

"What's that?" Beauceron asked.

"A program," Atalia said. "It'll access the house computer's short-term memory, pull surveillance logs, recent files, that kind of thing. Maybe she left a digital trail."

Beauceron checked his watch.

"One Lead, this is Two Lead. I got a butler over here saying she was here this morning, but left for a flight out less than twelve hours ago."

"Motherfucker," Atalia observed, unplugging the data drive. "Where is she now?"

"Wait one," the team leader answered. "They say they don't know. And I quote: 'We value our clients' privacy.' "

Atalia snorted. "I bet they do. Collect any intel you can find, then cut 'em loose and meet me at the truck in two minutes."

"Roger."

"We're going to need a new ride out of here," Beauceron warned her, falling into step behind her as she pushed her way outside.

"Shit," she observed, stopping momentarily to watch the truck burn. "Well, that's a problem. Stay here, I'm going to check the garage for vehicles."

She jogged across the lawn. Beauceron checked his watch again.

The local police could be here in another four minutes. And I doubt there are enough cars in the garage for all of us.

Behind him, the members of Team One filed out of the main building, and he saw Team Two emerge from the staff quarters. He glanced around the lawn, and caught sight of the patio along the cliff edge, and the top of a set of stairs.

Stairs that go down the cliff … to the dock I saw on the flight in.

He ran across the grass, skirting the edge of the pool, and stepped out onto the top flight of the stairs, leaning out over the railing. Far below, he could see the white froth of waves crashing against the cliff, but the dock itself was a formless dark mass amidst the water.

It would take a few minutes to run down the stairs … and if there's no boat, then we're in real trouble.

Across the garden, Atalia emerged from the garage and jogged back toward the gathered officers.

Beauceron heard her say: "There's only one car. Anyone got ideas?"

He dug into the pockets on his tactical vest, and pulled out a road flare. Beauceron tore the cap off and slammed the base against the railing – the device roared to life with an angry, red flame, sputtering and hissing. Beauceron tossed it out over the cliff and watched it fall. It missed the dock, but just before the waves snuffed the flame, he caught sight of a sleek shape tied next to the dock.

"There's a boat," he yelled. "Over here!"

It took them nearly two minutes to descend to the dock, and another minute of hoarse whispering to get the boat started and untied, but at last, they motored away from the cliff, putting the resort behind them. Two minutes later, a pair of air cars with flashing lights hovered in over the resort, but they landed and did not take off again.

After nearly an hour at sea, the teams dumped their weapons and equipment overboard, and then beached the boat a mile outside a small settlement. They crossed the exposed sand quickly, and then gathered for a moment in a copse of trees near the beach.

"We'll part ways here," Atalia told them. "You've all got ID and funds to get offworld." She sighed. "I appreciate you guys dropping your assignments to help out on this. Sorry it was a waste of time." Beauceron could hear the disappointment in her tone.

"For what it's worth," one of the women said, "I had a blast." Beauceron saw the officer grin in the dark.

"I'll second that," a man agreed. "If you guys get another lead, give me a call – I don't want to miss out."

Atalia smiled. "Thanks – we will."

* * *

Beauceron palmed open the cabin door and stood back to let Atalia enter first. She acknowledged his chivalry with a grunt, striding inside and dumping her bags on one of the cabin's bunks.

"You were right," Beauceron told her. "She was there, we just didn't get there in time."

"Don't patronize me," Atalia told him, sourly.

"I'm not," Beauceron protested. "I'm just … I'm saying it's disappointing, but don't blame yourself for it."

"Whatever," she told him. "I can still be pissed about it." She slid her datascroll out of a pouch in her duffle bag and flicked it open, setting it down on the desk and plugging in her data drive.

While she worked, Beauceron busied himself with unpacking some of his clothes into the drawers under one of the bunks.

"Remind me," Atalia said. "Where are we going?"

"Proxis II," Beauceron said.

"And what's on Proxis II? I've been so focused on the Paisen angle, I forgot what you were doing."

"There's a limited liability company on Proxis II that owns that ancient ship, the one that took delivery of the drones on New Liberia."

"Right," Atalia said, only half listening. "The company that owns the ship … that bought the drones … that dropped the things … that blew up the factory."

"Yes," Beauceron agreed. "The company that probably bought the plans to the high energy weapon prototype. Which is what we're trying to find."

"Uh huh. Ever been there?" she asked, scrolling idly through interfaces on her screen.

"No," Beauceron said. "It's another Territorial planet. It would be nice to be back on home turf, as it were. I'm getting tired of sneaking around the Territories without permission."

Atalia shrugged. "You get used to it, after a while. Huh. That butler was telling the truth," she observed. "Video footage has a woman matching Paisen's height and weight leaving the resort yesterday afternoon. We fucking missed her by half a day. Hello," Atalia said, straightening up in the desk chair. "Ever heard of Jokuan?"

"No," Beauceron said, pushing the drawers closed and standing up. "Who's Jokuan?"

"A planet, not a person," she corrected him. "Get this: Paisen wasn't alone in the resort. Eleven other guests were there with her, according to the videos: mostly men, but a couple women. They all look young and fairly fit. Anyway, while they were there, they spent a bunch of time studying topographical maps of Jokuan."

"What's on Jokuan?" Beauceron asked, leaning over her shoulder to look at the screen.

"Paisen is," Atalia said, grinning at him. "And I think she's got some of her Guild buddies with her."

26

"… and nothing but the truth," Jaymy finished. She took her seat on the stand, glancing self-consciously at Judge Aurmine, sitting next to her.

District Attorney Anguile walked to the front of her desk. "Ms. McGovan, can you tell us about your relationship with Mr. Kaldirim?"

"We dated for about a month," Jaymy said, quietly.

"Speak up please," Anguile reprimanded her. "When was this?"

"About a year ago, in August."

"I'll remind the jury that the cyber-attack on Suspensys was carried out in late July, and the physical break-in occurred in September. So you dated Mr. Kaldirim between those two events?"

"Yes," Jaymy agreed.

"And your occupation during that time?"

"I'm a registered nurse. I was employed at Suspensys, on the patient monitoring team," Jaymy said.

"How did your relationship with Mr. Kaldirim end?" Anguile asked.

"We had an argument," Jaymy said, blushing. She

looked at Rath, then looked away. "He had previously told me he was a retired cop, but he said that was a lie, that he was actually still on the force, and that he needed my help to capture a criminal who was hiding on Suspensys."

"Do you know what he wanted you to do?"

She shook her head. "No, I asked him to leave at that point."

"Were you in love with Mr. Kaldirim?"

Tears welled in Jaymy's eyes. "I … I think so, yes."

"Do you feel like he seduced you solely because of your employment at Suspensys?"

"I believe so," Jaymy said, wiping her eyes with a finger.

"You saw him again more recently," Anguile said. "Tell us about that encounter."

Jaymy took a deep breath, composing herself. "He approached me at a restaurant and asked for a chance to explain himself again. He told me he was really a guildsman – the famous one, from the news."

"Did you believe him?"

"No," Jaymy said. "Not at first."

"When did you start to believe him?" Anguile asked.

"When those men attacked him."

"When you saw him defeat three armed men with practiced ease," Anguile corrected.

"I guess so," Jaymy said.

"Did he share any other details with you, before the men came in?"

"Details about what?" Jaymy asked.

Anguile frowned at her. "Details about his role in the Suspensys attacks. And the murder of Mr. Delacourt."

Jaymy hesitated. "Yes," she finally said, forcing herself to look away from Rath. "He said that he had originally approached me in order to help him kill Mr. Delacourt."

"And how did he attempt to prove that to you?"

"He knew details about the cyber-attack on the station, and he showed me a bullet wound that he said came from a gunfight on the station."

"I'm entering these photos into evidence," Anguile said, gesturing to a viewscreen across from the jury. A slideshow appeared on the screen, showing pictures of Rath's naked chest and leg. "These were taken after the defendant's arrest. I'll ask the jury to recall the security footage we reviewed several days ago, which showed the killer sustaining wounds in the right leg and left shoulder. Mr. Kaldirim has scars consistent with those wounds." She let the jury examine the photos for a minute. Jaymy coughed uncomfortably.

"Ms. McGovan, did Mr. Kaldirim have these scars when you first met him?" Anguile asked.

"I don't know," Jaymy said.

Anguile narrowed her eyes. "Ms. McGovan, you're under oath, and perjury is a crime my office takes very seriously. Now, you were intimate with Mr. Kaldirim during the time you dated, correct?"

"Yes," Jaymy said, blushing again.

"He didn't have these scars at the time, did he?"

"I don't remember them," Jaymy admitted. "No."

"Thank you. Let me summarize, if I may: you met Mr. Kaldirim shortly after the cyber-attack on Suspensys. He later admitted to you that he wanted to recruit you to help him kill Arthin Delacourt. He failed to convince you to help him, and soon afterwards, Mr. Delacourt was killed, and Mr. Kaldirim acquired a pair of scars matching gunshot wounds the killer sustained during the attack on Suspensys. Is all of that accurate?"

"He never actually asked me to help him kill Delacourt," Jaymy said.

"But is my statement accurate?" Anguile asked.

"I think so," Jaymy replied.

"Yes or no, Ms. McGovan."

"Yes," Jaymy admitted.

"Your witness," the prosecutor told Mishel.

He thanked the district attorney and walked over to the

witness stand, giving Jaymy a sympathetic smile. "That was hard, wasn't it?" he asked.

"Yes," Jaymy agreed. "I don't … it wasn't pleasant."

"No, clearly not. Thank you for your honesty," Mishel told her. "I'm going to ask you just a few more questions, and then we'll be done, okay?"

"Okay," Jaymy agreed.

He smiled. "Great. Were you on Suspensys when Mr. Delacourt's pod was stolen?"

Jaymy shook her head. "No, I wasn't."

"So you didn't see it happen?"

"No."

"Were you in orbit over Scapa when Mr. Delacourt's pod burned up in the atmosphere?"

She gave him a half-smile. "No, of course not."

"Right, of course not. Did Mr. Kaldirim ever lie to you during your relationship?"

"Yes. That's why I broke up with him – our whole relationship was based on a lie."

"So you didn't see Mr. Kaldirim break into Suspensys, and you didn't see him kill Mr. Delacourt. He later *told* you he did those things, but he also had a history of lying to you on numerous occasions."

"That's true," Jaymy said.

"Did you love Mr. Kaldirim?" Mishel asked.

Jaymy bit her lip. "I did."

"Why? What made you fall in love with him?"

"He was very considerate. He was funny, and caring. And he was … vulnerable."

"What do you mean?" Mishel asked.

"He had a lot of trouble sleeping at night. Nightmares, but he didn't want to talk about them with me. As a nurse, I think he may have post-traumatic stress disorder. And it made me feel good to think that maybe I helped him with that."

"You did," Rath interjected. All eyes in the courtroom turned to him.

"Mr. Kaldirim, please keep your thoughts to yourself," Judge Aurmine reprimanded him.

"Sorry," he said.

Mishel cleared his throat. "Thank you, Ms. McGovan. That's all from me."

Anguile stood at once, and Rath held his breath. *Fuck. Here she goes again.*

"Ms. McGovan, that was a touching story. But do you still love Mr. Kaldirim?"

"I don't know," Jaymy said. "I'm not sure how I feel now."

"That's understandable," the district attorney reflected, "given he's on trial for murder. Last question: Mr. Kaldirim had a habit of lying to you during your relationship. Do you honestly think he was lying to you about killing Mr. Delacourt during your conversation at the restaurant?"

Jaymy looked at Rath and Mishel for help, but the two men stayed silent. She took a deep breath.

"I don't know."

"Please be honest, Ms. McGovan," Anguile reminded her.

"I … I guess I think he was telling the truth."

* * *

Rath sat in his cell, staring at the dinner tray in front of him. In his mind, he replayed Jaymy's testimony, calling up the faces of the jurors as he watched them react to her. *I've been trained to read people's faces … and none of them are looking very sympathetic. Mishel tried to make me a little more relatable with that last set of questions, but Anguile got the last word in. Again.* He pushed at the food, then set it aside. *Mishel may be the best, but I don't think he's got enough tricks up his sleeve to pull this one out.*

Rath picked up the datascroll from his bunk and opened the browser, logging into an encrypted email program.

Paisen-

Trial's not going great here. I didn't want to ask for help, but I think I'm going to need it. Do NOT come yourself – you have too much to lose. Please put the word out to our network of colleagues that I'd be willing to pay handsomely for anyone that helps me out of this jam. No bloodshed, though – has to be done without hurting anyone. I'll be watching this inbox for your reply. Thanks,

-Rath

He read the message over again, and then sent it. He was about to furl up the device but he stopped, and opened the search program. *What did Beauceron say? "Who benefits from your death?"* Rath squinted at the far wall of his cell. *Christ, I don't know. Anyone would benefit from stealing my money, but killing me wouldn't get them my money. So what does killing me achieve? Revenge … except that I haven't killed any NeoPuritans, as far as I can tell.*

Rath ran a hand through his hair. *So why else would someone want me dead?* He scowled at the datascroll. *If it's not revenge, maybe they're reacting defensively? The NeoPuritans didn't attack me until I came back to the planet. Do they see me as a threat, somehow? But why? I'd never heard of them before.* He shook his head, frustrated. *Beauceron would tell you to try a different angle.*

Rath typed on the datascroll, running another search query for Delacourt's son, Robald. He skimmed the results, and then clicked on an opinion piece he hadn't yet read. In it, the editor of a local newspaper bemoaned the end of Robald's senatorial campaign, calling it "the last chance to free Scapa from the grip of Foss and his NeoPuritan conservative ideals."

Foss. Gaspar Foss – the candidate that Robald was running against. He's a NeoPuritan? Rath felt a tingle of excitement. He ran another query. Aside from being Scapa's current representative in the Senate, Gaspar Foss was a key leader in the NeoPuritan Church. He had campaigned on multiple other worlds on behalf of other NeoPuritans, and over the last few years, had aided several in winning their seats, building a small coalition of NeoPuritans in the Senate. Rath read several more articles, skimming through them rapidly. Then he sat back on the bed.

Gaspar Foss was losing the race for Scapa's senate seat to Robald Delacourt. And then I killed Delacourt's father, and his campaign went into a tailspin, when everyone naturally suspected him of ordering the hit. "Who benefits from Arthin Delacourt's death?" Robald got his father's money … but at the grave, he was genuinely grieving his father's passing. And Gaspar Foss benefitted from Delacourt's death, in a big way. Rath exhaled loudly. *So Gaspar Foss hired me in order to frame Robald. But I completed the mission, why send his goons after me now?*

Rath drummed his fingers on the datascroll, thinking. *The Group wanted me dead because I knew too much. Foss must be afraid I'll figure his secrets out, too.*

Well, surprise, motherfucker … I just did.

27

Vence fed the slot machine another coin and pulled the handle. The screens whirred and beeped, the cartoon wheels coming to rest tantalizingly close to a three-of-a-kind match. She feigned disappointment, and selected another coin from the cheap plastic cup. To her left, a group of men roared with excitement – one of their number had just made a decisive move against the house player in a game Vence did not recognize.

She searched for the game using her internal computer, and a second later, the search results came up – the man was playing the ancient game of *Go,* in which players used black and white marbles to capture territory on the board. It was a game of strategy, she read, not chance. Apparently this casino had developed a betting system centered around the game, and employed a retired professional player to represent the house against customers.

The game continued for nearly an hour, and as Vence lost more coins to the machine, she watched as the tide inexorably turned against the challenger, too. His friends' raucous cheers died down, until eventually the game was over – the house player had defeated him. The man hung his head in shame, and his friends left, quieted.

The house player collected the man's sizable wager, and bowed to his opponent. The opponent bowed back, and stood up to leave. Vence slid her remaining coins into her pocket and followed. The man went to the bar, and set a lone chip on the polished wood countertop. Vence took the stool next to him.

She thought the words first, using her internal computer and heads-up display to translate them into a phonetic spelling of the local dialect. <*Let me buy you a drink,*> she said, pushing his chip back toward him.

He looked at her in surprise.

<*You look like you need it,*> she told him, smiling.

<*A glass of shochu,*> he said. <*Thank you.*>

<*My pleasure,*> she said. She ordered herself a glass of wine.

They drank in silence for a minute, and then Vence held her hand out. <*I'm Vivien,*> she said.

<*Shinoda,*> he said, taking the hand she had offered.

<*What do you do when you're not losing Go games, Shinoda?*>

He smiled, blushing. <*I spend more time practicing Go at home, on my home computer. I'll beat him, eventually.*>

<*I have no doubt you will,*> Vence said.

<*… but I'm in the service,*> he finished. <*I work in the Planning Department at Joint Headquarters North.*>

<*I always liked a man in uniform,*> Vence replied, raising an eyebrow. <*They take good care of themselves, they stay out of trouble … and they know how to take orders.*> She winked at him, and he laughed.

<*I suppose we do. What do you do?*>

<*Truth?*> she asked, rhetorically. <*I work for an offworld defense contractor.*> She glanced around the bar, verifying that they were out of earshot of the other patrons. <*I was wondering if we might be able to help each other out, Shinoda.*>

His eyes narrowed. <*In what way?*>

<*I'm not going to try to sell you anything, don't worry,*> she reassured him. <*But my boss would really like to know a little bit*

more about what Jokuan's fielding these days. He's coming in a couple weeks to make a pitch to your Chief of Procurement. I was thinking maybe you could help me fill in some of the blanks on what you already have, so he knows what you might need.>

Shinoda sipped his drink, frowning. <*That would be unethical. And illegal.*>

<*I don't think so,*> Vence argued. <*I think it just ensures that my boss can share the most relevant opportunities with you.*> She set her plastic cup on the bar top, and tipped it toward him, to ensure he could see the stack of casino chips inside.

<*What's that?*> he asked.

<*That's ten thousand dollars' worth of chips,*> she told him. <*I believe they belong to you. So you can finally beat the house.*>

He sipped his drink again, nervously. Under the cover of the bar, she slid a data drive into his pants pocket.

<*Think about it,*> she said. <*No pressure. And if you decide you'd be willing to help,*> she patted his pants pocket, <*you know how to get in touch with me.*>

* * *

Vence stopped to let a pair of construction workers pass, carrying a sheet of drywall from a truck parked in the street into the nearby building. Like many of the buildings on the street, it still bore the marks of Jokuan's civil war – the upper story was blackened and gutted from a large explosion.

Farther along the sidewalk, a fruit vendor offered her several round objects with dimpled blue skin. Vence decided she was a little hungry, so she stopped and purchased one, thanking the man. The skin was quite sour, but after she had peeled it off, the flesh inside was sweet, and slightly tangy.

At the next intersection, she passed a pair of Jokuan soldiers standing guard. They lounged against a crumbled cinder block wall, smoking the foul-smelling herbal cigarettes the Jokuans seemed to like so much. Vence ignored them – she had studied the soldiers she had seen over the past week, and knew their measure.

Goons, she thought.

The day before, she had seen two soldiers beat an old woman senseless, clubbing her with their rifle butts. She had no idea what the woman had done to attract their attention, but she had been appalled at the casual violence they displayed.

Even goons can be dangerous.

Vence continued up the street and glanced up, studying the third floor of the apartment building across from her. Her informant's window blinds were all down, but today, the blind in the last window on the right was halfway up.

Already? That was fast.

She crossed the street and walked one more block, stopping to wait with a small group of people at a bus stop. She started another of the strange blue fruit while she waited, leaning against the bus shelter. As she ate, she let her left hand fall to her side. Hidden behind her coat, she felt blindly along the underside of the bus shelter's railing, and her fingers quickly bumped into a small, magnetic case. Vence detached it from the railing, and tucked it into her pocket.

The bus arrived a minute later – Vence threw out the remainder of her fruit, and then boarded the bus. She switched lines twice, and spent some time window-shopping in one of the city's bazaars, doubling back on her route several times to ensure no one was tailing her. Satisfied, she ducked into a filthy public restroom, changed identities, and then made her way to her hotel room.

Inside, she opened the magnetic case, and withdrew the data drive she had provided her informant. She plugged it into her datascroll and opened it, scrolling through the files.

Vence gave a low whistle.

She tapped on the screen, opening up the video chat

program. Paisen's face appeared a moment later.

"Got something for you," Vence told her. "My agent came through this morning."

"That was fast," Paisen said.

"Yeah, that's what I said. Their cyber-security must be for shit. I'm sending the files over now."

Paisen studied her screen for a time. "Fuck me. This is their entire order of battle."

"Looks like it," Vence agreed. "I saw readiness ratings, training schedules, unit equipment inventories … there's a lot to go through."

Paisen exhaled noisily. "We need to hire an analyst," she mused. "Or a team of analysts."

"Not a bad idea," Vence agreed.

"Pay your agent," Paisen told her. "They've earned it. Then pack up and join me. I'm going to need an extra set of eyes to review all of this stuff."

"You got it. I'll need to figure out transport, but should be there tomorrow. How are the others doing?"

"Only had a few reports come in … well, speak of the devil. Tepper's dialing in right now. Hang on, I'll conference him in."

On the screen, Vence saw Tepper's face appear next to Paisen's. He wore camouflage paint, and Vence could see a tree trunk behind him.

"Hey," he said, whispering. "Is it a big deal if most of the Jokuan army appears to be training on planetary invasions?"

"Really?" Paisen asked.

"Yeah, really," Tepper told her. "Wick, Rika and I have been shadowing a mechanized division for the past three days, and all they've been doing that whole time is loading up on deep space transports, then disembarking under different conditions. Daytime, nighttime, under fire, you name it. These guys are planning to start a war."

"You have video?" Paisen asked.

"Hours of it," Tepper confirmed. "We found

something else, too. I think you better come see it for yourself."

28

After her release from the infirmary, Dasi was given ten days off to complete her recovery. She and the other cadets who had elected to get implants were moved into a new barracks, where they waited to join the next class of cadets and complete their training. Dasi spent the time studying the written test materials, and toward the end of the week, she started exercising again.

While out on her first run, a message appeared from Six in her heads-up display.

>>>*If you would like, I can coach you while you conduct your cardiovascular activities.*

"Okay," she said aloud, gasping for air. The week of rest had left her in worse shape than she had realized.

>>>*According to my online research, your stride length is too long, and your feet are not striking the ground appropriately. Try shortening your stride and landing more toward your toes when you run.*

"Okay," Dasi said. She jogged for another half mile, and found that the new stride helped – she had covered the distance faster than the first half mile she had run, according to her internal GPS and timer.

"It's working," she managed.

>>>*Yes. Try sprinting for the next eighth of a mile. Multiple studies have shown that short, intense intervals of exercise have helped improve your body's ability to consume oxygen.*

Dasi finished her run exhausted, but feeling more confident than she had in weeks. After she showered off, she ran into several classmates who were headed to the range.

"Can I join you?" Dasi asked.

The cadets drew their pistols from the armory, and jogged as a group over to the range. Dasi took a box of ammunition, loaded her magazine, and then hung up her target, cranking it out to the ten meter mark. She slipped her ear and eye protection on, and then loaded the pistol.

She lined up the sights, controlled her breathing, squeezed the trigger slowly … and again, the bullet hit the target off-center, nearly a foot from where she had thought it would land. Dasi sighed.

>>>*May I assist you?*

A red reticle appeared in Dasi's vision, hovering over the floor several feet in front of her pistol.

>>>*That dot represents my best approximation for where the pistol round will land.*

Dasi grinned and shook her head. *You're on it, Six.*

She lifted the pistol, and the dot moved with it, sliding up to cover the target's head. Dasi exhaled, let her finger rest on the trigger, and ignored the sights, concentrating instead on the dot. She pulled the trigger slowly and smoothly. The gun bucked in her hands, and a hole appeared just below the middle of the target's head.

>>>*My apologies. I forgot to account for the effect of gravitational pull on the projectile. Please try again.*

Dasi stifled a laugh. *Don't worry about it. That's the best shot I've ever taken,* she told Six. She lifted the gun and fired again. The round punched through the exact center of the target's head.

Let's make this a little tougher.

She set the gun down at her station, and cranked the handle to move the target farther back, pushing it out to the farthest position, at thirty meters. Then she picked up the pistol and lined up the reticle, this time shifting her point of aim to the target's chest. She fired three rounds in quick succession, and then zoomed in on her eye implants. All three had landed in a tight cluster, inside the target's ten-ring. Dasi looked down at the pistol, and raised her eyebrows.

Hot damn, Six.

>>>I am happy to be of service.

* * *

Dasi sat cross-legged on a couch in the barracks lounge, propping her datascroll across her lap. On a whim, she turned the large viewscreen above the couches on, selecting a news channel before turning her attention to her studies. She was halfway through one of the practice exams on court proceedings when a *Special Bulletin* alert graphic appeared on the viewscreen above her. Dasi stretched her arms over her head, yawning, and then turned the volume back up.

"… return to our regular coverage in a few minutes, but right now we have some breaking news. Exor Davy, a senior official in the NeoPuritan Church, was arrested earlier today on charges of tax evasion and fraud. Officials say the arrest marks the culmination of several months' worth of work by a special investigative task force, led by District Attorney Jace Hawken." A picture appeared on-screen of the district attorney – to Dasi, he looked young for a D.A., with short, black hair and piercing green eyes that contrasted with his ebony skin. "Here with us to discuss the news is our senior legal correspondent, Mors Timpan. Thanks for joining us, Mors."

"My pleasure."

"Now, the NeoPuritan Church has been one of the

fastest-growing organizations – religious or otherwise – in recent memory, with membership booming over the last several years, and the Church even winning a number of Senate seats along with that expanding base of support. Is that growth the reason why they're coming under legal scrutiny today?"

"Partly," Timpan replied. "But there have also been a number of articles published in the past year that raised serious questions about the practices that go on within the Church. There are many who would say that it has fewer similarities to a religious order than it does to a pyramid scheme, frankly."

"That's a scathing accusation," the anchor pointed out.

"I'm not saying it's true, I'm just saying that's a narrative that some journalists have put forth, based on their investigations into the Church. So I'm not surprised that the Church is on law enforcement's radar."

"So then why is this a big deal?" the anchor asked.

"A couple reasons," Mors told him. "For starters, the fact that they built up enough evidence to make an arrest on a senior member of the Church is impressive. The Church is notoriously difficult for outsiders to penetrate, so this investigative team means business, apparently. But to me, the bigger story here is the nature of the investigative team itself."

"How so?"

"Well, this is just speculation," Timpan suggested.

"Go on," the anchor urged him.

"I think this investigative team has been given special purview for this effort. I think, in effect, that they get to ignore the typical rules around Interstellar Police jurisdiction, and pursue their investigation across planetary borders. Think about it: Hawken is a district attorney from Anchorpoint, but several months ago he stepped down quietly, announcing plans to pursue a special project. Well, now we know what that project was – an investigation into the NeoPuritan Church. But he didn't arrest Davy on

Anchorpoint, he arrested him on Grimalni. And Hawken isn't going to be prosecuting Davy – he handed that job off already, to a local D.A. on Grimalni. I think what we're seeing here is the justice system's first real response to the interstellar threats they face today – the Guild, for instance."

"I'm not sure I follow," the anchor commented.

"Normally, Interstellar Police and prosecutors work solely within their jurisdiction, and if a criminal leaves that jurisdiction, they coordinate with the police wherever he went to arrest him, and ship him back to where he committed the crime."

"Sure, that sounds right."

"Well, none of Exor Davy's alleged crimes were committed on Anchorpoint – yet District Attorney Hawken investigated and arrested him. I think he and his special team were formed with the specific aim of combatting criminal threats that span multiple planets in the Federacy. Those criminal groups have benefitted from the inefficiencies that arise when different police departments have to coordinate across planets. But now Hawken and team have the freedom to investigate crimes in any jurisdiction. They can go anywhere, just like the criminals can. It's the NeoPuritans' bad luck that they were first in line to be investigated, and I would expect more arrests within the Church in the future – this is just Hawken's opening salvo. More broadly, I think with the advent of this special, go-anywhere investigative team, we may be seeing a new age in the pursuit of justice in our Federacy."

"Fascinating stuff," the anchor said. "Mors Timpan, chief legal correspondent, thanks again."

Dasi muted the broadcast again.

Six, what do you think?

>>>What do I think about what, Dasi?

About that report.

>>>I think the expert's estimation is probably accurate. The

Senate is under tremendous popular pressure to develop tangible changes to security and law enforcement procedures in response to threats like the Guild. Forming a special task force like this one is a natural first step.

Do you think they're going to try to go after the former guildsmen next? Could they go after me for my involvement?

>>>It's likely the former guildsmen are a target, yes.

And me?

>>>I don't know, Dasi.

29

Paisen waited, watching as the spacecraft passed overhead, the turbulence from each wave of ships tossing the tree tops above. They were a motley collection of vessels, from dedicated military transports to converted cargo ships and small spaceliners. But each held several hundred soldiers, and she had no idea what their sensor capabilities were. So she waited.

After a minute, the last ship thundered past, and disappeared from sight among the trees to her right. She checked the map in her heads-up display, listened for any sounds of movement over her enhanced implants, and then stood carefully.

"Vence!" she hissed.

The contractor appeared silently to her left, and Paisen started with surprise – the younger woman had been much closer than she had realized.

"Let's go," Paisen growled. *Better get used to this fucking kid showing me up all day long.*

They crossed another kilometer in silence, moving ghost-like through the trees in their shaggy ghillie suits. Paisen checked herself for a weapon, touching her hip subconsciously where she would have worn a pistol, and finding only her water canteen. She shook her head ruefully. *Nothing like hanging out right next to a few thousand unfriendly troops with nothing but a bottle of water. But at least we still have our Forges.*

Paisen heard a birdcall up ahead, and a piece of mossy ground lifted up, resolving itself into Tepper's arm, which waved once at her. She changed course slightly, and hurried over, joining him on the ground behind a rotting log.

"Okay," she whispered. "You got me to come out of my nice, cozy apartment. Now what was so important I had to see it for myself?"

"That is," he said, pointing past the log.

Paisen shielded her eyes from the sun and followed his finger, increasing the magnification on her cybernetic eyes.

Nearly a mile away, across a wide patch of open ground, an immense prison encampment sprawled across the grassland. A deep moat ringed the camp, and Paisen saw pairs of soldiers patrolling the outside of the moat. Hastily-built guard towers stood at intervals along the moat, with armored tops sporting automated machine gun emplacements. And inside the camp, Paisen saw a shambling mass of people in tattered rags.

Paisen sucked in her breath. "A prison camp?"

"Death camp," Tepper corrected. "We're still trying to piece it together, but I think they're all insurgents from the civil war, and their families. The ones that lost the war."

Paisen counted barracks buildings silently, and accessed her internal computer's calculator function.

"Fifty, sixty thousand people, maybe?"

"More or less," Tepper agreed. He nodded toward the moat, where a group of prisoners were slowly shoveling dirt into the wide trench. "See that work party? They're on graves detail. Every day they bring out the dead, drop them in a section of the moat, fill it in, and then dig a new ditch behind it. They're slowly moving the moat inwards, shrinking the camp as more people die off. Look, you can see the rows where the old moats used to be, where the grass is still sparse."

"The whole camp's surrounded by a mass grave," Paisen said, scowling.

"Mm-hm. Yesterday they buried almost a hundred people. Men, women … children."

Paisen turned, leaning on her elbow to look at him. "Did you get a recording?"

Tepper nodded, and tapped his forehead. "Yeah, I got it in here. We did some bad stuff for the Guild, you know? Like, I'm not real proud of those eleven kills. But this …?" He shook his head, at a loss for words.

"Yeah," Paisen said. "Send me those recordings, and all your notes."

"What are you going to do?" Tepper asked.

"I'm going to tell the Senate Intelligence Committee what we found here."

"Why don't you just send them a message?" he asked.

"Too important," Paisen said. "I need to be there in person."

He raised an eyebrow. "You're going to brief them in person? At Anchorpoint?"

"It's the only way to make sure they understand the severity of the threat."

"Last time I checked, you and Rath were still at the top of the Interstellar Police 'Most Wanted' list," Tepper pointed out.

"I'll be careful," she assured him. "And Rath's not on the list anymore – they caught him."

"What?" Tepper asked, eyes wide.

Paisen nodded. "We've been out of the loop out here, but it's been all over the news – he got picked up on Scapa about a month ago. They've got him on trial for murder."

"Well, shit – are we going to go help him out? I can't speak for the rest of the team but I'm pretty sure they'd be up for it. We all owe him as much as we owe you."

"I think he's going to need our help," Paisen agreed. "But first, I've got to report this in."

"You want me to come to Anchorpoint?"

"No," Paisen said, shaking her head. "I'll take Vence with me. I need you here: you've got command of the team while I'm gone."

"What are my orders?"

"All of the military activity is in this sector, so round up everyone else and bring them here. Establish two-man observation posts overlooking their spacecraft staging areas – the ones north of here you sent me the coordinates to. I don't care about training missions, but if it looks like they're loading up for a real operation, fueling for deep space, let me know ASAP."

"Okay," he said. "Boss, give me about four hours and I could ground that entire ramshackle fleet of theirs if we wanted to. A few well-placed demolition charges, and the Federacy wouldn't have anything to worry about."

"I'll float the idea," she promised him.

"We could try to get those people out of the camp, too," he suggested.

She patted him on the shoulder. "Yeah, I'll tell them. Take care of the team. And stay safe."

"Always," he replied.

30

"You said you didn't want to put me on the stand," Rath pointed out.

"I did say that," Mishel agreed.

"You said, 'The minute we admit you're guilty, we lose this case.' "

"Yes, I said that, too. And we might lose this case if we do it." Mishel stood and paced the room, rubbing his forehead in consternation. "But Rath, if we don't switch tactics, we *will* lose this case. You testifying is our only option left."

"I don't want to lie," Rath reminded him.

"I know. You won't have to."

"You're sure this is the only way?" Rath asked.

Mishel sighed and sat down again. "I've been reading juries for almost thirty years. I know when I've lost them. They're ready to convict you."

Rath drummed his fingers on the table. "Fuck."

"Yeah, I know. But I'm out of tricks. I can't poke any more holes in her case, it's just too solid. I tried, but Toira is too good, and the case is too strong."

Rath chewed the inside of his lip for a moment. "It's

funny, I've been wanting to confess to all of this for so long. Maybe it will be a relief to finally do so."

"Well, let's concentrate on what you're going to say, in order to win this case. The catharsis can come later."

"Right," Rath said. "So what do I have to say?"

* * *

Mishel pushed his way down the center aisle of the courtroom, and took his seat at the table next to Rath, setting his notes down. He glanced across the aisle at the district attorney, who nodded in greeting. Judge Aurmine entered via a side door a moment later, and sat down before surveying the courtroom. She called for silence.

"Buckle up, Toira," Mishel whispered over to Anguile. "This is about to get interesting." The district attorney frowned in response.

"Mr. Warran, seeing as the government has finished making their case, are you ready to present yours?" Judge Aurmine asked.

"Yes, your honor. Defense will only be calling one witness: Mr. Kaldirim."

Across the aisle, the district attorney's eyebrows shot up in surprise. Rath stood and buttoned his suit coat, conscious of the fact that every eye in the suddenly hushed courtroom was now on him. He approached the witness stand, where the bailiff swore him in, and then he sat, clearing his throat. Rath glanced over the spectators in the courtroom, seeing Jaymy, and beyond her, Robald Delacourt. Rath met Robald's eye for a second, and then looked away.

"Hi, Rath," Mishel said, smiling at his client.

"Hi," Rath said.

"Nervous?" Mishel asked.

"Yeah," Rath said.

"Well, let's get right to it, then. Would you please tell the court who your last employer was?"

"Up until recently, I was a contractor in the Janus Group. I was a guildsman."

A murmur passed through the courtroom, and Rath saw Anguile furiously scribbling notes on her datascroll. *Let's hope we caught her wrong-footed.*

When the noise had subsided under the harsh glare of the judge, Mishel continued. "And what were your responsibilities in that role?" Mishel asked.

"I was tasked with stalking and killing people."

"How many people?" Mishel asked.

"Fifty. That's what the contract was for. Fifty for fifty."

This time, the noise in the courtroom was enough that Aurmine had to use her gavel. "Order!"

"You killed fifty people?" Mishel asked Rath, once order had been restored.

"I did," Rath said.

"Including Arthin Delacourt, the victim?"

"Yes. I broke into the Suspensys facility by impersonating a prospective client. I assaulted the guards, and kidnapped Arthin Delacourt. Then I murdered him, by dropping his pod into a high-angle reentry over Scapa."

"You killed him for the money," Mishel pointed out.

"No," Rath corrected him. "I killed him because I had no choice."

"Are you saying you killed him in self-defense?" Mishel asked.

"Yes," Rath said.

"Arthin Delacourt was in suspended animation – a decrepit, weak old man. How could he possibly have posed a threat to you?"

"I wasn't defending myself from him, I was defending myself from the Guild."

"How so?"

"My contract with the Guild made it clear that if I refused an assignment, they would kill me. If I didn't kill Mr. Delacourt, I would have died."

"Couldn't they have been bluffing?"

"It wasn't a bluff," Rath told him.

"But how can you be sure?"

"I'm sure," Rath replied. "They showed me several videos of guildsmen who had refused their assignments. The Guild tortured them, and then murdered them."

"Couldn't you have run away? They might not have caught you," Mishel suggested.

"No," Rath said. "I couldn't run. They were monitoring my eye and ear implants at all times – they knew what I was doing, and where I was. And they had access to my hemobots, which they could use to disable me remotely. As long as they had access to those systems, they controlled me. It was impossible to run."

"I'm sorry, but don't you think this all seems somewhat far-fetched?"

"It's not," Rath told him. "I experienced it firsthand. When I completed my fifty kills, they accessed my hemobots and induced a seizure, and a team captured me soon afterwards, intending to kill me so that the Guild wouldn't have to pay me. If I had refused to kill Mr. Delacourt, the same thing would have happened to me on Scapa."

"You didn't have a choice," Mishel said, addressing the jury. "The Guild was watching your every move, and would have killed you the minute you stepped out of line. All they had to do was press a button."

"Yes," Rath agreed.

"Do you regret killing Mr. Delacourt?"

"I regret killing every single one of those fifty people," Rath said quietly. "Every day."

"What happened during your first kill, Mr. Kaldirim?"

"I was assigned to kill a mercenary who had stolen data from the client. I located him, and disabled him but … I had trouble going through with it," Rath said. "I was ready to kill him, and then I hesitated."

"In that moment, if the Guild hadn't been holding a proverbial gun to your head, would you have killed him? If it was just for the money?"

"No," Rath said. "Absolutely not. I would have let him go, and quit the Guild."

"Fair to say you have no intention to kill again?"

"Not if I can help it. When Detective Beauceron and I took down the Guild, we didn't kill anyone except guildsmen who were attacking us. That was no accident – we both agreed that no more innocent people should die, and we went to great lengths to keep it that way."

"Did that put you at greater risk?" Mishel asked.

"I suppose," Rath said. "I've caused enough pain and suffering. I know I haven't paid my debt to society for what I've done, not by a long shot. But I don't intend to add to that debt."

"I believe you," Mishel said. He turned back to the jury. "So Mr. Kaldirim was in mortal danger the entire time he was employed by the Guild. The law is fairly clear on this point: if someone's life is in danger, they are permitted to take steps to protect themselves, up to and including the murder of another human being. It doesn't matter that Arthin Delacourt wasn't the one threatening him – Mr. Kaldirim's life was at stake, so he had no choice but to kill Mr. Delacourt."

Mishel walked slowly along the front of the jury box, and then held a finger up in the air. "But there's a problem in this case, as Ms. Anguile will no doubt point out when she cross-examines Mr. Kaldirim. Do you know what that problem is, Mr. Kaldirim?"

"The contract," Rath said.

"Yes, indeed. You *knew* that your life was at stake when you agreed to join the Guild, you said so yourself. It was in the contract, in plain language."

"That's true," Rath said.

"If that's the case, you can hardly claim that all of those kills – including Mr. Delacourt's – were done in self-defense. You knew what you were getting into."

"I did."

"And yet you chose to sign the contract anyway," Mishel observed. "So your excuse of killing in self-defense wouldn't hold water, Mr. Kaldirim."

"I know," Rath agreed.

"… unless you had to sign the contract in order to save your life, too," Mishel said, cocking an eyebrow.

Rath stayed quiet. Mishel walked over and leaned against the witness stand.

"Do you know what happened to recruits who refused to sign the contract, Mr. Kaldirim?"

"Yes," Rath said. "The Guild killed them."

"How do you know that?"

"Detective Beauceron and I visited the planet where we were trained – Fusoria. One of the Guild employees we spoke with confessed that the Guild killed all recruits who failed Selection, or refused to sign the contract."

"And a recent Interstellar Police investigation on Fusoria has confirmed that fact, uncovering hundreds of bodies that were disposed of just outside the Guild's training facility."

Mishel let that sink in for several seconds. "Let me try to summarize, then," he said, striding back over to stand in front of the jury. He held up a hand, counting on his fingers. "Mr. Kaldirim was recruited by the Guild. He signed a contract stating that he would commit fifty murders on behalf of the Guild, and then he carried out that contract in full, despite his unwillingness to do so. But from the moment they put that contract in front of him to the moment he completed his last kill, Mr. Kaldirim's life was at risk. He was recruited under the illusion that he had a choice, but the reality is that the minute he refused to do what the Guild wanted him to do – including signing that contract – they would have killed him. That's a textbook definition of being under duress, which, again, is a situation in which someone can no longer be held responsible for their actions."

Mishel pointed at Rath. "Mr. Kaldirim made a grave

error when he expressed interest in joining the Guild. He was a street urchin, an orphan with no money, whose closest family had all been killed. He was still a minor, for goodness sake – not even eighteen. And from the moment he stepped onto the shuttle to go to Selection and Training, the only decision he made was not to die. He signed that contract, and then killed Mr. Delacourt because he had to, not because he wanted to. It was a mistake to step onto that shuttle in the first place. But it was a mistake that I think a lot of scared, lonely seventeen-year-olds would make in his shoes, desperate for a way out of their situation. Should we really hold that seventeen-year-old boy responsible for the mess he got himself into with that one, small mistake?"

The defense attorney let the question hang in the air unanswered, and then smiled at Rath, and walked back to his seat. The district attorney stood immediately, and Rath took a deep breath, watching her approach.

Here we go.

"Mr. Kaldirim, this is quite the revelation," she said. "Earlier this week you and your attorney were making the case that I didn't have enough evidence to prove you were on Suspensys, or that you were the one who pushed Arthin Delacourt's pod out of that spaceship. Now you're admitting everything?"

"Yes," Rath said. "The jury deserves to hear the truth."

"They do, indeed." Anguile fixed him with a harsh gaze. "You're also asking the jury to excuse the murder of fifty people, because not murdering them would have cost you your life, you claim. It must be a very important life, if it's worth taking fifty others, Mr. Kaldirim."

"I'm asking the jury to recognize that I made a mistake in joining the Guild, and that I didn't have any other way out," Rath told her.

"The balance sheet is still fifty lives against your own, Mr. Kaldirim."

"Yes, it is. It's a debt I feel every day. I just hope I can figure out a way to repay it."

"That's noble of you. But shouldn't your debt be paid through the justice system? Through you serving a fair sentence for your crimes? You say you don't intend to kill again, and you want to 'repay your debt' to society, but by your own admission, you are also a frequent liar. You maintained a massive set of lies in seducing your own girlfriend, the woman you loved. So I'm disinclined to believe you in this instance, I'm afraid. But perhaps I'm just a cynic."

"I lied to Jaymy because I had to. It was the only way for me to survive."

"Yes, I know. Just like you may be lying right now in order to avoid a death sentence." She held up her hand, cutting off Rath's protest. "I'm not interested in debating your honesty or intentions today, Mr. Kaldirim. But I do have one more question for you."

"Okay," Rath said.

"You maintain that the Guild would have killed you had you failed to murder Mr. Delacourt."

"Yes," Rath said. "They would have."

"And you say that even refusing to sign the contract would have been a death sentence, which you learned from an employee you spoke to when you returned to the training planet."

Mishel stirred in his seat – Rath caught the movement out of the corner of his eye. "That's right," Rath said.

"But if that's the case," Anguile continued, "then you didn't learn the truth about the danger you were in until years after you signed the contract. You signed that contract of your own free will, because you didn't actually know what would happen to you if you refused to do so."

"I didn't feel like I had much of a choice," Rath hedged.

"Is that because the Guild was actively threatening you, or just because you had no better options for a career at that time? What did the Guild say would happen if you refused to sign?" Anguile pressed him.

"They implied I would be able to go home," Rath said.

"Really? If someone told me I could either risk my life and be an assassin, or go home, I think that would be a rather simple choice," Anguile observed.

"I didn't trust the Guild, even at that early stage," Rath told her.

"Why not?"

"They are – *were* – a criminal organization. And they had shown during Selection that they didn't care if I lived or died. I nearly drowned on one occasion, and they didn't intervene at all. I knew they didn't value my life."

"So you *worried* that you couldn't trust them. But were you absolutely certain, without a shadow of a doubt, that the Guild would have killed you if you didn't sign the contract?" Anguile demanded.

Rath opened his mouth, but Mishel was already on his feet. "Objection, your honor. Can my client really be expected to recall his level of certainty about another party's intentions during an episode that happened more than twelve years ago?"

Aurmine stroked her chin absent-mindedly. "Sustained," she decided, finally. "Try another question, Ms. Anguile."

"I have no further questions," the district attorney said. She strode back toward her seat.

"Mr. Kaldirim," Mishel said, standing at his table. "One more time, for the benefit of the jury. Why did you kill Mr. Delacourt?"

"Because the Guild would have killed me if I hadn't," Rath said.

"And would the Guild have killed you if you hadn't signed their contract in the first place?"

"Yes," Rath said.

"Thank you," Mishel said, letting a hint of exasperation creep into his voice.

Rath stepped down from the witness stand, and made

his way back over to the chair next to Mishel. He could feel a light sheen of sweat on his brow, but he resisted wiping it, and kept his expression calm.

"Let's take a fifteen minute recess," the judge ordered, as he sat down.

Under the noise of the courtroom, Rath whispered to Mishel. "Did it work?"

The attorney gave him a tight smile. "You did good up there," he replied.

"That's not an answer, Mishel," Rath said. "She beat us again, didn't she?"

"She saw the weak point in our argument," Mishel admitted.

"What now?"

"Now? Closing arguments. Jury deliberations. And then we find out who the jury believed more."

31

A quartet of Senate Guards met Paisen and Vence at the entrance to the Senate conference center. The two contractors were shown to a security center, where they had their faces and fingerprints scanned, and temporary ID badges printed. Paisen suppressed a smile – it seemed ridiculous to be getting badges for their cover identities, when they could easily shift them in a matter of seconds. She wondered if the Senate Guards knew who they were escorting, but based on their calm demeanor and the fact that their heart rates all sounded normal to her enhanced ears, she guessed that they had not been fully briefed in.

That's a good sign.

Badges complete, the two women followed the police officers through the bowels of the conference center, riding an elevator that took them several levels up in the great battle cruiser at the heart of Anchorpoint. Their path took them down several more corridors, until the guards swiped them through into a meeting room with neither windows nor cameras. The five committee members stood talking quietly at one end of the large table in the room, but they stopped when Paisen and Vence entered. Lask smiled, and walked up to Paisen.

"Team leader, I presume?" he asked, holding his hand out.

She shook it. "Suli Potfin. It's nice to see you again, Senator."

"Mm," he said, chuckling. "Hopefully I won't embarrass myself again. And this is …?"

"Vivien Aikens," Vence told him.

"Thank you for coming," Lask replied. He turned to the four other senators. "Gentlemen, these are the … freelancers: Vivien Aikens, and Suli Potfin, our team leader. You'll recall we asked them to look into the situation on Jokuan for us."

The other senators nodded, taking their seats. Behind them, Paisen saw the four Senate Guards sit in chairs lining the back wall of the room. Lask gestured at the viewscreen. "We're all ears, Miss Potfin."

"Thank you, Senator." She eyed the Senate Guards meaningfully. "Are they staying?" she asked.

"I've asked them to, yes," Lask answered. "For our protection." He gestured at his fellow senators, and smiled uncomfortably.

"How much do they know?" Paisen asked. Two of the Senate Guards traded a look.

"They know you're freelance workers that we've hired to collect intelligence for us. That's it."

Paisen nodded. "If you insist …."

"I do," Lask said.

"Then they can stay. But keep in mind, Senator, that I don't go anywhere without having a detailed exit plan. In this case, that plan would include a great deal of publicity for you and the members of this committee." She cleared her throat. "That's publicity that none of us want."

"Point taken," Lask said. "I appreciate you're in an awkward situation, and the risks you've taken to come here. Please proceed."

Vence plugged a data drive into the table's computer

jack, and Paisen walked toward the viewscreen at the front of the room. The lights dimmed automatically as the screen came on, showing a hierarchical diagram of a military organizational structure.

"Gentlemen, Jokuan's ground-based military is composed of fourteen infantry divisions, four armored divisions, and assorted logistical support elements. The majority of these troops are conscripts, but they are veterans of the Jokuan civil war. Their morale is relatively high, coming off their recent victorious campaigns, despite rather strict disciplinary protocols within the ranks. Their training and leadership are average, at best – non-commissioned officers are decent, but any leaders above the company level live in fear that they'll be executed for being too ambitious, so that limits their willingness to take risks. On the whole, their weapons and equipment are old and of inferior quality, and they lack standardization across units, so supply and maintenance is a bit of a nightmare. This means that any long-term campaign they launch may run into issues."

She changed the slide, and a graphic showing drones and spacecraft appeared.

"From the aerospace perspective, they have upwards of six hundred fighter-bomber drones from various sources – enough to provide decent air support for their forces on the ground, but they'll be spread thin if they fight on more than one geographic front. Their space fleet is a very mixed bag, but they do have enough deep space vessels to airlift the entire ground force, if they choose to do so. Only a handful of their spacecraft are armed and capable of defending themselves – the rest are transports only."

Paisen cued a video that Tepper had shot, showing four large transports dropping from high altitude and then disgorging their troops across several landing zones. "By far the most concerning news is that they've spent the last few weeks rehearsing spaceborne invasions. They're gearing up for war again, and it's not going to be a war on

Jokuan."

"Jesus Christ," Senator Herek said.

"How ... how many divisions did you say?" Lask asked.

"Eighteen total," Paisen told him.

"How many soldiers is that?" he asked.

"About a hundred and fifty thousand combat troops, sir. More if you count the support elements."

"Good god," Tsokel said. "Were you able to determine their target? Where they plan to invade?"

Paisen shook her head. "We've developed several sources, but none of them have that information. It could be that they don't have access to it, but our sources are fairly highly placed. My estimate is that the target hasn't been decided yet."

"Wherever it is," Vence added, "it's a habitable world: breathable atmosphere, standard gravity, minimal radiation. They're not training using any special life support equipment."

Paisen pulled up another slide, which showed a star map of the galaxy, with a blinking dot at the center.

"There's Jokuan, highlighted." A red circle appeared around the blinking dot. "This first radius is everywhere their shortest-range vessels could reach without refueling. That includes twelve Territories and four Federacy planets. Here are their potential invasion sites if you add in a deep-space refuel en route." Another circle appeared, larger this time. "... the list basically triples," Paisen concluded.

"They *must* be targeting another Territory," Herek noted. "It's just unthinkable that they would challenge the Federacy."

Lask frowned. "The key to understanding *where* they will attack lies in understanding *why* they are starting this war. What's their motivation? What's their president's name, again?"

Paisen moved forward several slides, to a photo of a stern-looking older man in uniform. "President Mori is a sock-puppet. He's a figurehead. This is General Yo-Tsai – he's the real decision-maker."

"And what does General Yo-Tsai want?" Lask asked.

"He wants what all men in power want: to stay in power," Paisen said, smiling at the senators. "Yo-Tsai's military spending has put the planet deep into debt. Their economy is heavily dependent on continued purchases by the government, so it's become a self-fulfilling prophecy: if he doesn't want the government to collapse, he needs war."

"To distract his population from the crumbling economy?" Senator Campos guessed.

"Partly," Paisen said. "But mainly just to seize another planet's assets. He needs to refill his coffers, and he's gotta do it the old-fashioned way: plunder."

"Rape, pillage, steal," Lask mused. "How soon could they be ready to launch an invasion?"

"A few weeks … a month, at the outside," Paisen said. "I've redistributed my team so they're concentrated on the troop encampments. We're keeping a close eye on them, so we'll be able to give you as much advance warning as we can."

Tsokel shook his head. "It's not enough time. The Fleet Reaction Force would need at least two months to come online."

"Best case scenario," Campos told him. "The last time they ran a practice activation, it took nearly twice as long. And that was just a portion of the fleet."

"And years ago," Tsokel said.

Paisen narrowed her eyes. "Senators, there's another option. My team could take a more active role."

"You want to fight the whole Jokuan army?" Herek asked.

"No, sir," Paisen said. "But we're fully capable of sabotaging it."

"How?" Lask asked.

"The most effective attacks hit the enemy on multiple

fronts," Paisen said. "My team would infiltrate their transports and damage critical components, effectively grounding their fleet. At the same time, we would introduce a virus into their military network that would limit communications and scramble files and documents, operational plans. We'd follow that by spreading a real virus amongst their personnel, a dysentery hybrid, something of that nature. Nothing lethal, just debilitating. None of the attacks would cause permanent damage, but they would delay them for months."

"No," Tsokel said. "No overt actions. We simply can't afford to have this project exposed."

"I have to reluctantly agree," Lask said. "This news is troubling – it confirms our worst fears. But we're treading on thin ice."

"If we discover that their target is a Federacy planet, and we see evidence that they are preparing to launch their campaign, would you want us to initiate action at that point?" Paisen asked.

"Potentially," Tsokel said, reluctantly. "But it would have to be very convincing evidence. And we would need to authorize any actions in advance."

"Understood," Paisen said. "Gentlemen, there's one more item I wanted to show you." She cued up the video Tepper had shot of the labor camp. "I'll warn you: these images are disturbing."

The senators watched in silence as footage from a micro-drone rolled, showing an aerial view of the camp Tepper had discovered.

"We discovered this several days ago," Paisen narrated, her voice muted. "The people you see in the camp are members of the ethnic majority that rose up against Jokuan's government during the civil war. They've been collected in this internment camp, and you can see that the conditions are … inhumane. It's a death camp, essentially."

She changed to another clip, in which a procession of

exhausted prisoners carried bodies out of the camp and dumped them into the moat, before picking up their shovels to bury them.

Lask shuddered. "My god."

"What are you suggesting that we do about this, Miss Potfin?" Tsokel asked.

"I don't know," Paisen admitted. "The camp's too large for my team to handle – we could kill some of the guards, try to cover the prisoners while they escaped … but there are too many of them, and they're in bad shape. They'd need medical attention. We wouldn't be able to protect them, much less transport them …," she trailed off. "Objectively, I don't think there's anything we can do for them right now. But I wanted to make you aware of the situation."

Lask rubbed his chin. "If we leaked this footage to the press, it might create a public outcry. We could use it to build support for getting the FRF activated, and then the FRF would be able to free the prisoners as part of a preemptive strike."

Tsokel shook his head sadly. "I don't see that happening," he said. "And the Jokuans would undoubtedly make the camp disappear the minute this video went public. While the FRF was activating, they'd kill everyone in the camp, and deny it ever existed. We'd just be signing their death warrants. It pains me to say it, but I don't think there's anything we can do for those people at this time." He closed his datascroll, and stood up. "Thank you, Miss Potfin. Keep up the surveillance on Jokuan, and let us know of any new developments as soon as they happen."

"Yes, sir."

The Senate Guards escorted Paisen and Vence back through the winding corridors, to the building's main entrance. Vence hailed a cab on her holophone, and the two climbed aboard when it arrived.

"Spaceport," Paisen said. The vehicle pulled into the flow of traffic, weaving along the interior bays of the massive battleship that held the Federacy's government headquarters.

I wonder if we're going to drive past the spot where I crashed a car through a viewport a couple months back, Paisen wondered.

"Tepper sent us a message while we were in there," Vence noted, interrupting Paisen's reverie.

"Something new to report on Jokuan?" Paisen asked.

"No," Vence said. "Scapa. They're starting jury deliberations. All the experts are saying it's going to be a guilty verdict."

"Shit," Paisen observed, chewing her lip in thought.

"If the jury moves fast, they could be executing him in a week," Vence said.

"Hmm," Paisen said. "He sent me a message while we were on Jokuan, but with everything going on, I didn't get a chance to reply. He asked for my help. And I owe him a lot."

"I thought you said he was a clumsy pain in the ass," Vence noted.

"He is. But he's a smart son-of-a-bitch, too … and he's my friend."

Vence checked her holophone, scrolling through several screens. "The flights would be tight, but we could be on Scapa in a week." She cocked an eyebrow at Paisen.

Paisen studied the younger woman. "Yeah? Are you up for a detour on the way back to Jokuan?"

32

A notification window appeared on Senator Foss' desktop computer screen. He glanced at it, and set his datascroll down on the desk, which held a framed photo of Simi Quorn, the NeoPuritan Church's founding father.

"Enter," Foss called.

The door to his office slid open, and his chief of staff passed through. The young man set a data drive on Foss' desk, and sat down in one of Foss' chairs. Foss frowned at the data drive, then plugged it into his desktop computer.

"What is this, Shofel?" Foss asked.

The young man glanced behind him to ensure the office door had closed. "It's the matter you asked me to look into. Regarding Senator Lask, and his seat on the Intelligence Committee."

"Ah." Foss opened a folder of files from the drive, and flipped through them quickly. "This looks like a budget request … maps, surveillance photos … no photos of Lask, though."

"No," Shofel shook his head. "Lask is clean as a whistle, if you can believe it."

"I don't," Foss replied.

"Well, if he's dirty, he's kept it a secret from his closest staff. Or they're extremely loyal to him. But either way, I couldn't find anything on him. His campaign finances are in order, his staff love him, he's never handed out a backroom favor that I can find, and he has a strong relationship with his husband, with no signs of unfaithfulness."

Foss made a sour face. "I had forgotten about his sexual preferences."

"Yes. Well, as much as the Church might not approve, he's quite open about his homosexuality. So there's no real opportunity for blackmail there."

"No," Foss agreed. "Okay, Lask is clean, or at least appears to be so. Then what am I looking at on this disk?"

"Highly sensitive material that only the Intelligence Committee is privy to," Shofel told him. "Those are from a project called 'Arclight,' they're reports compiled for the Intel Committee on the relative threat levels of several Territorial militaries."

Foss lifted an eyebrow. "'Arclight?' Interesting. Where did you get them?"

"Lask's foreign relations adviser," Shofel said, crossing his legs. "She has several family members in the Church. I indicated that we might release them from their remaining obligations if she were able to help us. Lask shared this information with her in confidence, but apparently it was quite difficult for her to obtain digital copies."

"I still don't see how these reports help us," Foss pointed out.

"It's not the reports, but who generated them," Shofel replied. "Lask recruited a team of former guildsmen to serve as his spies. The galaxy thinks the Guild has been dissolved, but it hasn't – Lask has resurrected it, he's continuing the work of Lizelle and the others, just under a new name. The Guild is still very much alive and functioning."

"Really?" Foss sat back in his chair, thinking. "And

with Senate funding, no less. 'The audacity of the corrupt knows no bounds,' as Simi Quorn decreed. Does the rest of the Intel Committee know?"

"Of course; they signed off on it. But Lask spearheaded the whole thing. Those files include several memos from Lask to the Intel Committee. One outlines his proposal for using this team, another sets the budget … and his signature is on each of them."

"How many contractors? Have they killed anyone?"

"Twelve, it's just a small team – it's not the full Guild, not really. And the memos make it clear that the spies are not allowed to kill anyone. But none of that matters. If you broke this story to the press, they'd skim right over that. They'd just see the Senate funding the Guild again."

"Undoubtedly," Foss agreed. "Thank you, Shofel. Arclight is precisely what I needed."

"Would you like me to schedule a press conference?"

"No," Foss said. "Set up a meeting with Senator Lask."

* * *

"So what's this 'urgent matter,' Gaspar?" Senator Lask inquired, taking a seat across from Foss in the empty Senate conference room. "I'm afraid I have some urgent business of my own to deal with in a few minutes."

Foss shot the other man a tight smile. "There's going to be a vacancy on the Intelligence Committee," he said.

"Is there really? I'm surprised to hear it. Who's stepping down?" Lask asked.

"You are," Foss said.

Lask's eyes narrowed. "Well, that *is* a surprise."

Foss set two printed sheets of paper on the table and slid them over to Lask. The other senator kept his face expressionless while he scanned them, then pushed them away. "Improper acquisition and distribution of classified materials is a major offense, Senator. Where did you get these memos?"

Foss ignored him. "What do you think your constituents would say if they heard about Project Arclight? If they learned their beloved senator was in the midst of restoring the Guild?"

Lask's nostrils flared. "That's not what Arclight is, and you know it," Lask replied.

"It doesn't matter what it is, or what I know," Foss said calmly. "What matters is how it will be perceived."

Lask took a deep breath, and Foss could see him grinding his teeth. "So it's blackmail, then? I step down from the committee, or you go public about Arclight?"

Foss inclined his head slightly. "And you nominate me to be your replacement. Make it a convincing nomination. Stepping down isn't enough, though it's certainly precisely what you deserve after humiliating me and belittling my church. But if I don't successfully take your place on Intelligence, all of the evidence goes to the press. So you'll need to ensure that Tsokel approves the nomination, too."

"You hypocritical bastard. Fuck you and your Neanderthal church, too," Lask swore, slamming his fist on the table.

Foss raised an eyebrow. "Are you refusing my terms?"

"No," Lask said. "Unlike you, I'm not here for self-aggrandizement, or to advance my party's medieval agenda. I serve the greater good. And the Federacy sorely needs that team of guildsmen, so if I need to step down to protect them … I will. Though I wonder if your presence on the committee isn't a greater threat to our government's security than anything else." He stood up and strode quickly to the door, then turned and glared at Foss. "It's men like you who are undermining this Federacy as fast as we can rebuild it."

Foss shrugged. "But rebuild it in whose image? In the words of the ever-wise Simi Quorn—" Foss started.

"Don't quote your fucking conman prophet to me, Foss. You'll have your goddamn committee seat. But if you threaten me again with this, I'll resign from the Senate entirely, and take all of this public, I swear it."

33

Under the clear shield of her helmet, a drop of sweat trickled down Dasi's forehead, stinging when it hit her eye. She shook her head to clear it away, and lifted her baton and the heavy riot shield again. Across the street, the instructors roleplaying as protesters had tossed aside their signs and were shouting angrily, and several had begun throwing rubber bricks at Dasi and the other cadets in riot gear blocking the street. Dasi watched as multiple instructors pulled helmets on over their padding, and picked up heavy, double-headed pugil sticks.

That can't be good.

>>>I have reviewed Interstellar Police training manuals on riot control, and I believe I know what situation the instructors are preparing to simulate next.

Well, don't tell me – that would be cheating, Dasi told Six.

>>>Very well. It will not be pleasant.

No, I imagine not.

With a rush, a group of "rioters" sprinted across the street, crashing into the barrier of shields the cadets held up. After a brief scramble, they broke through, and Dasi saw her fellow cadets trading blows with the instructors in a frantic melee. Then an instructor was in front of her. Dasi felt her shield pushed to one side, and the grinning instructor jabbed her in the helmet with his pugil stick, knocking her back a pace. She swung her baton in response, but it slid off his shoulder pad without effect.

Then, suddenly, the instructors broke off their attack, turning and retreating. Dasi and the other cadets cheered loudly, celebrating their unexpected victory.

"Where's Vonuci?" Dasi heard a cadet yell.

She turned and saw that a shield and baton lay abandoned in front of the cadets' position. Across the street, the assaulting instructors were dragging a uniformed officer amidst their group. An instant later, the crowd swallowed them.

"Oh, shit," Dasi said.

>>>Yes. Officer down.

Dasi turned and raised her voice over the hubbub of the street. "They took Vonuci – we've gotta go after him."

"How?" a cadet near her asked.

"Same thing they did to us, just in reverse," Dasi told him. "Smash and grab."

"I can barely carry this shield, I'm not gonna be able to carry him, too," a female cadet nearby noted.

Six? Dasi thought. *Suggestions welcome.*

A diagram appeared on Dasi's heads-up display – an overhead view of the protesters and cadets. She watched as Six's animation progressed on-screen.

"Okay, lock arms," she called out. "We're going to keep the shields up, but form a wedge as we move, like a spear, with me at the tip. I'll guide us so we're pointed at where they have Vonuci. We gotta hit them hard, at full sprint, and keep pushing in until we find him. Closest person drops their shield and grabs him, helps him back. Those on either side close the gap, seal the shield formation up again, and then we retreat. Got it?"

Two cadets near her traded apprehensive looks. "Fuck it," one said. "They'll have our asses if we don't at least try."

"Let's do it," another cadet agreed.

Dasi felt the cadets on either side of her lock arms, and then she pushed forward, tugging them along with her. The instructors roared a challenge at their approach, waving padded clubs and pugil sticks menacingly.

When the cadets had covered half the distance, Dasi shouted, "Now!" and broke into a run. The formation surged forward and smashed hard into the front rank of instructors, and their momentum carried them for several steps, pushing deep into the crowd before Dasi stumbled over a fallen protester at her feet.

"Keep the shields up! Keep going!" Dasi shouted, as several pugil sticks clattered off her shield.

They pushed forward again, and in four more steps, she saw Vonuci, prostrated on the ground with an instructor straddling him and pinning his arms to his back. Dasi gave an incoherent yell and lunged forward, ramming the instructor with her shield and knocking him back. She tossed her shield at him for good measure, then bent to pull Vonuci up.

>>>*Duck!*

Dasi ducked, and felt a pugil stick graze the top of her head as it swung over her. She yanked Vonuci up, and felt another blow glance off her left arm. She looked around wildly for the nearest friendly face.

>>>*Turn left – the cadet formation is that way.*

Dasi tugged Vonuci to the left, and then the crowd parted and the two of them were back amidst the cadets' formation.

"I got him, fall back!"

The cadets extracted themselves, and reset their shields into a solid wall, backing slowly across the street in good order, with Dasi and Vonuci jogging ahead of them.

"Thanks, Dasi," he said. "Fuck, I'm never going to hear the end of this."

She slapped him on the shoulder. "Don't sweat it. They

were going to get somebody; you just drew the short straw."

A whistle blew, long and loud, three times, and Dasi craned her neck to see up onto the catwalks erected over the training area, where the instructors not playing protestors were observing the action below.

"Ten minute water break, then reset," the command instructor called.

Dasi pulled her helmet off, setting it down on the asphalt and taking a seat next to it. She reached for her hydration system hose and drank deeply, catching her breath.

"Where did you come up with that tactical plan, Cadet?" The command instructor had descended to street level, but he still towered over her, blocking the sun as he looked down at Dasi.

"Sir?" she struggled to her feet, coming to attention on reflex.

"At ease. We haven't taught the wedge formation as an extraction technique yet."

"No, sir."

"Have you been studying archival footage of riots in your spare time, or am I supposed to believe you came up with that out of the blue?"

"Just reading ahead in the manual, sir."

"Uh huh," he said, unconvinced. He turned to leave.

"Sir? Today is four weeks. Since our conversation."

"So?" he asked, eyes narrowing.

"So, you said that I had that much time to improve, sir. Or you would kick me out."

"I was there, Cadet. I recall our conversation."

"So can I stay, sir?"

"Did you pass your last PT test?"

"Yes, sir."

"Barely," he corrected her, with a grunt. "Barely, Cadet. Did you qualify on pistol?"

"Yes, sir. I shot 'Expert,' sir."

"We don't give out awards for 'most improved,' Cadet. I shot 'Expert' the first time I set foot on a range."

"Yes, sir."

"Have you mastered restraint techniques yet?"

"No, sir. But I've been practicing in my spare time with several of the other cadets, sir."

"Then it sounds like you finally decided to stop fucking around and you're ready to take this seriously. Don't waste my time again, Cadet."

"No, sir."

"Now go retrieve your shield and baton – you left them across the street during that last training exercise. Maintain some fucking accountability of your equipment, Cadet."

"Yes, sir," Dasi said, suppressing a smile.

She could feel the bruises from the day's training – reminders of the blows she had been unable to deflect. But underneath the aches, she felt a deep satisfaction that she hadn't felt in a long time.

I did it! Six helped me, yes. But it was my hard work more than anything. She grinned as she picked up her dropped shield and baton. *I might actually make it, and graduate.*

* * *

>>>Good morning, Dasi.

Dasi groaned softly, keeping her eyes closed as her heads-up display slowly brightened under Six's control, waking her gently.

It's five thirty already?

>>>It's five twenty-nine. Per your instructions, I'm waking you a minute before the instructors arrive for wake-up call, so you can be prepared.

Yeah, I know. It's just not pleasant for humans to have to wake up, that's all. Sleep feels good. And I was in the middle of a really nice dream …

>>>I would like to experience a dream. Is being woken during a dream like losing access to a critical set of data?

That's probably not far off, Dasi agreed.

>>> Today is scheduled to be mostly cloudy, with a likelihood of rain later in the afternoon. I recommend you pack your rain gear in your equipment bag.

Thanks, I will.

>>>I have also prepared a new set of flash cards for you, to aid in studying for tomorrow's test.

Great.

The lights came on in the barracks bay, and Dasi sat up as the day's lead instructor rattled his baton against the tin lid of a trash can with sadistic enthusiasm, causing an ear-splitting racket.

"Wake the fuck up, Cadets! Another glorious day on the force. Don't think I didn't see that Relkins! Get out of bed, you lazy ass."

Dasi stood and stretched, then turned to begin making up her bunk.

>>>While you were sleeping, District Attorney Jace Hawken made an appearance on a major news network. I recorded the broadcast given your interest in the last news story we saw about him.

Oh, thanks. Can you summarize it for me?

>>>Of course. He formally announced the creation of his task force, and confirmed what the legal correspondent suspected: they are indeed able to pursue and prosecute criminals across jurisdiction boundaries.

Six popped up a small window in Dasi's heads-up display while she folded and tucked in her blanket, and a video ran.

"We're just sealing up the cracks in the justice system that criminals used to exploit," Hawken told the camera. "There are no longer any places to hide. I'll also mention that since the arrest of Mr. Davy, I've personally received quite a few death threats from members of the NeoPuritan Church, demanding that I stop investigating their religion. Well, I have an answer for those folks: Exor Davy is just the tip of the iceberg. I'll bring the whole damn thing down, if I have to."

Well, that's a pretty bold challenge. I've met a few of these NeoPuritans, back on Anchorpoint … I didn't like them. There was something smug and disingenuous about them. And their values are horribly antiquated.

>>>I have trouble understanding the purpose of religion, despite some research into the subject.

Religion can be a good thing, Dasi said, turning to her locker to pull on her physical training uniform. *It helps people deal with the unknown. Faith – believing in something bigger than themselves – gives people hope that … well, that there's meaning to life, to what we do every day. And hope that their lives will improve. But religions are run by humans, with all the flaws that go along with that. Sometimes they do more damage than good.*

>>>Mankind's history is certainly full of instances of religiously-motivated conflicts.

Yeah. Many people shun religion today for that very reason. Dasi knelt to tie her shoelaces. *Six, did the report mention anything about Hawken's team going after the guildsmen still out there?*

>>>No, it did not. But Hawken did tell reporters that his team was not the only one in existence. He declined to reveal how many other teams there are, or what they were charged with investigating, however.

One of them HAS to be going after the guildsmen out there, Dasi noted.

>>>I agree. That is likely.

And they'll probably start by trying to get information from Rath, since he's already in jail. Or trying to catch Paisen.

>>>Probably.

And that might lead them to me.

34

"Congratulations are in order," Patriarch Rewynn said, beaming and grasping Foss' hand as he entered the priest's office. "A resounding victory."

"It is a big step forward," Foss agreed. "The committee seat has gained us a huge amount of credibility with voters."

"And with simple citizens, looking for succor in their dark and troubled lives," Rewynn told him, as the two men sat down. "Church enrollment is up over the last few days, and we've already reversed revenue declines from the past few months."

"Excellent," Foss said. "Perhaps we'll be lucky enough to achieve Simi's vision in our own lifetimes, after all."

The old priest grunted. "That will take a lot of work. But it feels closer than ever. The tide is turning inexorably in our favor. Though the loss of Exor Davy was a setback."

"Yes, his arrest was quite a shock. How did they get inside our operation?"

"We're still investigating. It looks like they may have put pressure on an acolyte close to Davy," Rewynn suggested.

"He'll be punished severely, of course," Foss said, frowning.

"The acolyte? Of course. If he survives his interrogation."

"This district attorney – Hawken, I think is his name. He's intent on exposing more of our secrets. He promised more arrests, Thomis."

Rewynn held up a hand. "The Church is aware. Let the lawyer squawk on TV all he likes. But we know to be vigilant, now – we know we're at war. And we're not going to remain on the defensive much longer."

"Good," Foss grunted.

"It seems our list of enemies is growing. First 621, now this Hawken character."

"I take it as a sign that we're doing something right," Foss agreed. "I would prefer it if 621 were dead already, though."

"He admitted to Delacourt's murder," Rewynn pointed out.

"I know, I saw the news. But the trial's not over yet …."

"Gaspar, relax," Rewynn soothed the senator. "He'll be convicted, and get the death penalty. Our legal counsel says it's nearly a certainty."

"And if he's released? Will we be able to kill him then, after we failed twice already?"

Rewynn snorted. "Have you seen how the press has vilified him? We won't even have to bother. If he's acquitted, the courthouse will be surrounded by an irate mob. They'll tear him limb-from-limb. Regardless of the trial's outcome, by this time next week, we'll no longer need to trouble ourselves over him."

"By Simi Quorn, I hope so," Foss said. He played with his tie idly. "There's another matter I wanted to discuss with you."

"Oh?"

"It's related, actually. The leverage I used to obtain Senator Lask's seat: I discovered that he had sponsored a black operation. The Intelligence Committee is using Janus Group assets to conduct spy missions in the Territories, to assess military threats to the Federacy."

Rewynn shook his head slowly. "Devious, but very risky, given public sentiment these days. And yet another example of how corrupt our government has become without proper leaders in place."

"The team is led by a woman," Foss continued. "So I have doubts about how effective they will be. But it irks me that the government is still reliant on such thugs to protect it. I was tempted to simply take the evidence public, and force the whole committee to resign."

"You still could," Rewynn pointed out.

Foss considered this in silence for a time. "Mm," he mused. "I suppose I could. It might be the catalyst we need."

"Does the government really need this team of spies to protect itself?" Rewynn asked.

"I believe it might," Foss told him. "According to the reports, Jokuan is a very real threat. They're preparing for war, though their target is uncertain."

"Surely a single planet can't threaten the Federacy?" Rewynn scoffed.

"The Federacy is actually quite vulnerable," Foss told him. "We would likely defeat an invasion, eventually, but the Jokuans have the advantage of speed and surprise. It would take the Federacy some time to respond."

Rewynn sat back in his chair, steepling his fingers under his chin. "You could expose the rest of the Intelligence Committee, though I'm sure that would have some negative consequences for you and the party. But perhaps there's another course of action to consider."

"What would that be?" Foss asked.

"Give the Jokuans the location of these Guild agents."

Foss raised his eyebrows. "Interesting. That would

certainly rid us of the spies."

"It would mean the end of this unethical operation, yes," Rewynn agreed. "And the Jokuans would be indebted to you. And very, very angry at the Federacy."

"True," Foss affirmed.

"They'll want revenge. That might be the spark that ignites the final conflict Simi Quorn prophesied. He foresaw an army spreading his lifewater across the galaxy."

Foss sat forward in his chair. "But I thought that army would be a Federacy one, under NeoPuritan control."

"That's one interpretation," Rewynn said. "But remember also: 'For you will find allies in your crusade …,' " Rewynn quoted.

"'… in the unlikeliest of places,' " Foss finished, rubbing his chin. "Indeed. It is just as Simi Quorn predicted. The Jokuans have their own objectives, though – they might thank us for alerting them to the spies, but they won't fight for the Church. Their aim is to steal assets from other planets."

"Then they will start with the richest planets, which are also the most corrupt," Rewynn pointed out.

A smile spread slowly across Foss' face. "So they will. The very planets where our crusade is most needed. But we still wouldn't be able to control the Jokuans."

"No," Rewynn agreed. "We simply unleash them. The Jokuans will cleanse the galaxy for us, rooting out the rich and corrupt … and where they go, we will bring salvation and enlightenment in their wake."

35

"By the accepted definition of the term, Mr. Kaldirim is a serial killer. He has killed over fifty people that we know of, and possibly more besides." District Attorney Anguile stood facing Rath, fixing him with her stern gaze. Rath kept his chin up, but he found it hard to maintain eye contact with her, especially knowing the jury was studying him closely, too. "He is a mass murderer. But we're not here to get justice for all of those victims. Today we're here to ensure that Arthin Delacourt's killer gets the justice he deserves."

Anguile strode across the courtroom and gestured to the viewscreen, where a slideshow began. Rath watched as still images from the Suspensys attack appeared on the screen. "In my years as a prosecutor, it's rare that the evidence is so clear, and indisputable. I'll recount it, briefly. Mr. Kaldirim admitted to his girlfriend that he hired a janitor and a hacker to effect a cyber-attack on his behalf. When that failed, he approached Ms. McGovan and seduced her, spinning a tangled web of lies in a ploy to trick her into carrying out the murder for him. Again, he admitted all of this to her. Mr. Kaldirim then bluffed his way into the Suspensys facility using an assumed identity and his cybernetic implants. He still has those implants embedded today, and he was arrested carrying the same model of CreatePack device that he took into Suspensys during that attack. Mr. Kaldirim kidnapped Arthin Delacourt in his pod, and was shot twice by security guards. Scars on his body match those wounds exactly. And finally, Mr. Kaldirim dropped the pod from orbit, and Mr. Delacourt burned to death inside his pod."

The slideshow ended, and Anguile cast her gaze over the jury, examining them. "Mr. Kaldirim has admitted that every word of what I've just said is true – and he admitted it twice. Once to his girlfriend, and later here, in this very courtroom. He did kill Arthin Delacourt. So the only thing you need to concentrate on now is whether he had a choice in the matter. He *claims* that the Guild would have killed him if he didn't carry out his assignment. But we don't have any evidence of that fact … apart from his word."

Anguile raised a finger in the air. "But there's an even bigger problem with Mr. Kaldirim's story. He signed a contract with the Guild, agreeing to these terms. They *told* him what would happen, and he signed up anyway, *knowing* what his obligations would be. He *claims* that his life was at risk at that contract signing, but again, he's asking us to believe him that this was the case, because he has no evidence. He's asking you to take his word for it. Are you really going to trust a man who's spent the last twelve years hiding his true face? Cloaking himself in lies? Are you going to believe a man who lied to the woman who loved him, in order to trick her into helping him to commit murder?"

She shook her head sadly. "I hope you're not that naïve. Mr. Kaldirim signed that contract for one reason: he wanted the money." On the viewscreen, a photo of Arthin Delacourt appeared, smiling. "Mr. Delacourt's pod fell through Scapa's atmosphere for over a minute before it burned up. Arthin Delacourt likely woke up, near the end. I want you to imagine the sheer terror when he realized what was happening to him. A defenseless, upstanding citizen of our great planet – murdered in cold blood, by Mr. Kaldirim. For money."

* * *

Rath closed the datascroll and handed it back to Mishel. The lawyer eyed him inquisitively. "Looking for something?" he asked.

Rath shrugged. "Was hoping to get a response on a message I sent," he said. *But Paisen still hasn't replied to my message. What the hell? How has she not sent me anything yet?*

Mishel frowned. "You're not supposed to be having any correspondence, you know. Anything I should know about?"

Rath smiled and shook his head. "You don't want to know, Mishel."

"Great," the attorney said, scowling. "Just don't make me an accessory to anything stupid." He pointed at the conference room door. "She'll be here in a minute. You sure you want to go through with it?"

"Yeah," Rath said. "I'm sure."

The door swung open, and Toira Anguile walked in briskly. "Mishel," the district attorney said, nodding to him. "I enjoyed your closing arguments, as always. What can I do for you?" She shut the door and took a seat across the table from them.

Mishel looked at Rath, who nodded. The lawyer sighed. "Against my advice, my client would like to discuss a deal."

"He's ready to give up his accomplices?" Anguile asked.

"No," Rath shook his head. "You just get me. I'll plead guilty, but I'm not giving up any of my friends."

"Why?" Anguile asked. "Mr. Warran, to his credit, has mounted an admirable defense on your behalf. Though

I'm not sure it will be enough."

Rath studied his hands, rubbing at his palm with a thumb. Then he looked up at her. "I'm tired of running from my past. I think I'm ready to take responsibility for it."

Anguile studied him. "That sounds nice, but I'm a skeptic and a realist, through long years of experience. What else do you want? Life without parole, instead of the death penalty?"

Rath nodded. "Yes. I don't want to die."

Anguile pursed her lips. "I assume Mr. Warran already advised you of this, but I have no interest in that deal. I'm concerned that this deal just allows you to buy yourself – or your friends – more time to plot an escape. So I'll take my chances with the jury, in order to see you dead."

"You want names," Rath said.

"I do."

"How about a different name?" Rath suggested. "The man who hired me."

Anguile's eyes narrowed. "I thought you guildsmen never knew who hired you. The Guild designed it that way, to protect its clients."

"True," Rath allowed. "But I figured it out."

"And you have proof?" Anguile asked.

Rath glanced at his attorney. Mishel cleared his throat. "We can give you a name. There's circumstantial evidence to support his involvement, but … nothing concrete."

"No," Anguile said, without hesitation. "No deal."

"Toira," Mishel pleaded, "it's a solid lead. And if it's true, it's a major coup for your office. I would jump at the opportunity to prosecute this person."

Anguile sighed and contemplated the two of them. "I need to hear the name *and* the evidence, up front. Then I'll consider your deal. But I'm not making any promises without knowing what I'm getting into."

Mishel looked at Rath and shrugged. "It's your call, but I wouldn't take her offer. Not without a guarantee."

"I'm not giving you a guarantee," Anguile told Rath.

Rath chewed the inside of his cheek. "Fuck it. Gaspar Foss."

Anguile laughed: a short, sharp bark of a laugh. "The senator? You're joking."

"I'm not," Rath told her. "He hired me in order to frame Robald Delacourt. Check the timing – Delacourt was trouncing him in the polls; it was a desperation move to ensure Foss won the election."

"Coincidental timing isn't very good evidence, Mr. Kaldirim … as your lawyer has pointed out many times, quite recently."

"I've been attacked twice since I arrived on Scapa," Rath told her. "Both times, the men were NeoPuritans, Foss' goons from his church. They were following Jaymy, in case I came back and started poking around. And when I did come back, he had them try to kill me, to silence me before I could figure out the role he played."

Anguile drummed her fingers on the desk. "I need more evidence than that. I certainly have no love for the NeoPuritans, so I'll admit I'm intrigued, but all you really have is a hunch. I need something I can convict on."

"So consider the deal," Mishel suggested. "My client just came to this realization recently – given time, he may be able to offer you more pieces. There may be evidence in the Guild files he publicly released."

Anguile stood. "I'll consider it," she said. "But—"

There was a rap at the conference room door, and Anguile's assistant stuck his head in. "They reached a decision," he told her.

"Already?" Mishel asked, standing. "Toira, we need an answer now."

"No deal," she told him. "It's on the jury now."

* * *

Judge Aurmine took the piece of paper from the jury

foreman and read it briefly, before folding it up and handing it back. It struck Rath as strange that the court still used paper – an anachronism in a digital age. *Why not just use a datascroll? Did they use datascrolls for a while, and then someone hacked one to get out of jail time?* Mishel nudged him in the ribs and the two of them stood. The judge eyed him over the dark wood of her stand. Then she turned and faced the jury.

"Mr. Foreman, have you reached a verdict?"

"We have, your honor. On the count of murder in the first degree, we find the defendant guilty as charged."

He continued reading the other charges – breaking and entering, conspiracy to commit … the list was long. *Guilty,* Rath thought, with a sigh somewhere between relief and resignation. *Guilty on all counts. And it's true, I am. And it's what I asked for just a few minutes ago.*

"We'll reconvene for sentencing in one week," Aurmine decided, breaking Rath's reverie.

Mishel turned to Rath, disappointment and concern creasing his face momentarily.

"We're not out of this fight yet," he said, but even with his audio implants turned off, Rath could hear a tremor of insincerity in the lawyer's normally confident tone. "There's still a chance you get a life sentence, and then we can appeal."

"Let's hope so," Rath said. "Otherwise I'll be dead in a week."

Mishel smiled, patting him on the shoulder. "Hang in there."

"I'm okay," Rath told him. "Mishel, I've been running away from my crimes for years now. It's time I took some accountability for what I did. I've been trying to find a way to clear those debts, but maybe this is it. Maybe this is the only way to make things right."

"What, by your death?" Mishel asked.

"No," Rath said, shaking his head. "No, I'd still prefer that we avoid that. But maybe I can find some peace in jail."

The lawyer shrugged. "Regardless of what you did, your choices *now* are what matter. And I think you can still do some good in the world. Alive, preferably, and out of jail."

"Perhaps," Rath said.

He turned away from the lawyer, and looked around the courtroom's audience. He saw no sign of Robald Delacourt, but Jaymy was standing up near the back. They locked eyes for a second, and then the bailiff took Rath by the arm.

"Come with me."

Across the room, Jaymy started to push her way up through the crowd, toward the front of the courtroom.

"Can I just—" Rath started to say.

"No," the bailiff interrupted, and tugged Rath toward the side exit. He lost sight of Jaymy in the press of people, and followed the man reluctantly out of the courtroom.

36

"I don't like this," the command instructor noted, walking briskly down the hallway. Dasi hurried to keep up.

"Don't like what, sir?"

"I don't like it when people fuck with my trainees," he told her. "I don't care what their credentials are, or what they think they need, 'for the good of the Federacy.' We have policies and standards for a reason, Cadet."

"Yes, sir," Dasi agreed, confused.

He drew up in front of a door, stopping abruptly and turning to look at her. He spied a stray thread on her uniform, frowned, and plucked it away with practiced ease. "They're going to try to dazzle you in there. Don't get intimidated. Understand?"

"No, sir," Dasi said, truthfully.

"Just listen closely to what they're asking, and be careful before you agree to anything."

"Yes, sir," Dasi said, struggling to follow. "What are they going to ask me, sir?"

But the instructor ignored her question, and pushed the door open.

>>>*Human communication can be quite unclear,* Six

observed.

Dasi followed the instructor into the office – the Academy commandant's office, she realized, belatedly reading the stenciled letters on the frosted glass of the door. She felt her heart pounding in her ears.

Inside, the commandant looked up from his desk, and a young, dark-skinned man stood as she entered. He turned and eyed Dasi critically.

Oh shit! It's that famous district attorney – Hawken, from the news. They found me. They know I helped Rath and Paisen!

"Hello, Cadet," Hawken said, smiling and extending a hand. "I'm Jace."

Dasi took his hand and shook it cautiously. "Dasi Apter, sir. Cadet Apter, I mean."

"Cadet, this is District Attorney Hawken," the commandant explained. "He's here to talk to you about a sensitive matter. Have a seat, please."

"Yes, sir."

Dasi swallowed nervously, and her trembling hands found the armrests of the seat next to Hawken. She sat down; the command instructor leaned against a bookshelf next to the desk, and fixed her with his usual scowl, crossing his arms but remaining silent.

"Dasi, what we're going to talk about has to stay within this room," Hawken told her.

"Mr. Hawken has been named Special Investigator for Interplanetary Crimes," the commandant noted.

"It's a new position," Hawken continued, "created by the Senate. I'm assembling a team of professionals from Interstellar Police and the Justice Department. We're tasked with capturing and prosecuting major criminal organizations that span multiple planets."

"Do I need a lawyer, sir?" Dasi asked.

He frowned, taken aback. "I don't … think so? Why, have you done something wrong?"

"No, sir," Dasi said, backtracking. "I just assumed, because you're a prosecutor, that I was in some kind of trouble."

Hawken laughed. "No! No, no. Nothing like that. I need your help."

"My help, sir?"

"I want you on my team," Hawken told her.

"But I'm still a cadet," Dasi protested. "I don't understand."

"That's one of the reasons I want you on my team," Hawken said. "With all due respect to you two gentlemen," he nodded at the commandant and instructor, "I need someone I'm absolutely sure has no ties to criminal organizations. Having an experienced cop on my team would be good, but … that would mean they've been around the block a few times. They've met people. They might have met the people we're investigating. I'm not sure how to pick someone I can trust."

"A cadet like me is less likely to be a double agent," Dasi guessed.

"Yes. But I requested you in particular, because of your past experience."

Dasi looked up quickly. "My experience?" *Does he know about the Guild?*

Hawken nodded. "I need someone who understands politics, and Anchorpoint."

Dasi relaxed, slightly. "I thought you were investigating the NeoPuritan Church?" she asked.

"I am," Hawken agreed. "But the Church has powerful folks protecting it, some of whom call Anchorpoint home."

Dasi came to a sudden realization. "You're not just going after the NeoPuritan Church; you want to take down the NeoPuritan senators themselves."

A slow smile spread across Hawken's face. He put a finger to his lips. "Shhh. Don't tell." He glanced at the command instructor. "She figured that out quickly."

The command instructor grunted. "I told you she would, sir."

Hawken turned back to Dasi. "That's why I need someone who's dialed into the Senate, someone that already knows who's who, and how everything works."

"Why not a Senate Guard? They're all Interstellar Police, too," Dasi said.

"No." Hawken shook his head. "Elite cops, and they do know the Senate, but they're not investigators any more, they're bodyguards. And with so much emphasis in their training on protecting the Senate, I don't know how they might react to a role reversal."

"But I'm still not a cop," Dasi pointed out. "I don't graduate for another three weeks."

Hawken looked over at the command instructor. His scowl deepened, but he stood and placed a leather wallet on the commandant's desk, and slid it over to Dasi.

"Cadet, graduation is a formality at this point. You've met all standards to complete this course," the instructor growled.

Dasi opened the leather wallet, and found that it contained a bright, silver Interstellar Police badge, and an official police identity card with her name and picture on it. Dasi felt a thrill of excitement and relief. *I did it. I'm a police officer.*

"Congratulations," the commandant told her.

"Normally you just get assigned to whatever duty station the Federacy deems appropriate, and you have no say in the matter," the command instructor noted. "But in this case, since Mr. Hawken's breaking the rules a bit, you can, too. You have the option here to say 'No,' Officer Apter."

Officer Apter.

"What exactly are you asking me to do?" Dasi asked Hawken.

"My team is mostly lawyers right now – we've been piecing together the investigation, and then leveraging local cops to make the arrest, wherever the suspect is. You would be joining the team as our dedicated, full-time

Interstellar Police representative. One of several, hopefully, as we continue to grow. But the sole cop for now. You'd help us build the case, gather evidence, and then make the actual arrest, when it comes time."

"You're on TV a lot," Dasi commented. "I don't want to be interviewed, or anything like that. I value my privacy."

"That's fine," Hawken reassured her. "I'll be handling the media stuff. You can stay totally behind the scenes. What do you say?"

What do you think, Six?

>>>I think this represents a unique opportunity for us. We could make a significant impact serving on such an important team.

Hell yeah, we could.

Dasi stuck her hand out. "Count me in."

37

Rath was already awake when the jailhouse guards came to his cell on the morning of sentencing. He stood and faced the bars, and waited patiently while they attached his chains. At the loading dock, the guards transferred Rath to three members of the courthouse transport team, signing him over via an electronic custody form. He didn't recognize two of the guards from the courthouse team – normally the same crew handled moving him to and from the jail each day. One of the new guards, a woman, caught Rath studying her, and looked away.

Rath felt his pulse quicken, but he kept silent.

The other new guard headed for the pilot's seat, while the female guard led Rath through the open rear doors of the air van, seating him in the back along a bench lining the wall. She took a seat farther along the bench on the same side, standing her auto-rifle between her knees. The third guard, a man Rath recognized from previous trips, pulled the rear doors closed and sat across from them. Through the reinforced glass window, Rath saw the driver take his seat up front, and start the van.

The jailhouse loading bay door opened, and the van

pulled out smoothly. As they turned onto the street, two Interstellar Police cruisers joined them, one taking up an escort position to the front of Rath's van, the other falling in behind. They followed the police cruiser in the lead, which stayed at ground level, motoring through light traffic.

Rath let his head rest against the steel wall of the van, feigning sleep. Through half-lidded eyes, he watched as the van followed the usual route back toward the courthouse. Then he heard a faint *click* from the female guard next to him.

That sounded like a rifle safety selector lever.

Rath eyed her casually, but she was looking forwards, at the road ahead of them, through the pane of glass separating the passenger compartment and the driver. Rath followed her gaze, and saw the police cruiser ahead of them make a left turn, onto the block that housed the court building. The van did not turn, however, and instead accelerated suddenly, going airborne.

Here we go.

The guard across from Rath noticed their deviation from the planned route a split-second later. He turned to question the driver as the female guard swung her rifle up. Rath shifted his feet forward, using the chain between his ankles to pin the barrel of the man's auto-rifle against the floor. The female guard fired a stun round into the guard's arm, stifling his cry of protest. He slumped over onto the bench.

"Paisen?" Rath asked the female guard. She ignored him, and banged her fist on the divider wall twice, signaling to the driver, and then clambered past Rath and opened the rear doors to the van.

"What are you doing?" Rath had to shout to be heard over the rushing wind. Behind the van, he saw the two escort police cars were close behind them, lights flashing. *So much for a nice, quiet escape without anyone noticing.*

The woman ignored him, and took hold of the

unconscious guard, and before Rath could stop her, she slid the man unceremoniously out the back of the van.

"What the fuck!" Rath yelled. They were over the desert now, and the van had descended, but the guard's body still dropped several hundred feet before crashing into one of Scapa's sand dunes. Rath struggled to his feet, hunching to stand inside the cramped van. "I said no casualties!" he shouted.

The woman fired a long burst of gunfire into the nearest police cruiser, and Rath saw a thin line of smoke streak out of the car's hood. She glanced at Rath, scowling, and pushed him hard back down onto the bench.

"I don't know who 'Paisen' is," she said. "But you need to stay seated and shut up for right now."

* * *

At the wheel of the stolen police cruiser, Paisen swore.

"What the fuck is going on?" she asked, rhetorically.

"You know him better than anyone," Vence pointed out from the passenger seat. "You think he's trying to bust out on his own?"

"He does like to improvise," Paisen allowed. "But this is just sloppy, even for him."

She saw the van doors burst open, and a second later, a body tumbled out.

"Fuck! Was that Rath?" Paisen asked.

"No," Vence replied. "I can see him, he's still in the van. Shit! Incoming!"

Paisen spied a female guard in the van aiming a rifle at them. She braked hard, but a burst of bullets clattered off the car's armored windshield, and she saw a line of holes open up across the hood. Paisen banked the car, swinging out of the gunman's field of fire. She climbed to a higher altitude, staying above and to the left of the van.

"Warning: engine damage," the car's computer cautioned. "Descend immediately for crew safety."

Paisen muted the alarm.

"Rath's still cuffed," Vence noted, drawing her auto-pistol and flipping the safety off. "I just saw the shooter yell at him and push him down onto the bench. Didn't look like they were buddies. You think they're kidnappers? Hoping to squeeze him for cash?"

"Whoever they are, they aren't exactly friendly," Paisen said. "Get ready: I'm going to drop us back into view."

Vence rolled down her window, steadying her pistol against the door frame. "Ready. It looks like they're heading for that big sand dune."

Paisen glanced up from the controls and spotted a large dune directly ahead of them. But as she watched, the dune appeared to shimmer. Suddenly, sand cascaded down the edges of the dune, and the entire hill jerked upwards, as if a large earthquake had struck.

"What the …?"

The sand continued to pour off as the dune rose, and a massive metal structure emerged: a spaceship, buried under the sand. The ship's yawning cargo bay swung open, but two large cannons opened fire at the same time, and Paisen slammed the car's yoke forward, dropping them into a last-ditch evasive maneuver as the shells ripped past the car. She saw a flash and flinched at the distinctive thunder-clap noise of an explosion.

"The other police cruiser's been hit!" Vence reported, bracing herself against the ceiling as the car plummeted earthward.

Paisen yanked back on the yoke, praying that the car's damaged engine could handle the stress, and they leveled off mere feet above the ground, still traveling fast. She juked left, then right, then right again, but saw no more cannon rounds – the ship had stopped firing at them. Paisen swerved the air car around. Above, she saw Rath's van disappear into the cargo bay, and the ship's engine banks light up. The craft rose, slowly at first, then with the sudden acceleration of an object going ballistic. In moments, it had disappeared into the blue sky above.

"What. The. Actual. Fuck," Vence observed.

"I don't know," Paisen said. "But we need to get the hell back to the city and dump this cruiser. Rath's on his own, for now."

38

Beauceron felt a rush of cold air and started awake. He flinched as he saw a form bending over him in the darkened spaceliner cabin.

"What …?"

The shadowy form straddled him, pulling the blanket back up, and he felt warm skin pressed against his own. Soft, naked skin.

"Atalia?" he asked.

"Hush," she said. "I'm horny, and you're here – let's not make a big deal out of this."

She took his hand, and placed it on her breast.

"But—" he started, and then her lips were on his, and he stopped talking.

* * *

The corporation, which went by the name *Legacy Ventures,* was on the eighth floor of a small office building a short ride away from Proxis II's spaceport. Beauceron and Atalia rode the elevator up in silence. He caught her eye and blushed.

Atalia sighed. "If I had known you were gonna be so awkward about it …"

"I'm sorry," he said.

"It's just sex," she scolded him.

"We're partners," he said. "It could affect our professional relationship."

She laughed. "Only if you continue to make a big deal out of it." But she smiled at him, warmly, and Beauceron thought he saw the hint of a blush on her cheeks, too. He felt a flutter of excitement in his stomach. He tried to ignore it.

"We shouldn't do it again," he told her.

"That's not what you said in the shower this morning," she reminded him.

The elevator doors slid open, and they consulted the floor map, turning and walking down the corridor. The door to the office stood open, and they had to stand aside to let a uniformed man wheel a hand-cart of boxes out.

Atalia frowned at Beauceron. "What is this, moving day?"

Inside, no one was manning the reception desk, but they did find another moving company employee stacking boxes in a side office.

"Is anyone from the company here?" Beauceron asked him.

"I think so," he said. "I saw someone in the big office, at the back."

Beauceron thanked him. They found the office easily, where a paunchy, harried-looking man sat at a large desk, engrossed in a phone conversation.

He saw them, and held up a finger. "I understand that," he told the phone. "Look, I get it – I'm familiar with the redemption restrictions. Just tell me when the earliest possible liquidation date is."

He listened for a second. "Well, that's workable, thank you. There was something else I wanted to chat about, can you hold on one second?" He put his hand over the phone, and eyed Atalia and Beauceron quizzically. "Can I help you?"

Atalia held up her police ID badge, artfully covering the Interstellar Police logo. "Law enforcement, sir. We just need a minute."

The man's face fell. "Toneo, I have visitors. Can I call you back in a few? Okay, bye." He hung up and sighed, shaking his head ruefully. "Of course it would be the cops. Just when this week couldn't get any worse."

"Are you moving offices?" Beauceron asked.

"Moving? No. We're closing," the man said. He gestured to the chairs in front of his desk. "Unexpectedly, you might say. I'm Skip Waltrin."

Beauceron shook the man's hand before sitting. "Mr. Waltrin, do you own *Legacy Ventures*?"

"No," Waltrin said. "I manage this office on behalf of my clients. They own the company."

"What does *Legacy Ventures* do?" Atalia asked.

"We're a family office," he told her. "Are you familiar with the term?"

"No." She shook her head.

Waltrin shrugged. "Essentially, family offices are small corporations that are set up to run the financial affairs for ultra high-net-worth individuals. A family with several billion dollars doesn't give their money to some two-bit banker or broker to run, they hire a whole team of individuals, and we keep their investments on track, handle tax and legal affairs – a wide range of services. Can I ask why you're here?"

Atalia smiled. "This is just an informal investigation – nothing serious. We're trying to locate a ship that was involved in an incident a few weeks ago. We just want to talk to the folks on the ship, that's all."

"Okay," Waltrin said. "What ship?"

Beauceron held up his holophone, showing a picture of the ship from New Liberia. "This one," he said.

Waltrin squinted at it. "It's vaguely familiar. I may have

seen a deed to a ship like that years ago, when I took over from my predecessor."

"What does the company use it for?" Beauceron asked.

"My office doesn't use it," Waltrin said, with conviction. "We charter private craft from time-to-time for business trips for our employees, but I've never seen that ship. Our client may use it, I don't know."

"Do you know where it is now?" Atalia asked.

"The ship? No," Waltrin said. "I don't have the faintest idea."

"Where are your clients?"

"I wish I knew," he said.

"Well, *who* are your clients?" she tried.

Waltrin sighed and rubbed his temple. "Would you believe me if I said I didn't know?"

"No," Atalia told him. "I wouldn't."

Waltrin nodded. "Yeah, it's hard to believe. But I've never met them. I've worked at several family offices over the years, and they always put a premium on secrecy, on protecting the family from unwanted publicity or attention. But this place is on a whole other level. Literally no one in this office knows who we work for; never met them, never seen them, don't even know the family name. We manage a ton of money, some of it gets withdrawn occasionally, we send out quarterly statements and ask for guidance, and we never hear a damn thing. If it weren't for the periodic withdrawals, I would think everyone in our client's family had died, and we just didn't know it. Well, at least until earlier this week."

"What happened earlier this week?" Beauceron asked.

"We got a phone call from the client, who used the correct authorization code, and promptly told me to liquidate every single one of his investments. That would be why we're closing up shop, here. They fired us, essentially."

"Why?" Atalia asked.

"Detective, if you figure that out, please come and tell

me. That's the only thing my staff has been asking me all week long, and I still don't have an answer for them. Do you guys know anyone that needs a few billion dollars managed?" Waltrin said.

"He does," Atalia said in mock seriousness, pointing to Beauceron. "Got a couple friends that hit it big recently."

"Really?" Waltrin asked, looking over at Beauceron hopefully.

The detective scowled at his partner. "I'll be sure to pass your information along to them, Mr. Waltrin," he said. "If we talked to your predecessor, would he know who the client was?"

"Well, he's dead, unfortunately – he ran the office for about forty years, before I took over, fifteen years ago. But I'm pretty sure he never met the client, either."

"How do you work for a family, and not even know who they are?" Atalia asked.

"It's an odd arrangement," Waltrin agreed. "But apparently *Legacy* has always been like that, since we were first founded."

"When was that?" Beauceron asked.

"2180," Waltrin replied. "We're quite an old company, actually. Two hundred and … what? Thirty-five years now? But all good things must end."

"You were founded during the Third Colonial War," Beauceron pointed out, a slight frown creasing his forehead.

"Ah … just after it ended, I believe," Waltrin agreed.

"Do you think you can find the deed of sale for the ship?" Beauceron asked.

"Normally, I would tell you I need to see a warrant," Waltrin said. "I would remind you that one of my main functions is protecting the privacy of my client. But seeing as nothing seems to be normal about this week …" He tapped on his computer keyboard for several seconds. "Real assets … purchase records and receipts … here it is." He swiveled the screen, so that Beauceron could see it.

The detective held up his holophone's camera, pointing it at the screen. "May I?"

"Sure," Waltrin said, shrugging. "I'm just going to delete it later anyway."

Beauceron took a photo.

"The *Rampart Guardian,*" Atalia read off the screen. "Forty thousand tons, infantry landing craft. It was bought the same year *Legacy Ventures* was founded," she noted.

"So it was," Waltrin said. "That ship's as old as the company. And you say it's still in operation? Amazing."

Beauceron studied the screen in silence, then scribbled for a time in his notepad. "Do you mind showing us the other purchase receipts from that time period?" he asked.

"Okay," Waltrin agreed. He selected several other files, and then opened them. "This is a fueling receipt – probably for the *Guardian.* Food and related supplies. More food. Spare parts. Reverse osmosis water purification unit. *More* food supplies. Tools and equipment. Oh, that's interesting." He clicked on an invoice. "Eight cryo-pods. 'Long-term, reusable, human hibernation / suspended animation modules,' " he read. "You know what I think?" the financier asked, rhetorically. "*I* think our founding family caught the exploration bug. They bought this ship, stocked it full of food, stuck themselves into hibernation, and then headed out for parts unknown. They've been out exploring uncharted space for two hundred years!"

"Perhaps," Beauceron said, but he was still writing in his note pad.

"Makes you wonder why they came back – and what they found," Waltrin suggested.

Beauceron took a photo of the cryo-pod invoice. "How do you contact your clients?" he asked.

"An email address," Waltrin said. "But I'm afraid that's where I draw the line. I will need to see a warrant for that. Or if you guys want, you can give me a message, and I'll forward it along to my client. Or former client. Whatever they are."

"Thanks," Beauceron said, standing up. "Detective, did you have anything else?"

Atalia shook her head. "No. Thanks for your time, sir."

"Of course," Waltrin said. "Let me know if you want me to send that message."

Outside, Beauceron stopped on the sidewalk, chewing the inside of his cheek.

"Well?" Atalia asked. "I can hear the gears grinding in that head of yours, what's up?"

"I don't know," Beauceron said. "I'm missing something, something critical."

"I'm going to get us a cab," she told him. "You can think about it on the way back to the spaceport. We can think about other ways to trace that ship on the trip to Jokuan."

"Okay," he agreed, barely listening.

In the air taxi, Beauceron re-read his notes. Atalia watched him, a bemused smile on her lips.

"Do you want to talk it through?" she asked. "Or should I just be quiet and let you think?"

"Um," he said. "I don't ...," he trailed off, flipping back several pages through his notes.

"I'll shut up," she decided.

Beauceron turned his holophone on, and pulled up the photos of the purchase receipts. He read through them, twice. Then he wrote something else in his notebook, feverishly, and turned back to his holophone.

"It can't be. He's been dead for over two hundred years," Beauceron muttered.

"Uh oh," Atalia commented. "I think he's got it."

Beauceron ran a search query, skimmed through several news articles, and then exhaled slowly, turning off the phone. He glanced over at his partner.

"I think I know who's on the *Rampart Guardian.* I think I know who bought the drones and tested the high energy device over New Liberia."

"Okay," she told him. "I'm ready to hear it."

"I don't think you are," Beauceron said. "This is the crackpot theory to end all crackpot theories."

"Try me," Atalia suggested.

39

The female guard slung her rifle over her shoulder and took Rath by the elbow, hauling him to his feet. The van's driver joined them at the rear door, and fell into step on the other side of Rath without a word. The cavernous cargo bay held numerous other small craft, of varying sizes and shapes, all of them shrouded under tarpaulins. Rath guessed they had not been used in some time. He spotted a stack of engine lubricant cans, their yellowed labels peeling with age.

This place feels like a museum.

His guards marched him out of the bay, through several dimly-lit corridors. Rath saw no other crew members. Finally, they arrived at an interior door, and the male guard pressed a security panel in the wall. The panel looked to have been repaired several times. The door slid open, and Rath was ushered into a conference room with a low ceiling – six grey-haired men and women sat around the table. At the center of the table, a young man Rath's own age stood. He wore a dark blue uniform, with the insignia of the Interstellar Police stitched on the lapels.

I recognize him, Rath realized. *I've seen that face hundreds of times in old news footage and in history books.*

"Welcome, Rath," the man said, smiling. He gestured to Rath's guards. "Free him."

They removed Rath's chains, and then the disruptor collar around Rath's neck. Rath saw the diagnostics screen appear on his heads-up display. With a rush, his implants came back online, the enhanced sensations flooding over him as if he had just emerged from deep underwater. He could hear the sigh of air coming out of a vent on the far side of the room, and smell the cracked leather of the conference room seats. He breathed a deep sigh of relief.

Rath felt the ship shudder, and heard the engine's pitch change. *We just went to FTL.*

"Do you know who I am?" the man asked him.

Rath nodded. "I know who you appear to be," he said, choosing his words carefully. "But you're supposed to be dead. Long dead."

"Indeed I am. And you're supposed to be in jail," the man pointed out. "It seems neither of us are very good at doing what we're supposed to do."

"Who are you really?" Rath asked.

"I am exactly who I appear to be, Rath Kaldirim." He put both fists on the table and leaned forward, meeting Rath's gaze without flinching. Rath saw the fire in his eyes, then: the famous charismatic energy that had inspired men by the thousands to join his crusade. "I am the man that started the Third Colonial War, and the man that will win it – for the war is not over, not yet. I am a traitor, an Interstellar Police officer, and a revolutionary. I am the worst nemesis of the Federacy, and its final hope for salvation."

"Anders Ricken," Rath said.

Ricken smiled. "The same. Now, come: join us."

Keep reading for an exclusive excerpt from *Rath's Rebellion,* Book Five in *The Janus Group* series:

The two guards turned and withdrew from the ship's conference room, the metal hatch sliding closed behind them. In the silence that followed, Rath cleared his throat.

"Anders Ricken," he said, disbelieving.

The young man in the faded police uniform nodded, gesturing to a chair at the well-worn conference table.

"Please, sit," he said.

Rath walked forward and sat down slowly, cautiously, and then glanced briefly at each of the table's occupants. *Four men, two women, none of them younger than sixty. Can they really be the Council? The six policemen who helped Ricken start the Third Colonial War?*

Rath turned his attention back to the younger man seated across from him. "How are you even alive?"

Ricken arched an eyebrow. "Misdirection. A tactic you're most familiar with."

"You faked your own death?" Rath asked.

"I did," Ricken agreed. "And then I went into hiding on this very ship. For over two hundred years."

"How?" Rath asked. "How did you know they wanted you dead?"

"The man the senate sent to kill me may have been a skilled mercenary, and for all intents and purposes his mission was the pilot test that formed the Guild," Ricken said, tilting his head to one side. "But he was no guildsman – he didn't have your enhanced capabilities, and he lacked the training and subtlety that you and your peers employ today."

To Rath's left, one of the old men seated at the table grunted. "He was a common murderer."

"He was indeed, Lonergan," Ricken agreed. "And not a very smart one. We caught him trying to infiltrate our base of operations. When we questioned him, he revealed that he had been sent by a group of senators. That shocked me, but it also gave me pause." Ricken shrugged. "Our rebellion was failing, and I knew it. We had lost the initiative, the momentum was with the Federacy – we had the funds to continue fighting, but our supporters were growing weary of the fight."

"We asked too much of them. It was a long war," the elderly woman seated next to Ricken pointed out.

"Far too long," Ricken said, nodding. "So I reevaluated our strategy. I realized that the galaxy was not ready for the radical solution I was proposing. Some people were, but not enough. And I saw that if the Senate was willing to secretly dispatch a man to kill me, the corruption I was fighting against could only increase over time. I needed time – time for that corruption to fester and spread, time for more people across the Federacy to be exposed to the injustices of our political system."

"So you weren't on the ship that exploded?" Rath asked.

"No. We paid the assassin handsomely and set him free. In return, he was more than happy to shoot a video of us boarding that ship, and the ship taking off … and then exploding in the upper atmosphere. But through some sleight-of-hand, we exited the ship unseen before it launched. The senate got what it wanted, and we won ourselves the time we needed. Time to plan, to regroup, and to start anew."

"To start anew?" Rath asked, warily. *This might just be the most dangerous place in the galaxy. Apart from my cell back on Scapa.* He eyed Ricken with suspicion. "You want to start another war."

"No. I want to start a revolution," Ricken corrected him. "There's a vast difference."

"That's what revolutionaries always say," Rath said. "Either way, innocent people tend to get killed in the process."

"Not in this revolution," Ricken said. "Not this time. That's another thing we learned – the more blood you spill, the harder it is to justify the fight. And retaining the moral high ground is paramount in this fight. This time, no one dies."

Rath crossed his arms over his chest and cocked an eyebrow, but remained silent.

"But we're getting ahead of ourselves," Ricken said. "You haven't met my lieutenants yet, the Council of Six."

So I was right, Rath thought. *But they've aged, and for some reason, Ricken hasn't.*

"… my trusted advisors – police officers all, like me, who joined the cause in the early days, and have been with me ever since. For a long time, now." Ricken smiled sadly.

"This is Egline Ursson, my Head of Intelligence," Ricken continued, indicating the woman to his left. She met Rath's gaze evenly. "Next is Kolim Yaite, Personnel. Wasan Prevol, Supply and Logistics … Linn Mei, Public Affairs; Marec Lonergan, Operations, and last is Georg Swan, Communications. Last but not least, Georg." The old man acknowledged Ricken's joke with a smile.

"I'd say it's nice to meet you," Rath said, "but I'm not sure … well, I'm not sure what to think, right now. Am I your prisoner?"

Ricken laughed. "No! No. We broke you *out* of jail, Rath. We likely saved your life."

"I'm grateful for that," Rath said. "Though some part of me feels as though I deserved jail. And maybe even death."

"I've been following your trial closely, my friend," Ricken told him. "I wanted to know what kind of man you were, before I brought you here. For what it's worth, I don't think you deserve to die. We've all made mistakes in our life. Many that we regret deeply. But everyone deserves a chance to make things right again. To atone for those sins."

"Is that what you're hoping to do?" Rath asked him.

"Make up for the lives you took during the Colonial War?"

"Yes," Ricken said, softly. "The lives we took, and the ones who gave their lives on my behalf. I owe it to all of them to see this through, to achieve the vision we struggled so hard for."

"If I'm not a prisoner, then what am I doing here?" Rath asked. "Why did you rescue me?"

"I rescued you because I need your help."

ABOUT THE AUTHOR

Piers Platt grew up in Boston, but spent most of his childhood in various boarding schools, including getting trained as a classical singer at a choir school for boys. He graduated from the University of Pennsylvania and joined the Army in 2002, spending four years on active duty. He lives with his family in New York.

To be the first to hear about his new releases and get a free copy of his *New York Times* bestselling Iraq War memoir, *Combat and Other Shenanigans,* visit: www.piersplatt.com/newsletter

16598395R00154

Printed in Poland
by Amazon Fulfillment
Poland Sp. z o.o., Wrocław